Also available from
Susan Andersen
and Harlequin HQN

Susan Andersen

That Thing Called Love

HARLEQUIN®

entertain, enrich, inspire™

Recycling programs
for this product may
not exist in your area.

ISBN-13: 978-0-373-77691-7

THAT THING CALLED LOVE

Copyright © 2012 by Susan Andersen

Dear Reader,

I am so excited about my new series. This first Razor Bay book stars Jake Bradshaw, a man who's made a lot of mistakes, and Jenny Salazar, the take-no-crap woman who holds his full attention. And I got to plunk the fictional resort town down on Hood Canal, an area that holds a lifetime of memories for me.

Most people hear the word *canal* and picture man-made waterways. This canal is actually a natural sixty-five-mile saltwater fjord in western Washington. I was just a baby when my folks discovered it. Every summer for two weeks, I ran wild with my brothers and cousins, swimming in icy, superbuoyant water until my fingers and toes were pruney, playing until the sun sank behind the soaring Olympic Mountains, roasting marshmallows and hot dogs over blazing bonfires. When I was nine, my folks bought land on the beach and built a little cabin on it. This, to me, is the most beautiful, peaceful spot on earth.

It's likely a no-brainer to tell you I consider Razor Bay a character in its own right. So trust me when I tell you it's my dearest wish that you enjoy it, too, alongside Jake and Jenny and the folks of Razor Bay.

~Susan

This is dedicated, with love,
to my friends in the industry, both old and new.

To

Jen Heaton, who, despite a crazy busy life,
always carves out time to brainstorm with me,
to haul me back on track and make my work better,
and is just an all-around really good friend

To

The M&Ms—Meg Ruley and Margo Lipschultz—
my wonderful, marvelous, world's best agent and editor

To

Robyn Carr, Kristan Higgins and Jill Shalvis,
for daily posts, a host of laughs and shared tears

And to

all you readers, without whom I'd be writing this stuff
just for myself. Thank you for your loyalty,
lovely emails and Facebook friendships

Plus a special thanks

to

the brilliant Robin Franzen, R.N.,
who allowed me to have my chicken pox and excuse it, too.

That
Thing
Called Love

PROLOGUE

February 23
Razor Bay, Washington

"JEEZ, JENNY, are they *ever* gonna go home?"

Jennifer Salazar heard the half angry, half plaintive query beneath the rise and fall of conversation coming from the dining room. Outside, gusts of wind, howling down out of Canada, chased rain from the Olympic Mountains rising across the water to ping and rattle against the venerable old Craftsman on the bluff.

Turning around from the momentary break she'd taken to watch raindrops fracture into prisms against the leaded glass porch light, she looked down the hallway.

Thirteen-year-old Austin stood between her and the doorways to the kitchen and dining room. He was curved in on himself, and his newly wide shoulders in that grown-up black suit coat looked out of proportion to the rest of his verging-on-skinny body—even hunched up around his ears as they currently were.

Moving quickly, she reached out to pull him into her arms. He hugged her tightly in return.

"They will," she assured the teen. "And pretty soon, I imagine, given how fast the weather is turning." She pulled back to smile into his tense face. "But Emmett was an institution, pal. People want to pay their respects."

Austin was the closest thing she had to a brother, but lately she hadn't known quite how to deal with him. It killed her to see his pain as he struggled with the loss of the grandfather who'd raised him. Emmett Pierce's death had tromped on the heels of Austin's grandmother's, who had preceded her husband just a few short months ago, blasting the barely turned teen with a double whammy.

But he was so volatile these days. A well-adjusted kid one minute, unhappy or angry the next. And he rarely shied away from mouthing off the rest of the time. Emmett and Kathy had spoiled him shamelessly, up to and including buying him a brand-new Bayliner Bowrider—a boat she'd argued against—for his thirteenth birthday.

"I swear I'm gonna pop the next person who calls me 'you poor boy,'" he muttered. "And Maggie Watson pinched my cheeks like I was four years old or something!"

She didn't know whether to commiserate over the misguided insensitivity or laugh at the indignation in his voice. "I imagine they just want to express their sympathy but don't know what to say."

"And they think I do? I mean, am I supposed to say it's okay or somethin' when they tell me Gramps's in a better place? 'Cause it isn't. Plus, what genius thinks I'd jump at the chance to be 'you poor boy' to a bunch of people who've known me since birth? And I'm sure as hell not gonna talk about how it *feels* to lose him." His voice cracked and he cleared his throat angrily. "My feelings are— They're…"

"Yours and no one else's," she supplied with an understanding nod when he stalled. She had experience with the phenomenon. She'd only been a few years older than he was now when her own world had fallen apart.

"'Zactly," he mumbled.

Realizing she'd stepped back to give her neck some relief from looking up at Austin, Jenny dug at the bunched muscles in her nape and gave him a rueful smile. "I'm still not used to you being bigger than me—let alone so much bigger. The last time I checked you had maybe three, four inches on me. But I'm wearing four-inch heels today and you're still way taller!"

For the first time since Emmett's passing last week, Austin flashed her the wholehearted smile that until recently had been his default expression— the endearing grin that crinkled his pale green eyes and carved little crescents around the corners of his lips. "I hate to break this to you, Jenny, but *crickets* are way taller than you are."

"Why, you little smart-ass." She smacked his arm, but refused to be sidetracked. "When did you get to be, though? I swear you weren't this tall yesterday."

She had begun to fear he might, in fact, turn out as height challenged as she. Heaven knew *she* wasn't thrilled to have ended up a scant five-two in a default thirty-two-inch-inseam world—and that only if she practiced really excellent posture. She couldn't help but think the same outcome for a boy would be even harder.

But considering the kid had apparently grown three or more inches overnight, her worry would probably be better directed at something that actually required it.

Austin's momentary good humor visibly fading, he merely shrugged at her question. "What's gonna happen to me now, Jenny?"

"Well, for starters, since Emmett's will assigned me temporary custody, you'll continue living with me at the resort. Or, if you'd rather…" She faltered a moment, hit with her first uncertainty. "I suppose I could move in here with you."

"God, no!" He shook his head emphatically. "It was hard enough staying here when Grandma died— and we'd at least been kinda prepared for that."

True. The elderly woman had been failing for the past couple of years.

"But with Gramps…" Austin surreptitiously knuckled away a tear, then scowled at her when he saw she'd noticed. "I keep expecting him to show up every time I turn around, ya know? I'd rather be at your place."

"Then my place it is." Jenny wouldn't mind a good

bawl herself. She missed Kathy and Emmett like crazy. They'd been so good to her, and losing them almost back-to-back had been a one-two punch to the heart.

She needed, however, to be strong for Austin.

"I went to the estate lawyer to talk about permanent custody, but he wanted to wait a bit." She hesitated, then admitted, "He's doing his best to contact your father." Much as she'd prefer to keep that information to herself for the time being, Austin had a right to know.

His mouth flattened and his eyes went hard. "Like *he'll* give a shit."

She didn't have the heart to chastise him for his language, because in all the years she had known him, she had *not* known his father to show a speck of interest in him.

Still. "Apparently he's on a *National Explorer* shoot somewhere. No one seems to know quite where at the moment, but Mr. Verilla said he hopes to track him down soon."

"Yeah, I'll be sure to hold my breath waiting for him to show up." Austin's voice resonated with knife-sharp teenage sarcasm. But his angry eyes had taken on that stricken cast they adopted whenever the topic of his father came up.

And for one red-hot minute Jenny wished she could get her hands on the man who had disappointed this boy so many times over the years. It just sucked so bad that she couldn't.

What she could do, however, was run interference as Kate Ziegler stuck her graying head out the kitchen door, focused faded blue eyes gone watery with sorrow on Austin and said, "Oh, you poor, *poor* b—"

Jenny strode right up to Kate with such authority she cut herself off midword and took a startled step back.

"Mrs. Ziegler!" Jenny exclaimed warmly, grasping the older woman's arm to firmly guide her to the crowded dining room across the hall. "I've been meaning to compliment you on that wonderful ambrosia salad you brought. Why, if I'm not mistaken, it was the very first thing to go."

As the woman bustled over to check out the table, Jenny shot Austin a half smile over her shoulder.

It broke her heart that, although he tried to smile back, he couldn't quite manage it.

CHAPTER ONE

JAKE BRADSHAW BLEW INTO TOWN almost two months later, at a quarter to three on a blustery, sunny April afternoon.

Not that Jenny was keeping track or anything.

Hell, who kept track of those things? She was busy minding her own business, washing the window over her kitchen sink and thinking the shutters on the Sand Dollar—the luxury cottage across the shared parking lot from her small bungalow—would benefit from a new coat of paint, when the doorbell rang. She just happened to check her watch. Then, looking down at her seen-better-days cropped T-shirt and raggedy jeans, she sighed. Why didn't anyone ever drop by unexpectedly when she was dressed to kill?

Murphy's Law, she supposed. Shrugging, she set aside the old tea towel she'd been using, paused her iPod, pulled out the earbuds and went to answer the summons. School had let out for the day; it was likely a friend of Austin's, although Austin himself wasn't home yet.

When she pulled the door open and saw the man on the other side, her mind went blank. Holy Krakow, how wrong could one woman be—this was no teenage kid. This was a total stranger, something you didn't see very often this time of year—unlike during the summer tourist season.

And the guy was a god.

Okay, not really. But he was definitely the next best thing. His hair, which she'd mistaken at first glance for blond, was actually a medium brown that had either been burnished by the sun or was the product of some world-class stylist.

She'd vote for the former, given that every man she'd ever known would choose castration before they'd be caught dead over at Wacka Do's wearing a headful of little tinfoil strips. And although she could honestly say she'd never met an actual honest-to-gawd big-city metrosexual, she was pretty sure this guy wasn't to be her first.

His tanned hands were too beat-up looking, his skin a little too weathered. He had muscular shoulders beneath a nice gray suit jacket, worn over an olive-drab hoodie and a silky, silver-gray T-shirt. And solid thighs that were molded by a pair of button-fly Levi's that had seen hard wear.

She couldn't see his eyes behind the shaded lenses of his sunglasses, but he had the most gorgeous lips she'd ever seen on a man, full yet precisely cut. If she were a different type of woman, in fact, she might almost be able to imagine lips like those kissing h—

"Is your mother home?"

"Seriously?" All right, not the politest response. But, please. She hadn't *almost* imagined what his

lips could do—Marvin Gaye had started crooning "Let's Get It On" in her head. And having him talk to her as if she were a child was like ripping the needle across a vinyl record, bursting her pretty, if where-the-hell-did-*that*-come-from, fantasy.

After a startled look, he studied her more closely. Those lips curved up in a faint smile. "Oh. Sorry. Your size fooled me for a minute. But you're not a kid."

"Ya think?"

His smile deepened slightly. "I'm not the first to make that mistake, I'm guessing."

Okay, get a grip, sister. What was her problem, anyway? She didn't lust after strange men. And she'd been in the hospitality business since she was sixteen, for pity's sake, so rarely, either, was her first inclination to unleash snide sarcasm on people.

At least not on people I don't know.

She gave an impatient mental shrug. Because even if she was in the habit of lusting or unleashing, this guy could be a guest at the inn for all she knew. It was the dead lowest part of the low season, which was why she'd felt comfortable enough leaving Abby to man the front desk while she took a rare day off. But Abs was still green, and it wasn't a stretch to imagine the girl blithely drawing directions on one of the resort maps to help a complete stranger find Jenny's place on the back grounds of The Brothers Inn.

Jenny plastered a pleasant expression on her face. "Is there something I can do for you?"

He looked down at her. "Yeah. I was told I could find a Jenny Salazar here?"

"You found her."

"I'm here about Austin Bradshaw, regarding his guardianship."

Jenny's heart picked up its pace, but she merely said, "You don't look like a lawyer."

"I'm not. But Mr. Verilla said you're the person I need to talk to."

She sighed and stepped back. "Then I guess you'd better come in. You'll have to excuse the mess," she said, leading him inside. "You caught me in the middle of cleaning day."

Her place was just under six hundred square feet of recently weatherized cottage, so it took a total of five seconds to reach the middle of her living room. She turned to face him and saw that he'd removed his shades and was hooking one temple arm into the neck of his T-shirt. Raising her gaze from his strong, tanned throat, she met his eyes for the first time.

Shock jolted through her. *Oh, God.* Only one other person in the world had eyes that pale, pale green—the exact same shade as the summer shallows in the fjord that was Hood Canal.

Austin.

Anger was deep, immediate and visceral. And it had her drawing herself up to her not-so-great greatest height. "Let me guess," she said with ice-edged diction. "You must be Jake Bradshaw."

When she looked at him now, she didn't see that

compelling face or the abundant sex appeal. Instead, she pictured all the times Austin thought his father might call, might show up, and the stark disappointment each and every time that didn't happen. Disdain she couldn't quite disguise tugged at her upper lip.

"Mighty big of you to finally decide you could spare your kid a minute of your precious time."

FOR OVER A DECADE, Jake had dealt with all manner of people. He'd long ago perfected the art of letting things slide off his back. Yet for some reason the contempt from this little female dug barbed needles under his skin.

It didn't make a damn bit of sense. The woman was all of five foot nothing, for crissake, and her shiny dark hair, plaited into two thick little-girl braids, with a hank of long bangs pulling free from the left one, didn't exactly promote a grown-up vibe. She had spare curves, clear olive skin and brown eyes so dark it made the surrounding sclera look almost blue-white in comparison. Dark eyebrows winged above them, and her slender nose had a slight bump to its bridge.

His brows met over the thrust of his own nose. "Who the hell do you think you are, lady?"

Okay, not what he'd intended to say. But being back in Razor Bay, the place he'd spent most of his teen years plotting to see the last of in his rearview mirror—well, it put him on edge. Plus, after the thirty-two-hour trip from Minahasa to Davao to

Manila to Vancouver to Seattle to here, he was so
dead on his feet he was all but punch-drunk. Not to
mention seriously tense at the thought of seeing his
kid after all these years. Of having full responsibility for him for the first time.

So excuse the hell out of him for reacting to the
contempt in her voice and his own flicker of temper
that here was yet someone *else* who thought they
could dictate to him about his son.

Stuffing down every negative feeling that arose,
however, he managed to moderate his tone when he
inquired, "And you think you have the right to judge
me, why?" God knew, he'd done enough of that on
his own. He didn't need some half-pint stranger's
condemnation on top of it.

He watched as she crossed her arms and raised
her chin. "Well, let me see," she said coolly. "Maybe
because I'm the woman who's been in Austin's life
for the past eleven years. And this is the first time
I've ever seen you."

Jake wanted to howl at the unfairness of her
charge. Except...was she actually wrong? He'd had
a series of come-to-Jesus talks with himself on the
endless journey back here and was forced to admit
that he'd been looking at his dad ethic through a
pretty skewed lens for a long time now. The admission made not defending himself to Ms. Salazar more
than a simple matter of pride, more than an ingrained
reluctance to plead his case to a stranger.

He couldn't in all conscience smear the memory of Austin's grandparents. Not only would it be too much like something his own father would have done—making it all about *him* and not giving a damn that his kid had loved the people he was trash-talking—but all that damn soul searching had made him realize that he'd spent too many years blaming Emmett and Kathy for doing the job he himself had abdicated.

They'd protected Austin. And if it cut to the bone that they'd felt it necessary to do so from *him*...well, *I guess it sucks to be you, Slick.*

Somewhere over Midway Island he'd dropped his defenses and admitted they had cut him a lot more slack than he'd deserved before they'd finally lowered the ax and banished him from Austin's life.

But that wasn't the central thing here—at least not right this minute. *That* would be that he was finally doing what he should have done a long time ago: stepping up.

So, go him.

Not that any of this prevented the woman standing in front of him from scratching at his temper. He took an involuntary step in her direction. "The fact remains, I'm Austin's father and I'm here now."

Apparently that wasn't what she'd expected to hear, because she blinked long, dense lashes at him, just a single slow sweep that lowered fragile-looking lids over her almond-shaped eyes, then raised them again.

The action ate up a couple of seconds tops, yet

somehow it was long enough to make him aware that he was standing a whole lot closer to her than he'd intended. It made him aware as well that, except for the blink, she'd gone very still. Had she seen his banked anger? Jake slowly straightened. Shit. She couldn't possibly think he was going to *hit* her, could she?

He took a giant step back, shoving his hands in his Levi's pockets.

In the sudden silence, the back door crashed open, and from the way little Ms. Salazar stiffened, he knew exactly who it was. Heart beginning to kick hard against the wall of his chest, he stared at the opening to the kitchen.

"Hey, Jenny," called a male voice from the other room. "I'm home." The refrigerator door opened, then slammed shut and the lid of something rattled against a hard surface. "Dude! Leave a cookie for me."

"Trade ya for that carton of milk," came a second youthful tenor.

"You better be using glasses!" Jenny raised her voice to warn. "If I see washback in my milk, you're dead men."

Glass clinked and a cupboard slapped closed. Silence reigned for a few moments after that, before being abruptly broken by the sound of stampeding feet. Two boys burst through the archway.

The boy in the lead was a gangly brunette who— *sweet mother Mary*—had the exact same all-bones-no-meat thirteen-year-old build Jake had had at the same age.

God oh God. All the moisture dried up in his mouth and his habit of being aware of everything around him—honed by years of knowing that otherwise he'd likely end up bitten by a snake, stung by an insect or mauled by an animal with way more tonnage, power and teeth than him—went up in smoke. The cozy little room and everything in it faded from his consciousness, leaving nothing but his son.

His.

Son.

Awash with joy, with terror, with a raft of pain and regret, Jake stared. An emotion he'd never experienced suffused his chest, while panic clawed at his gut. Jesus. He was shaking.

He hadn't thought it would matter so much, hadn't expected to be struck so hard. Was this what love felt like?

The thought snapped his spine straight. Hell, no.

It couldn't be. *A:* he was a Bradshaw and Bradshaw men's version of the Big L was so fucked it gave the sentiment a bad name. And *B:* a man had to actually *know* someone before he could start slinging that word around.

He drew a deep breath. It was probably just simple wonder that the kid could have gotten so big already. Jake'd had this image in his head of Austin at two, at four. Hell, at six even, which was how old Austin was the year Kathy had sent him the last picture.

But this was no little boy—this was an almost-grown teen. Not that Jake hadn't known how old he was, of course.

He just hadn't had a clear picture of it in his head.

He'd long ago convinced himself that he was doing the right thing—that Austin was better off with his grandparents, who could give him the stable, structured life that he himself could not. And he'd been right.

But now—face-to-face with what he hadn't merely let slip through his fingers but had actively thrown away with no more than an occasional second thought—his carelessness felt like shards of glass hacking his gut to shreds.

Oblivious to the thoughts and feelings that threatened to swamp Jake, the boy crossed directly to Jenny without even glancing in his direction.

"Can I spend the night at Nolan's?" he demanded. "His mom said it was okay." His gaze passed incuriously over Jake, returned to Jenny. "She's gonna order pizza from Bella T's, and Nolan has a new Xbox game we're gonna try ou—"

With a neck-snapping double take, the kid's gaze suddenly shot back to lock on Jake's. He took a step toward him, making Jake's overburdened heart leap into his throat.

Then Austin snapped upright and an ask-me-if-I-give-a-shit expression molded his young face. He looked at Jake through pitch-black narrowed lashes. "Who the hell are you?" he asked, even though his shuttered expression made it obvious to anyone with eyes that he knew.

Jake swallowed, fighting to sound calm in the midst of the fucking circus taking place inside of him. Automatically, he started forward. "Your dad. I—"

The teen made a wrong-answer-buzzer noise that stopped him in his tracks. "Like hell you are. In case you don't know…and I'm guessing you don't since this is the first time I've ever seen ya," he said, contempt coating his every word, "I'm thirteen. I don't need or want a daddy in my life." He turned back to Jenny, pinning her with angry eyes. "So can I stay the night at Nolan's or what?"

Jake watched as she reached up to stroke the boy's cheek, then visibly quelled the urge, clearly knowing he would hate the public show of sympathy. Instead she nodded. "Sure."

Without another word—or so much as a quick peek in Jake's direction—the teen turned and vanished with his friend into a room off the living room. When he reappeared less than a minute later, he was tucking a toothbrush into his jeans pocket. His other hand clutched a pair of flannel lounge pants.

"You need money for pizza?" Jenny asked.

"Nah," the other kid answered. "Mom's got it covered."

Still ignoring Jake, Austin headed for the kitchen, Nolan tight on his six.

"Hey, wait a minute!" Jake stepped forward, but the two boys were already slamming out the back door.

Jake didn't know if it was disappointment or relief that crashed through him. Whatever the sensation was, it nearly knocked him to his knees. God, he must have pictured this first meeting a hundred times since he'd received the news of Kathy's and Emmett's deaths, must have run as many scenarios through his mind. Not once, however, had he envisioned this. He'd been braced for his son's anger, for a barrage of pointed questions he wasn't sure he could answer to the boy's satisfaction.

But how did a guy brace himself to be so utterly... dismissed? He turned on Jenny. "Are you kidding me? You let him just walk out?"

"What did you expect?" Her voice was cool, her gaze even cooler. "Austin's just discovered that the man who fathered him, the man who was never here when he wanted him most, has finally deigned to show up. Don't you think he might need a little time to process that?"

Yeah. He supposed he did. The kid had said it himself: he was thirteen—not that many years from being grown. Jake had missed his opportunity to be a father.

No. He squared his shoulders. *The hell with that.* Austin was a good five years from the bare *minimum* of being grown, which was a helluva long way from full-out grown. Yeah, he was late to the party, but this was his opportunity to be the man he should have been. And the first order of business was to establish a relationship with his son.

Given Austin's reaction, though, it clearly wasn't going to be easy. Well, tough shit. He wasn't afraid of hard work.

Still. *It's a damn shame the kid's too old to buy a pony.*

He cleared his head and turned his attention to Jenny. "I agree, he does need time to process. But let me make myself clear. I've spoken with my lawyer, and matters are well in the works to have my parental rights returned to me."

"No." She stared at him as if he'd told her he got his jollies mutilating puppies.

"Yes. My attorney is drafting the documents as we speak. I only need to sign them when I get back to Manhattan. Once they've been filed, Austin will be where he belongs. With me." Okay, probably not smart to tell her that—she looked as though it might not be beyond her to stage an "accident" before that happened.

No. That wasn't murder in her eyes; she looked… crushed. Bereft. Sick to her soul.

And because he knew exactly how that felt, he gentled his voice. "Look, I don't intend to grab Austin and run." Okay, so his initial reaction when he'd heard both the Pierces were gone had been exactly that—to get back here, command Austin to pack up, then drag the kid back to where Jake had built a life for himself, at least for the part of each year he was in-country.

But he wasn't gonna be that guy. He wasn't going to be his father. "I'm not here to yank the rug out from under him that way. I know he needs time to adjust, to get to know me."

She sagged in patent relief, and it bugged him that he was so attuned to her, that he harbored an urge to relieve her mind. It would be better for all concerned if no one entertained any false hopes.

"Make no mistake," he instructed in his coolest voice, "my life is in New York and we will be moving there. I'll stay here to give my son time to get accustomed to the idea. While he does, I'll find out what, if anything, needs to be done about Emmett's estate."

Suspicion entered her eyes and he narrowed his own in response. "Don't even go there. I'm not after Austin's money—I've got plenty of my own."

"And I should believe you because…?"

God! Why did that look, that tone, make him want to loom over her, to step too close, crowd into her space and see how she dealt with it?

The urge startled him, because, really, where the hell had that come from? He'd never manhandled or acted threatening toward a woman in his life.

And looking into her fierce little face, he almost snorted. Mighty Mouse here would probably call the sheriff's department if he even looked like he was about to make a misstep. And rightly so, considering she was a woman alone in her house with him—a stranger she didn't know from Adam and mistrusted the little she thought she did know.

But wouldn't *that* just be the cherry on his fucking cupcake if his half brother Max showed up to arrest him? It would probably make the bastard's day to haul his ass to jail.

He drew a steadying breath. "I don't require that you believe me, but in the interest of playing nice with others, I'll give you a freebie." He pulled his wallet from his hip pocket and fished out a card, which he handed to her. "This is my assistant. Call her with your fax number and I'll have her send you my latest bank statement." He gave her a level look. "We have real issues to get through. Me stealing from my kid isn't one of them."

She folded her arms beneath little breasts. "What do you want from me?"

The reasonableness of her tone released some of the tension from his shoulders. "Austin clearly cares about you. I want you to be the conduit between us."

She laughed in his face. "Why on earth would you think I'd do that?"

"Because while I'm willing to stay here for the next two or whatever months to let him finish the school year, in the end we *will* move to Manhattan." He thrust a hand through his hair. "I'm going to be taking him away from everything familiar, and I don't fool myself it'll be a popular decision. If you care about him, you'll make the transition easier for him. Or you can keep your mad on going with me and make it hard. I guess it's up to you."

She looked at him a long time. "All right. I'll think about it." Her extravagant eyelashes lowered until her eyes were mere coffee-dark glints shining between them. "For Austin's sake," she stressed. "Whatever I decide, I won't be doing it for you."

"No shit," he muttered, but thrust out his hand to shake on the deal. Her narrow fingers were warm as she slid them across his palm, her grip firm.

He was caught unprepared for the spark of electricity that shot through him at the contact. But he buried his response, countering it with his all-purpose wry smile.

"Trust me, I didn't assume otherwise for a minute."

CHAPTER TWO

AFTER JAKE BRADSHAW LEFT, Jenny paced from the couch to the fireplace to the picture window, no sooner reaching one destination than lighting out for the next. The already small living room felt like it was shrinking decrementally by the minute.

She had no idea how much time had passed before her restless circuit finally ended back at the window. She stared blindly beyond the resort grounds to the peekaboo glimpse of The Brothers, the prominent twin peaks in the Olympic mountain range that the inn was named after. "Oh, God." Thrusting her hands through her hair, she knocked her forehead once, twice, three times against the cool glass. "What the hell am I going to do?"

Nothing came to mind. And wasn't that too whacked for words—she who had had a plan since her daddy was sent to the pen when she was barely sixteen? At the moment, however, her mind was nothing but white noise, her stomach awash in red-hot acid. And she couldn't string two consecutive thoughts together to save her soul.

She needed Tasha.

Just the thought of her best friend made her stomach a fraction less messed up, and she dashed into the bedroom, snatched her purse from the top of her dresser where she always left it, and headed back toward the door.

On the way, she caught a glimpse of herself in the full-length mirror on the inside of her open closet door.

"Holy crap." She'd forgotten she was still wearing her cleaning clothes. Not to mention that she was devoid of so much as a hint of makeup and her do was totally pulled apart in front from her ten-fingered grab-and-bang. "*That's* not pretty."

Tossing her purse back on the dresser, she toed off her Keds and kicked them into the closet. She shimmied her jeans down her legs and wrestled her T-shirt off over her head. She was in no mood to go primp crazy, but surely she could do better than this.

It took her no time at all to pull on a nicer pair of skinny-wale cords, a thin red sweater and her three-inch Cuban-heeled black leather boots. She swiped a sheer red balm over her lips and gave her lashes a cursory pass with the mascara wand. Then, removing the rubber bands from her braids, she pulled a brush through her hair.

And called it good.

Two minutes later she was out the door, pulling on a military-style jacket as she headed for the boardwalk that followed the curving shoreline into town.

The wind whipped her hair around her head when she rounded the inn, and she pulled a knit beret out of her jacket pocket. Stretching its back opening, she caught up the bottom of her hair, tugged the gray angora front band into place and tucked in stray strands blowing around her face. The day was more blustery than cold, and the upside to the gusty wind was the clarity of the air now that the earlier clouds had blown away. The Olympics soared out of green layer upon complex green layer of foothills, rising a scant two miles away across the choppy, white-capped water, their snow-blanketed peaks brilliant white against the clear blue sky.

Two blocks down the beach, the actual Razor Bay of the eponymously named town cut a deep, irregular half circle into the land. The boardwalk emptied onto Harbor Street, the face of the business district, with its brightly painted storefronts lining the long arc of the inlet. As Jenny walked away from the mouth of the bay, the winds dropped and the waters calmed within the protection of three sides of land.

Someone tapped on the window as she passed the orange clapboard Sunset Café, and she waved back at Kathy Tagart and Maggie Watson, who sat at a table on the other side of the glass. She strode past Razor Bay Jet Ski & Bicycle Rentals, darkened now as it was only open on Saturdays and Sundays this time of year. The neighboring aqua, blue and green building next door was Bella T's Pizzeria, where she was headed.

Jenny whipped the door open, and the rich scent of pizza sauce wafted from brick wood-burning ovens to wrap around her like a security blanket. It was a little early for the dinner crowd, but an older couple she didn't recognize sat at one of the window tables, and a group of teens, laughing and talking, crowded around two tables they'd pushed together near the game room. As she crossed to the order counter, the door to that room opened and closed, belching out the electronic beeps and clangs of the video-game machines behind it.

Tasha looked up from chopping something on a block below the sales counter—and broke into a wide smile. "Well, hey, girlfriend!" she said. "I didn't expect to see you this afternoon. Thought for sure you'd be spending your day off eating chocolate-drizzled popcorn and reading romance nov—" Her smile faltered and she lowered her voice as Jenny approached. "What's wrong? Is it Austin?"

"No, Austin's okay." A bark of laughter that threatened to morph into something else escaped her throat. "Well, 'okay' might be stretching it a bit, considering his father is in town, and he's determined to take Austin back to New York with him."

"What?" Setting aside her knife, Tasha wiped her hands on the white waist apron circling her narrow hips. Then she shook her head. "No, wait, let's go over to the far table where we'll have a little privacy. You want a slug of red?"

"Oh, God. That would be *soooo* appreciated."

"One glass of wine coming up then." She selected a wide-bowled goblet and filled it higher than usual with the house cab. "Here you go, sweetie." Pushing it toward Jenny with one hand, she poured a less generous portion for herself. Then she gave Jenny a quick but thorough once-over. "When's the last time you ate?"

"Breakfast, I guess." She honestly didn't remember.

Tasha was already turning away. "Let me make you a slice."

"I'm not sure I can swallow anything," she said, but her friend had already grabbed a section of dough out of the fridge, slid it onto a paddle and was ladling sauce onto it.

"If this is as bad as it sounds, you're going to need fuel. I've got some of that Canadian bacon and pineapple you like, although how anybody can eat pineapple on—" She waved the old argument aside. "Take our wine over to the table and I'll bring the food."

"Fuckin' *A,* dude!" A boisterous male voice suddenly rang through the room, making the elderly couple gape in shock at the table of teens.

Jenny didn't even turn. Instead, she watched as her friend reached for the big-barreled gun she kept on the lower counter. Then she slowly pivoted as Tasha took aim at the offender and pulled the trigger.

The ping-pong ball that fired from the gun hit dead center in the back of the cursing teen's head and bounced away to skip in decreasing hops across the linoleum floor.

"*What* the—" Slapping a hand to the spot, the

boy pushed back from the table and whirled to face Tasha, his face a study in indignation.

But once he had her in his sights, he appeared to promptly lose his train of thought.

For the first time since she'd discovered Jake Bradshaw's identity, Jenny experienced a trace of amusement. Tasha had that effect on the XY end of the chromosome pool. Jenny had always found it interesting because it wasn't her friend's body—Tasha was far from being built like a goddess. She was tallish and gangly, with average-size breasts and no hips to speak of. But with her gray-blue eyes, full upper lip and Pre-Raphaelite strawberry-blond curls, she had the more exotically striking than beautiful looks—and presence—of a model from a Michael Parkes painting.

It stopped males in their tracks every time.

The gaze she leveled on the teen at this moment lacked her usual warmth. "This is a place for families," she said without raising her voice. "So clean up your language or get out of my shop. You only get one warning."

He hesitated as if tempted to protect his machismo with the usual teenage, knee-jerk don't-tell-*me*-what-to-do 'tude. Instead, he swallowed, his Adam's apple sliding the length of his throat. "Yes, ma'am," he muttered. "Sorry."

"Yeah, sorry, Tasha," Brandon Teller called from his seat next to the boy who'd dropped the F-bomb.

"This is my cousin's first time here. He didn't know the rules."

"Now you do." Tasha granted the boy a smile. "And admiring as I do a man who's not afraid to apologize, I'll tell you that you handled it better than many. Welcome to Bella T's."

When she and Jenny took their wine and food to a table on the other side of the room a moment later, however, she demanded sotto voce, "Seriously? When did I become a *ma'am?*"

She made an erasing gesture before Jenny could respond. "Never mind. That's not what's important. I want to see you eat some of that pie."

"I really don't think—"

"Try."

So Jenny picked up the slice and took a tiny bite off its tip. She felt so sick at the thought of Jake taking Austin to the other side of the country, she was honestly afraid her stomach would rebel. But the pizza's flavors exploded on her tongue and she found the crisp golden crust, flavorful sauce and hot, soft cheese a comfort.

Pizza to her *was* Tasha, and Tash had been her best friend since Jenny's second day in Razor Bay High, when the other girl had put herself between Jenny and some kids who had thought it would be fun to torment her over the much-publicized statewide scandal from her father's exposed Ponzi scheme.

She'd come to learn that Tasha's mother made the strawberry blonde's standing in school even lower than her own. But that only made Jenny admire her more, because most teens already on the fringe—and likely a good percentage of adults, as well—would have covered their own ass rather than put it on the line for a total stranger.

So she smiled at her friend as she reached for her wineglass. "Have I told you lately how proud I am of you? You did it, Tash—not only do you make the world's best pizza, but you're making this place a complete success." Bella T's had only been open for ten months, but it had taken off from the beginning, not just with the tourists during high season, but with the locals, as well.

Tasha gave her a lopsided smile. "Toldja a hundred years ago I was gonna."

She had—the first time she'd made Jenny a homemade pizza in her mother's single-wide. The same night she'd divulged her dream to one day own her own pizzeria.

From the beginning, the two of them had shared a mutual determination to move beyond their circumstances. But Jenny had been in awe that her new friend, who was only six months older than she, had a full-fledged, neatly typed business plan in her underwear drawer. *She'd* been living day to day, just trying to keep her grades up in school and her mother and herself off the streets with the after-school maid job at The Brothers that had brought her to Razor Bay. She so honest-to-God admired everything Tasha had accomplished and was happy for her success. Because nobody worked harder.

Now, in the unspoken agreement of good friends, they chatted about everything but what had brought Jenny here until they finished their meal. Finally, reaching for the half carafe she'd brought to the table, Tasha topped off Jenny's glass and added a splash to her own.

"You look a little more relaxed," she said. "So take a few deep breaths and try to give me the details without getting yourself all stressed out again."

"Tall order," Jenny said, and admitted, "I don't know if that's possible." But she took the calming breath her friend advised and recounted everything that had happened from the moment she'd discovered who Jake Bradshaw was.

"Crap," Tasha said quietly when she finished. "What are you going to do?"

She blew out a breath. "I don't know. He's ignored Austin his entire life—it never once even occurred to me he *would* show up. But not only has he," she said with fierce indignation, "he's here with a plan to disrupt Austin's life by dragging him away from everything he knows! God, I just want to—"

She stared down at her hands and reached for another calming breath as she uncurled the white-knuckled fists she'd unconsciously tightened into her fingers. Then she looked up at her friend. Gave her a slight half smile.

"It would be nice if I could say I'm being altruistic

here, that my concern is strictly for Austin's welfare. But, God, Tash, I really thought I'd get permanent guardianship. I can't bear the thought of him going that far away!"

"Of course you can't. You've been in his life since he was, what, two years old?"

"Nearer to three and a half before I really got close to him."

The other woman shrugged. "Close enough." She reached across the table to give her hands a squeeze. "And maybe it won't come down to that. You said Bradshaw is staying here until school's out, right? Maybe he'll get bored with playing daddy and go back before June." She frowned. "Okay, that's a shitty thing to wish for, too."

"I know." Jenny ground the heel of her hand against the headache beginning to throb between her brows. "It's not like I haven't considered the same thing. But it's hard to forget how long Austin fantasized about having a father before he finally put that dream away." She growled with frustration. "This is such a no-win situation. It's pretty much guaranteed that one or both of us is going to wind up hurt."

She leaned into the table. "But I've got to think like an adult. Because as much as it'll kill me to lose Austin, I'm even more afraid that Bradshaw will win his forgiveness—will make him *care*—then do something exactly like what you said and stomp the kid's heart to paste."

The moment the words left her mouth, however, she

thought of that glimpse she'd caught of…something. Something that had seethed in Jake Bradshaw's pale green eyes when he saw Austin for the first time. She wasn't sure what it had been, exactly. But it had caught her by surprise because she hadn't expected a guy who'd ignored his son since birth to harbor such strong emotions.

Then she shrugged it aside. *So what?* It was probably just impatience at having to be here, at having to deal with her and Austin.

All the same, she sat up straighter. "If he's telling the truth," she said slowly, "Jake Bradshaw is going to have legal custody of Austin."

"I'm not sure why he'd lie about it, since that's something easily checked," Tasha said.

"That's my thought, too, because you can be sure I will check. But if it is so… Well, he's right when he said that if I care about Austin, I have to help make the transition easier for him." Acknowledging it made her feel like howling.

Tasha nodded. "I'm sorry, Jen. But I think you're probably right. Look." She leaned into the table. "You can't do anything about it tonight, and I don't like the idea of you going home to brood. You said Austin's sleeping over at Nolan's, right?"

"Yes. Part of me is so relieved that I don't have to pretend in front of him. But you know me too well. Because as much as I'd love to tell you you're wrong about the brooding, I have a feeling that rat-

tling around the house alone is going to make tonight
seem like a dog year."

"So don't go home. Things quiet down around
here after seven. You can hang around here until
then, or run errands or whatever and come back.
Either way, I'll have Tiff close for me tonight. You
and I are going to the Anchor. There's always some
distraction to be had there. We can get stinkin' or
we can just feed the jukebox and knock 'em dead at
darts. Whataya say?"

She really wasn't in the mood for the local bar. But
neither did she want to go home to take up pacing
again. Plus, if she knew nothing else, she could rely
on one thing: being with Tasha would help. "Deal. I
think I'll hang here until you're ready. That'll give
me plenty of time to decide whether darts or getting
stinkin' is the best way to go."

CHAPTER THREE

JAKE COULDN'T SETTLE DOWN. He'd driven around the area to refamiliarize himself with the spots he remembered and to check out the changes—surprised at how many of the latter there were. Back at the inn, he'd explored both his suite, which had taken all of five minutes, and the grounds of his former in-laws' resort, which had at least used up a little time. He'd called room service to deliver his dinner, because he was too wired to sit in the dining room.

But now it was only six-thirty and the walls were closing in. He had to get out of here.

Grabbing his hoodie, he pulled it on, zipped up, then wrestled his sport jacket on over it as he headed for the beach. He'd walk into town. See if he couldn't kill some more time.

He barely glanced at the rugged, panoramic mountain range across the water that stopped the tourists in their tracks. Head down in the wind, hands jammed in his pockets, he strode purposefully along the boardwalk, one of the additions that was new to him.

Moments later, he reached Razor Bay—only to discover they'd already rolled up the streets.

"Shit." How could he have forgotten that? It used

to be just one more reason added to the many that'd had him dying to get out of this backwater burg. There was bugger all to do in the low season. Hell, it only offered a limited selection of distractions during the high.

The Sunset Café, Bella T's Pizzeria and a new Vietnamese sandwich place were still open, and those likely only because it was Friday night. At least in the summer both Harbor Street and Eagle Road were jumping until eleven.

Remembering Austin talking about his friend's mom getting them pizza, he almost went into Bella T's. He tried to convince himself that he had an urge to do so simply because the place was new to him and he was curious. But he wasn't that good a liar. He knew damn well the fuel driving that machine was the off chance of seeing his son.

Even if Austin was in there this very moment— and what were the odds of that?—did he really want a public face-off with the kid? Jenny was right: he needed to give Austin time to get used to the fact that he was back in town.

He didn't know why just thinking her name made a vision of his son's guardian dragon pop into his head. But not only could he see her shiny hair, those big dark eyes and smooth olive skin, the damn mental picture was high-def.

He blinked the image away. Where the hell had *that* come from? She was so not his type.

He gave his shoulders an impatient hitch, looking

for a more comfortable fit in his skin. The more he thought about it, the more his earlier idea—to have li'l Ms. Salazar help pave the way with Austin—seemed like the way to go. At the time it had merely been one of those throwaway ideas that sometimes popped off the top of his head. But it was a solid plan.

Of course, it was also predicated on her agreeing to it. And given her opinion of him, that was one big-ass *if.*

Suddenly recalling the Anchor, he headed for the narrow walkway that was cut between the General Store and Swanson's Ice Cream Shack. The pedestrian shortcut led to Eagle Road, which paralleled the long curve of Harbor Street and comprised the rest of the town's business district, and to the parking lot behind that. As Razor Bay's sole bar, if you didn't count the one off the lobby at The Brothers—which tonight he definitely did not—The Anchor was one place still bound to be open.

He spotted the white-framed mosaic sign he remembered the instant he cleared the tiled walkway connecting the two streets. It spelled out the bar's name in sea-hued bits of tile on the bump-out over the marine-blue building's three front windows. The same twin neon anchors from his youth flashed yellow and blue on either end of the sign, and what he'd swear were the same neon beer signs dotted the windows.

He felt an edge of anticipation and had to admit he was curious. He'd left town before he was old enough to be allowed in the bar. Back in the day, he'd tried to lay hands on some fake ID with the thought of going there, but it hadn't panned out.

He snorted. Hell, even if he'd scored the best fake identification ever produced, it wasn't as if there'd been a hope in hell he'd have gotten away with using it. Not in the Anchor. In a town this size, everyone pretty much knew who everyone else was.

Pulling open the door, he walked in.

Dimly lit, the interior sported dark wood-plank floors scuffed from years of foot traffic, and matching, if less beat-up, walls covered in black-framed photos that appeared to be black-and-white shots of midcentury Razor Bay. He wouldn't mind taking a closer look at those.

A long bar with tall stools took up most of the back wall, and the two blackboards behind it, whose chalk menus were highlighted by art lights, showed a surprising selection of microbrewery beers and ales. A jukebox, pinball machine and a couple of dartboards took up a small slice of real estate down at the end of the front wall to his right. Tables and chairs took up the rest of the floor, and a few small booths occupied the wall opposite the gaming section.

He didn't know what he'd expected, but this was a bar pretty much like you'd find anywhere, if a touch more hip than he'd anticipated. But at least he could kill a little time here with a beer and those photos.

"Well, would you look at what the cat dragged in," a deep voice drawled from one of the booths.

Jake froze midstride, and for a single hot second he was a fourth-grade boy again, forgetting for a moment that his dad had walked out on him and his mom, because he was finally on the much-coveted big kids' fourth-to-sixth-grade upper playground at Chief Sealth Elementary. He'd had one perfect moment—until a boy two grades older came up to him, gave him a shove that almost knocked him off his feet and said, "Heard you got what you deserved. If your tramp of a mama hadn't got herself knocked up, my dad would still be with me and my mom."

It had been a shock on every level because how many darn families did his until-recently-adored father *have?* And Jake sure hadn't started the new school year expecting to be pushed around by his previously unknown half brother. A brother, he'd learned over a course of several school-yard confrontations, whom their mutual father, Charlie Bradshaw, had totally ignored even when they'd lived in the same town—the way Charlie ignored *him* now that he'd moved on to a new family.

But the little flash down memory lane was just that—there one second and gone the next. Shaking off the mix of confusion and rage that dealings with Max Bradshaw had always given him, he strolled over. "Well, hey, big brother," he drawled right back. "Long time, no see. I hear somebody thought it was a good idea to give you a gun. Tell me that doesn't scare the shit out of the general populace."

"Oh, most people don't have a thing to worry about."

Max gave Jake a pointed look. "You, however—" His gaze grazed Jake's chest as if visualizing a bull's-eye.

It was never easy to tell when Max was serious and when he wasn't, but Jake gave him the same cool look either case would garner. "So what number wife are you up to now? Three? Four, maybe? Any nieces or nephews I oughta know about?"

The words had barely left his mouth when he felt an odd regret. He and Max actually shared several traits, and when their father had waltzed out of town, they'd had a narrow window of opportunity to bury the hatchet somewhere besides in each other's skull. After all, they were probably the only ones in Razor Bay who truly understood how the wreckage Charlie left behind affected the other. It had been a rare chance to take comfort in having *someone* who got it, someone with whom you didn't have to pretend you didn't give a damn that Charlie Bradshaw was a great dad as long as you were his current favorite, but that he forgot you even existed the moment he moved on. And they might have.

If hating each other's guts hadn't been so well ingrained by then.

Even in the dim light he could see his salvo cause something dark to flash across his half brother's deep-set eyes. But the other man merely shrugged a big shoulder. "No wives, no kids. You're the one who started early and followed in the old man's footsteps."

You opened yourself up for that one, Slick. But,

ouch. It was a direct hit, and one that gouged at a long-festering guilt, more than a decade old.

Because as much as he'd like to blow off his half brother's potshot as the usual sour grapes, Max wasn't wrong. When Jake's high school girlfriend Kari had gotten knocked up in their senior year, he had started out with good intentions, fiercely determined to man up in a way that his own dad never had. And for a while, he had done just that.

In the end, however, he'd turned out to be nothing but a chip off the old block.

The knowledge rankled now just as much as it had back then, so instead of acting cool and shrugging off Max's remark the way he should have, he snapped, "You don't know a damn thing about me, *bro*. You didn't when I was nine and you turned the big kids' playground into a battleground, and you sure as hell don't now. When are you gonna get it through your head? My mom and I didn't make the old man leave you and your mother, any more than whoever that other woman was made him leave us. When it comes to Charlie's wives and kids, he's got the attention span of a fruit fly."

His half brother dug his knuckles into his forehead just above the bridge of his nose. Then, dropping his hand to splay atop the scarred table, Max looked up at him. And blew out a breath. "Yeah," he agreed, his deep voice a tired rumble.

Jake took a seat in the booth across the table from Max. "You know what?" he said in a low voice.

"I don't have the heart for this anymore. I've got enough on my plate just trying to make up for my past and hoping to hell I do a decent enough job to get to know my kid. I don't have enough energy to fight you, too."

Max gave him a puzzled look. "You do get that you're handing me a whole shitload of ammunition, right?"

Jake shrugged. "You're gonna do what you're gonna do—it's not like I can stop you. So fuck it."

"Right." Max shifted in his seat. "Fuck it. We're not in high school anymore." He leveled a look on him. "Don't get the idea you're ever gonna be my bud, little Bradshaw. But I can probably stomach being around you now and then."

Jake had to swallow a grin at the "little Bradshaw" crack. That was a good one. He wasn't particularly small: he missed the six-foot mark by a fraction of an inch. But Max was a good six-three and twenty pounds heavier. "Give me a minute," he ordered. "I'm kinda overwhelmed here. I'm not sure I know how to handle so much enthusiasm coming my way." He shook his head as he met the gaze of the man across the table. "The thrill of it all just may kill me."

"We can only hope."

A cardboard Anchor Porter beer coaster landed on the table in front of him and he looked up at a cheery, college-age blonde.

She gave him a toothy grin. "Well, hey there, new blood. Haven't seen you before. Trust me, I'd remember." Then she waved the mild flirtation aside. "Get you boys something?"

"Him another table," Max said.

Jake flashed the waitress a smile. "My brother's such a kidder."

She did a double take. "Shut the front door! You two are *brothers?*"

"Half," Max emphasized. "We're half brothers."

"Half, whole." Jake shrugged. "What's the diff? Blood's blood, right?"

Max gave him a disgruntled glare. "Give it a rest, Jake…before I'm tempted to spill yours."

"Whatever you say, my brotha." He winked at the blonde. "Give old Bradshaw here another of whatever he's drinking and I'll have a Fat Tire."

"One Bud tap and a Fat Tire coming up."

"Budweiser?" Jake asked, turning his attention back to Max as the girl headed to the bar. "Seriously?"

Max rolled his muscular shoulders. "It's a good American beer. And it doesn't have a stupid name. Hell, I could've given you a fat lip for free."

"And have, on more than one occasion. But it's Fat *Tire,* philistine. I'm guessing you don't get out of this burg very often."

"Why would I want to? I've got everything I need right here."

Jake shuddered. If he had to stay in Razor Bay a second longer than it took to make Austin trust him, he'd open a vein.

The waitress was back with their beer almost before their exchange ended, and he dug his wallet out of his hip pocket, paid for the order and dropped a hefty tip on her tray.

Max studied him. "It's easy to tell you live in a big city."

"Why? Because I tip?"

His half brother scowled. "I tip. Maybe not fivers for a four-dollar bottle of beer, but I tip. But I was talking about that metrosexual thing you've got going."

"The hell you say!" He might like the amenities of a big city but, he'd never had a manicure or facial in his life.

"I do say." Max gave him a feral grin. "You're a pretty boy."

"I'm ruggedly handsome." He bounced a fist off his chest. "A *manly* man." Then he shrugged. "Still, you're right about the big city. I own a loft in Soho."

"We talking New York City?" Max grimaced, then unknowingly echoed his own sentiments. "Christ. I'd open a vein if I had to live there."

"How do you know? Have you ever been?"

"Nope. I've never had my balls waxed either, but I can tell you without a doubt that I wouldn't like it."

Unable to help himself, Jake laughed even as he hunched in a little over his own *cajones*. "Yeah, because the two things have so much in common. You ever been anywhere, Max?"

"Sure." He hitched a shoulder. "California. North Carolina. Afghanistan. Iraq."

"Of course. What else would a law-and-order type do but join the—what?" A laugh escaped him. "No, wait, this is a no-brainer. You couldn't be anything but a jarhead. Or I suppose one of those Navy SEALS or Green Beret dudes."

"Please. Like I'd join either of those pussy branches of the service. I was one of the few, the proud, boy."

"And now you're the sheriff of Nottingham."

"Deputy of Nottingham. The sheriff's about a hundred years old."

But Jake was barely listening. Hearing a raunchy feminine laugh on the other side of the room, his head snapped up. That couldn't possibly be...

His gaze cut through the crowd that was beginning to fill the watering hole, tracking the sound to its source. And discovered that—*hell*—not only could it be, it was. Jenny Salazar was at the bar, laughing with the bartender and another woman.

She looked different tonight. Not at all like the little girl he'd first mistaken her for. Her lips were red and soft looking. Her hair without those braids was longer than he'd realized, a shiny rippling curtain of dark against the red sweater she wore. And her—

"What the hell are you staring at?" Max twisted in his seat to look over his shoulder. Then with a nod he settled back. "Ah. Tasha. She has that effect on guys. Not sure why—it's not like she's drop-dead gorgeous. Still, she's got a way of stopping the show."

Jake tore his gaze away. Gave himself a mental smack to get his head back in the game. And discovered that even then he didn't have any idea what Max was babbling about. "Who?"

"Tasha Riordan. The strawberry blonde? That's not who you're looking at? Who then—*Jenny?*" He narrowed his eyes. "You don't want to go there."

That got his full attention. "I don't? That is, I really don't—my interest in her isn't like that." *At least not much.* He gave his head a shake. "But just to clarify, *why* don't I? Is she yours?" He didn't question too closely why the idea bugged him.

But his half brother seemed almost appalled by the idea. "No!"

"Okay. Some other guy's?"

He shook his head.

"She's a nun, then."

Max gave him a *what-the-fuck?* look. "Here's a thought. How 'bout you try not to be any more of an idiot than you already are."

"I'm groping in the dark here, bro. She a lesbian?"

"Jesus. No. She's just…sweet. Loyal. A good friend to everyone. Not someone for a guy like you to be messing with."

"Yeah? Does she roll over and wag her tail when you scratch behind her ears, too?"

Max scowled, but Jake was too familiar with the expression to be intimidated. "What? She's a woman, big *B*. You make her sound like an old dog."

"You don't understand."

"No shit. I thought she was a kid when I met her this afternoon, but she herself disabused me of that notion right from the get. I take it she's single, so I don't see the problem if some guy—not me, but someone—wanted to slap the moves on her. So if she's none of the things I've already mentioned, what does that leave? Terminal?" He shook his head. "No, the conversation I had with her didn't leave me with that impression—she's not inward looking enough. Leper?" He was enjoying his brother's disgust at his guessing game, until a sudden thought turned his blood to ice and drop-kicked the smile right off his face. "Christ. *Rape* victim?"

"*No.* Where do you come up with this shit?"

He shrugged. "I'm a journalist. I've seen things."

"I thought you were some hotshot photographer for *National Explorer.*"

"I am. Well, a photographer anyway. The hotshot part's still a work in progress. But just because most of my work is told through the lens of a camera, doesn't mean I'm not a questioning kind of guy." Jake glanced over at the woman under discussion once again. She and her friend had migrated to a table. The friend, who had taken a chair facing him, did have something, he admitted. But it was Jenny, sitting in profile to him, who commanded his attention.

Well, of course she did. She held considerable sway over any relationship he might forge with Austin.

He looked back at Max. "I talked to her for all

of maybe fifteen minutes this afternoon. So tell me about her. How does she fit into Austin's life?"

"She's like his sister."

"Yeah, I got that. What I don't get is, how did that happen? No way in hell they're related. Kathy was an only child, and Emmett had one older sister who never married."

Max shrugged. "She came here when she was fifteen—" He paused for a moment, thinking. "Sixteen?" He shook his head. "The exact age doesn't really matter. She came here as a teen in the midst of a huge scandal. I was home on leave when she hit town."

That caught Jake's attention, but his brother immediately gave the air a negligent swipe with one big-knuckled hand.

"Not her scandal. It was her old man's. He'd been all over the news because of some big swindle that crashed down around his ears and landed him in Monroe. Jenny came here with her mother." Max's face hardened. "Who, as far as I could tell, planted her skinny socialite ass in bed from the shame of it all, while her underage kid kept the two of them off the streets by doing housekeeping at The Brothers after school and on weekends."

"And Emmett and Kathy just invited two strangers with a questionable past to move into their home?" In a way it sounded like something they'd do. But in other ways, it wasn't like them at all, especially in light of Kari's death, which couldn't have been more than a year or two before that time.

Max shook his head. "That was a while later. When they first got here, Jenny and her mother rented the Bakers' little place."

"Christ." He shifted uncomfortably. "That old rehabbed chicken coop?"

"Yeah. Where her mom just curled up and died. I'm talking literally. From what I heard, the woman couldn't live with her loss of status and just willed herself to die. But it took her a while. By the time she passed, Jenny was a senior and had been working for the Pierces almost two years."

"So—what? They just replaced Kari with her?" Even as the words left his mouth, he knew he was the last person with any room for righteous indignation.

But somehow that didn't stop him from feeling it.

Max gave him a look that suggested he was thinking the same thing. But he merely said, "The one time I went to their house to see Austin, I was strongly discouraged, so I'm hardly an expert on their mind-set."

That sidetracked Jake. "You wanted to see Austin?"

"I thought I should meet my nephew."

He simply stared at Max for a moment before admitting, "It never occurred to me you were his uncle. But you are, aren't you?"

"Not as far as Emmett and Kathy were concerned," Max said drily. "They said considering my background with you and the fact that the little dude didn't know me from Adam, they didn't see the point in my spending time with him—that he'd only be confused." He shrugged. "They were probably right. I mean, you and I never acted like real brothers. Why should my relationship with your get be any different? But I always wondered if maybe I shouldn't have pressed them a little harder. Done more. Hell, I put more effort into getting to know the boys over at Cedar Village," he added, naming the home for delinquent boys on Orilla Road outside town.

Then he shook his head. "That's not what we were talking about, though. Because one thing I do know about the Pierces is that they sure as hell mourned Kari. So I doubt replacing her with Jenny entered into the equation. I think they saw a hardworking girl who was the age their daughter had been when she died and who was struggling to make ends meet— and thought they could help. In the end, I believe they came to think of Jenny as the next best thing to a daughter."

"What about her? What did she get out of the relationship, besides the obvious?"

Max's eyes narrowed. "I don't like what you're implying, bro."

"She went from the Bakers' chicken coop to the Pierces' big Craftsman."

"Where she refused every enticement to live a life of leisure." Max looked him in the eyes. "And you know she could have. But Jenny kept working at the inn and, after graduating, put herself through college.

With no help from the Pierces, from everything I've ever heard. She earned her promotions with good, old-fashioned hard work. And she moved out of that big Craftsman. Bought the little cabin she lives in from Emmett." Max gave him a hard look. "So, you don't want to be calling that kettle black, pot."

Jake scrubbed his hands over his face. "I know. I know."

"I'll tell you what *I* think she got from her relationship with Emmett and Kathy. They were considerably older than her own parents, and I think she looked on them as sort of grandparents. You gotta know how they spoiled Kari—"

He nodded. God, did he ever.

"They did the same thing with Austin, but Jenny curbed it wherever she could. So the kid is less spoiled than his mother was. And she flat-out refused to let them spoil her."

"Yeah, she's a goddamn paragon," Jake muttered, staring across the room at her profile.

"Pretty much," Max agreed cheerfully. "A helluva lot more than you can ever hope to be."

Jake abruptly became aware that the strawberry blonde was watching him watch Jenny, and even as he noticed, she leaned into the table to say something to her friend. Jenny turned to look his way, a friendly, interested smile on her face.

It turned cool as the evening wind when she saw him.

"Shit."

Max glanced over his shoulder, then looked back at him with raised eyebrows. "And you call yourself a big-city sophisticate? Hell, even us rubes know if you stare at a female like a dog at a juicy bone long enough—"

"The hell I did!"

Max thrust an authoritative forefinger at him. "Dog." The finger thrust in Jenny's general direction. "Juicy bone." He shook his head. "Jesus, kid. I'm embarrassed to acknowledge some of the same blood runs in our veins. It was only a matter of time until you were busted."

CHAPTER FOUR

JENNY STROLLED INTO THE INN'S dining room the following morning, only to rock to a halt in the doorway when she saw Jake Bradshaw sitting alone at one of the window tables. How did he do that? How the hell did he manage to be everywhere she went?

Wasn't it enough that he'd thrown a monkey wrench into her get-away-from-it-all evening with Tasha last night? Now he had to invade her dining room, as well? This was *her* time of the morning, dammit, her territory, her inn.

Okay, maybe the latter wasn't hers in the legal sense, aside from the portion Emmett had so generously bequeathed her. But in all the ways that mattered, she claimed ownership. The Brothers Inn had been a major part of her life since she'd arrived in Razor Bay at sixteen. Hell, it was the reason she'd come to this town in the first place—the promise of a job when the pampered life she'd known had disintegrated in the wake of her father's arrest and incarceration.

And ever since Emmett had promoted her to general manager, she'd made a habit of coming to the dining room each morning at the end of the breakfast shift to eat that much-touted most important meal of the day. She'd found it particularly beneficial since Austin had moved in with her. Breakfast at the inn was her way of easing into the day, a transition between getting the teen off to school and diving into her busy shift at the inn.

Striding across the room, she smiled at or murmured hellos to the few guests still finishing up their meals, before stopping at Jake's table.

"What are you doing here?" Okay, so it was obvious, given the topped-off coffee cup at his elbow and the plate containing a smear of egg yolk, an untouched bunch of red grapes and a single crust of toast, which he'd pushed out of the way to accommodate the *Bremerton Sun* he was reading.

But it was the best she could do when she wasn't allowed to say, *You breathe, therefore you bother me—get the hell out of my dining room.*

"Hey." He looked up from the newspaper spread out on the table. Flashed her a million-dollar smile. "I'm having breakfast. You, too?"

She crossed her arms beneath her breasts and tapped the toe of a fabulous-if-she-did-say-so-herself Steve Madden Mary Jane. It reverberated a soft tattoo against the hardwood floor.

Jake's smile faded. "Is it a problem that I'm staying here? Do you want me to leave?"

Yes! The moment Austin had left this morning, she'd put in a call to the Pierces' lawyer to discuss her chances of keeping the boy with her now that his absentee father had stated a willingness to fight for custody. Already feeling ragged from the results of that conversation, learning that blood relatives are almost always chosen over a nonrelated contestant, she wished nothing more than for Jake Bradshaw to go far, far away.

And never come back.

But he'd made it pretty clear that wasn't going to happen. And she knew the bastard had been right when he'd told her that either she could make things easier for Austin, or she could stick to her guns and likely make them a lot more difficult. So she sighed and dropped her arms to her sides.

"No. We don't make a habit of turning customers away at The Brothers just because we don't like their looks." Hearing herself, she almost blew a pithy little raspberry, but managed to sink her teeth into her lower lip before she could follow through on the impulse. But, please. She doubted anyone had *ever* turned this guy away over his looks. "Or their history. Not if they aren't currently doing anything wrong."

He raised his eyebrows. "But it's just a matter of time, eh?"

"You said it, not me."

He laughed. "You're not shy about trying to kick my teeth down my throat, are you? I like that about you."

She gave him her politest GM smile. "Always happy to oblige."

"I bet you are." He kicked the chair across from him away from the table. "Have a seat."

The response that rose to her lips was very un-GM-like, not to mention an anatomical impossibility. *Austin,* she reminded herself firmly. *I have to consider Austin first and foremost.*

She sat. "Thank you. I'm not sure I've ever received an invitation so suave."

He grinned. "It's my big-city polish."

Dammit, she didn't want to like anything about this guy, but she couldn't stop the corners of her lips from twitching upward in appreciation. Then the decision she'd made after a night spent tossing and turning slammed front and center.

And the smile dissolved.

"I gave your request a lot of thought," she said. "And I've decided to do what I can to make Austin's transition as easy on him as possible."

He sat straighter in his seat. "*Thank* you."

"Like I told you yesterday, I'm not doing this for you. And you might want to hold the thanks, anyway, because I don't know if you'll like my take on how you should handle things."

"Lay it on me."

"For starters, I wouldn't tell him your plans to haul him back to New York yet, if I were you."

His brows drew together. "You don't think he should be prepared?"

A plate with scrambled eggs, toast and a ramekin of yogurt, blueberries and handmade granola was slid onto the table in front of her, and Jenny looked up at the waitress, giving her a smile. "Thanks, Brianna."

"No problem." The young woman turned Jenny's cup over in its saucer and filled it with coffee. "Can I get you anything else?"

"No, thank you." Glancing around, she saw that she and Jake were the only diners left—not that there'd been that many to begin with. "Go grab your own breakfast. And tell the crew to work around us if we're still here when they're ready to set up for lunch." A chore they performed as soon as the breakfast crowd cleared out and they'd eaten their meals.

The girl shot her a grin. "Will do."

She watched Brianna walk away, then turned back to Jake. "I absolutely believe Austin needs to be prepared," she said, picking up the conversation. "But if you lead off with the fact you're taking him from Razor Bay, he'll shut down on you so fast it'll make your head spin—and it will only take you that much longer to gain his trust. Look, you might be accustomed to packing up and taking off at a moment's notice, but trust me, Austin is not."

He studied her. "What makes you think I am?"

"Please," she said with dismissive scorn. "There's a wealth of stuff about you on the internet."

"You looked me up?"

"Of course." She tipped her head. "Do you find my assessment off the mark?"

He hitched one shoulder. "No, that's pretty accurate."

"So you're used to living life on the fly. You're also an adult. He's a kid who's lived in one place his entire life."

"And is probably dying for a change."

"Why, because you were at his age? That's something you should definitely discuss with him, but aside from longing for a daddy when he was younger, I can't say that I've ever witnessed signs of Austin being dissatisfied with his lot."

He started patting his chest and her eyebrows drew together. "What are you doing?"

"You slipped that knife in so sweet and slick, I want to be sure I don't bleed to death before I even realize I've been shivved."

She shrugged. "Put yourself in his place for a minute instead of trying to shoehorn him into yours. I know you're getting up there in years but—"

A bark of laughter interrupted her. "Jesus, you're a pisser."

Jenny ignored him. "—try to remember back to when you were thirteen. How open would *you* have been if a man you'd never met suddenly inserted himself into your life and, without giving you so much as a moment to get to know him, told you he was gonna haul you away from everything you knew to a life different from anything you could imagine, clear on the other side of the country?"

"In all honesty?" He gave her an ironic smile.

"I probably would've burned rubber packing my bag. But in the interests of that putting-myself-in-his-place thing, I agree that a different kind of kid might be pissed." He gave a grudging nod. "I'll keep my plans to myself until we get to know each other."

"And I'll work on trying to get him to spend some time with you."

"Thank you."

She shrugged and picked up her fork. She'd prefer to move to another table where she could eat her breakfast in peace, but for the sake of cooperation, she stayed put. But the sourdough toast and eggs in her standing Saturday order tasted like wood chips and glue.

He didn't try to talk to her while she forced herself to eat every bite. For a while she appreciated it. But as the silence dragged on, she felt an antsy need to fill it with something.

Anything.

She shifted in her chair. Set her fork down and looked at him across the table.

Got hung up for a minute on his eyes.

Stop that! Dammit, what *was* it about him? She'd never been one to go all crazy over a handsome face. Yet with him—well, it was scary how unlike herself she felt when she looked at him too long or too closely. She was so not the bubbleheaded *Ooh, what pretty eyes you have—what's your sign* type.

So why did she look at this man and feel darn near that vacuous?

Giving herself a mental head-smack now, she sat a bit straighter in her seat. "Why did it take you so damn long to get here after Emmett died?"

She almost crowed in self-approval, but managed to confine herself to a silent *Thatagirl. Put him on the spot.*

He leveled those glorious green eyes at her. "The phone call was made to my home rather than my assistant—"

"Maybe because no one knew you had an assistant," she snapped.

He sighed. "Look, I stipulate that everything is my fault, okay?"

Jenny reined herself in, because these knee-jerk reactions weren't helping. "I'm sorry," she said and put real effort into sounding as if she actually meant it. She gave him the slightest nod. "Go on."

"Said the queen to the peasant," he said drily.

Shooting him her snootiest look, she twirled her hand to urge him to get *on* with it.

He only laughed. "It was a perfect storm of lousy luck. The housekeeper had been with me less than a month when I left on this trip, so by the time it occurred to her to contact Lucinda—that's my assistant—the news was several weeks old. I was photographing the reefs and the Karangetang volcano in the Sangihe-Talaud Archipelago of Northern Sulawesi at the time. It's remote, it's freaking monsoon season, which our scheduler should have known before he set the damn trip up, and we only got access to a satellite phone when we came back to Minahasa about every third weekend or so." He shrugged. "Even when I heard about it, I was obligated for an additional six days. Then it took time to get a flight to the Philippines and even more time to get a flight from there to Seattle. I don't go to the most accessible spots in the world."

"So even if you heard right away, you wouldn't have been here any sooner?"

"I had a contract! Would you have left this inn in the lurch?"

"For Austin? In a New York minute."

His expression went blank. "I genuflect to your superior parenting skills. But I'm trying here, okay?"

And since Jenny had caught a glimpse of genuine pain cross his eyes before he slapped on a poker face, she nodded. For the first time she really saw that he was, indeed, trying—and that maybe this wasn't as easy for him as he'd made it appear up until now. "Okay. I guess the important thing is that you're here now. But you've gotta understand that this isn't going to be easy."

"I know," he said wearily. "Believe me, I get it that I've got a lot to make up for."

She pushed her plate away, sat a bit taller and reached for her coffee cup, wrapping her hands around it in an attempt to warm her cold, cold fingers. Despite the lip service she'd given, a part of her must have secretly hoped this was something that would simply disappear if she wished hard enough.

Instead, it was growing more real, more concrete, by the second. She drew in a deep breath, then quietly exhaled. Replaced her cup in its saucer and pressed her hands, fingers splayed, against the cool wood of the tabletop to disguise the faint tremor they'd developed.

"Give Austin time and don't bullshit him," she told him quietly, "and he'll likely come to love you. He adored the idea of you when he was little."

Jake leaned into the table. Slid his own long-fingered hands across its surface as if to touch her. But he halted their progress when his fingertips were less than an inch from hers.

She hated that the near touch set up a series of quivers deep inside.

"And you'll help me?" he demanded.

"I said I would, didn't I?"

He nodded.

"Then I will."

Even though it'd likely rip her heart right out of her breast to do so.

"BRADSHAW! GET YOUR head outta the clouds and pay attention!"

Austin literally jerked at the sound of Coach Harstead's brisk bellow—and raised a baseball mitt-encased hand to acknowledge the reprimand. "Sorry, coach!" Drawing a deep breath, he forced himself to refocus on the Bulldogs' Wednesday practice.

God, it was hard, though. His so-called father had been trying to pin him down for the past week and a half, wanting to talk and *bond* and shit. Austin had been doing his best to avoid the guy, but surprisingly, Jenny, who he'd assumed would be the last person wanting him to spend time with the man, hadn't been much help. She actually thought he should be—how had she put it?—*open-minded*.

My ass. Resettling his cap in front, he narrowed his eyes on the batter. His friend Lee was up. Dude was right-handed with a tendency to pull the ball, so ninety percent of his hits came straight to where Austin played shortstop, between second and third base. "Come to Mama," he murmured.

Yet even as he concentrated on being ready for it, he wondered where his "dad" had been when he'd actually *wanted* a father. Nodamnwhere, that's where. Or maybe, given the guy's big-deal job, everywhere.

Everywhere except Razor Bay.

The crack of a ball off the bat focused his attention once again and, seeing Lee's line drive arc to the left of him, Austin got himself in position. A second later he snagged the ball out of the air, feeling it hit his mitt with a satisfyingly meaty *thwonk,* and winged it to the second baseman to tag Oliver Kidd, who should have stayed put on first.

"Good work, Bradshaw!" Coach Harstead called. Then to the rest of the boys, he said, "That's a classic example of the double play that frequently happens when you hit to shortstop. So let's all work on not doing that, whataya say?"

Stoked over his play, Austin's concentration improved for the rest of the practice. He actually felt pretty good by the time Coach called it quits. It was a nice little break from the stress he'd been feeling this week with his dad back in town.

Nolan came up and slapped him on the back. "Nice play with Lee and Oliver."

He grinned. "Yeah, I did okay for once. Usually Coach catches me at my worst."

"Nah. He knows you're good. Maybe even all-star material—"

"Austin."

He stiffened all over at the sound of Jake's voice and, schooling his expression, turned to face him, giving a sullen shrug of acknowledgment. Making up his mind to play it cool, however, he tried real hard not to scowl.

But, jeez.

The guy didn't resemble *any* of his friends' dads. He was younger, for one thing. And even if he *wanted* to talk to him, it wasn't like he'd have the first idea what to say. Jake had like a billion-dollar camera slung around his neck—and between the hot-shit globe-trotting photographs he took for some famous magazine and the way he *looked*—like an action-movie guy or something—well, it could be sorta intimidating. If Austin gave a rip about that kind of stuff.

Which he didn't.

Jake turned to Nolan. "Your mother called Jenny," he said. "She had to take your little brother to the doctor. It's nothing for you to worry about," he assured the boy, "but because she's hung up, I'm here to give you two a ride."

Crap! Still, there wasn't a lot they could do about this plan—not when it had the parental stamp of approval. So by unspoken agreement, he and Nolan tumbled into the back of Jake's Mercedes BlueTEC SUV that everybody and his brother had asked Austin about, as if *he* would be the first to know anything about it—*not!*—and visited with each other, ignoring their driver.

When Jake pulled into the driveway at Austin's friend's house a short while later, Nolan opened the back door but stopped to say, "Thanks, Mr. Bradshaw."

Austin, who was damned if he'd thank Daddy Dearest for anything, simply nodded. "Yeah," he said, climbing out of the SUV in Nolan's wake. He met Jake's eyes when he reached back in to grab his pack. "Tell Jenny I'm doing my homework with Nolan," he said, and slammed the door shut. Then he turned and stalked away.

He refused to feel guilty over the flash of disappointment he'd spotted on the face of a guy he'd assumed didn't need anyone.

CHAPTER FIVE

JAKE WATCHED UNTIL THE KIDS disappeared through the front door of Nolan's house. "Well, that went fucking swell." Blowing out a breath, he put the Mercedes in gear and backed down the driveway. Now what did he do?

He'd expected to get a little more out of the opportunity Jenny had presented him in the wake of Rebecca Damoth's frantic phone call than to receive the invisible chauffeur treatment. Grumbling to himself to avoid acknowledging the hollow that had formed in his gut when his son resolutely ignored him, he drove aimlessly around Razor Bay.

He had to admire the irony. When he'd heard the news about Emmett and realized that this was his final chance to take responsibility for the parenting he'd abdicated so many years ago, what should have been a cut-and-dried decision wasn't. He hated to admit it, but part of him had been seriously tempted to simply continue doing what he'd been doing. In the end, however, *not a damn thing* wasn't an option. He was tired of the guilt. He might be able to shove it aside for blocks of time, but it always came back to haunt him.

Maybe he was like those chicks who were only drawn to men who treated them like shit. Because the more his kid ignored or tried to avoid him, the more fascinated he found himself.

Spotting the sign for the public access to the canal at the north end of town, he turned off the road into its long parking area and drove through the lot to the double-wide boat ramp, not stopping until his tires were a few feet shy of the water. The tide had turned but was only about halfway to high. He turned off the ignition and, tapping his fingers on the steering wheel, stared out at the canal.

Not only was it midweek with most people at work, the day was gray as a bucket of day-old fish guts, the mountains obscured by liverish rain clouds too dense and weighty to push beyond the stratum of those stacked upon them. The parking lot didn't contain a single vehicle with attached trailer, and Jake had his doubts that even the most intrepid, boat-happy sailor from Bangor—the naval station on the other side of Kitsap—would be hauling a boat down to the launch today.

He climbed out of the SUV, stepped off the paved launch and walked to the water's edge.

It had been windy during the week and a half he'd been in Razor Bay, but today not so much as a breeze stirred. The skies looked as though they might open up at any minute, but for now they were dry. Squatting, he selected a few flat stones from the rocky beach then surged back upright, took a step back with his right foot and skimmed one across the water's flat, mirrorlike surface. It skipped four times before sinking. He pulled another out of his jeans pocket and let it fly, as well.

He'd envisioned making at least a little progress with his son by now, but Austin avoided him like a case of the Asian clap. How was he supposed to get to know him if the boy was either impossible to find or faded like smoke in the wind the few times Jake could locate him?

It didn't help that he was getting that closed-in feeling Razor Bay inevitably generated in him and, agitation building, he abandoned the lightweight skipping stones and culled some honest-to-God rocks—several with razor-edged oysters attached—from the beach. He hurled them, one after the other, as far as he could throw them. Each made a nice, solid *kerplunk,* sending up a decent splash as they struck the water.

That was where his satisfaction ended.

At the rate he was going, Austin would be thirty before he was ready to move with him to New York. Jake needed to get things moving at a faster clip than he'd managed so far.

Frustration at his failure to make progress bit deep. Dammit, he was accustomed to dealing with problems in a brisk, competent manner. He spent a good deal of every year in far-off places where situations without easy solutions regularly arose. Yet, when faced with dilemmas, he was the guy you could count on to dig in and find ways to fix them.

That wasn't what he'd been doing here. And the hell of it was, whenever he bent his mind toward finding a way to break the ice with his son, instead of working with its usual efficiency, his brain turned into a barren moonscape.

Tires crunched over the scattering of pinecones that had dropped from the evergreen trees dotting the parking lot, but Jake had no interest in seeing who'd arrived. What did he care if someone decided to overlook the less than ideal weather conditions? Hell, as far as that went, why shouldn't they? It might be a butt-ugly day, but the canal was calm for the first time since he'd arrived in this godforsaken town.

Hunkering down on the beach next to the paved boat ramp, he culled a new arsenal of the largest rocks he could find. The mood he was in, he'd welcome the opportunity to lob a boulder or two, but the beach wasn't exactly littered with those.

He was aware in a disinterested corner of his mind that the vehicle hadn't swung around to back a trailer down the ramp alongside his SUV. Instead, a car door opened and closed behind him and, as he rose to his feet to throw the first rock, he heard the gritty sound of shoes kissing sand-dusted pavement. Ignoring it, he hurled another rock, then another.

"Tourists pay big bucks for access to that water," Max said from behind him. "They expect it to be there the next time they show up. So keep that up and

I'm gonna have to write you a ticket for reef building within twenty feet of the shoreline."

Hearing the deep tones of his half brother's voice
gave him the usual screw-you jolt of irritation—but
laced this time with a new, unexpected thread of pleasure. He shrugged off the latter as a fluke, since his
pleasure receptors and Max were a foreign pairing.

"Twenty feet?" he demanded, turning to face
Max. "Please. I could throw these babies thirty in
my sleep."

Max's mouth curved up on one side. "I'm guessing algebra wasn't your long suit."

"True." His own lips quirked. "Business majors
don't need no stinkin' algebra." A degree he'd pursued in order to prove he was the financial achiever
his father wasn't. Not that Charlie Bradshaw hadn't
provided for his family—whoever that might have
been at any given moment. But where he had been a
middling salesman, Jake had an intrinsic knack with
money. More important, he'd had an urge to be more
successful than his father. To be better in every way.

The recollection wiped the smile from his face.
Because look how well that had worked out for him.
His precautions had failed, Kari had gotten pregnant
and he hadn't stuck around to be a father.

He wasn't the least bit better than the old man.
And in some ways was maybe even worse.

He eyed Max as he approached. His half bro wore
a khaki shirt and black tie under a military-style
black wool V-neck sweater with reinforced shoulders,

elbows and forearms. Velcro-closure cotton epaulets decorated each shoulder, a badge was pinned to his chest, and gold, black and green shield-shaped patches, each sporting a spread-winged eagle and the Razor Bay Sheriff's Office designation, decorated the sweater's upper arms. He wore jeans and a black web utility belt that bristled with the tools of his trade—not the least of which was a serious-looking gun. "You following me, Deputy Dawg?"

"Yeah, because I live in awe of the wonder that is you." Max let the absurdity hang in the air a moment, then made a rude noise. "Get over yourself. I heard the navy's doing maneuvers out here this week, and I've stopped by every day to see if I can catch the show." He gave Jake a comprehensive once-over. "What's your excuse?"

Resurrecting as it did his many recent failures, the query made him want to snarl. Jake did his best, however, to shrug the mood aside. He intended to give Max's question the brush-off, as well. Their relationship was a long way from either opening an emotional vein in front of the other. He didn't share that kind of relationship with anyone.

So he was astonished to hear himself admit, "I'm trying to get to know my kid, but if he can't outright avoid me, he acts like I'm see-through." He looked over at Max. "Did you know he plays shortstop for the Junior League?"

"Yeah. I've seen him play." Jake must have looked as astounded as he felt, because Max said with cool authority, "I'm the deputy sheriff. It's my civic duty to keep tabs on the kids in this town."

Aw, man, he was *so* full of shit if he thought Jake bought that. But before he could call him on it, Max said, "He plays the same position as you, huh? I heard between baseball and your grades, you got yourself a full-boat scholarship to some fancy East Coast university." He hooked his thumbs in the webbed belt. "It can't be easy, following in your footsteps."

Jake looked at him in surprise, then wasn't sure why he was so bowled over. Both of them probably knew a great deal about each other. God knew that once upon a time he had kept close tabs on everything Max did, rationalizing that it was simply good business practice to keep track of the enemy. The truth was he'd always been unwillingly fascinated by this guy who shared the same blood but was a dedicated adversary.

"I doubt there was ever a comparison," he said now. "I was out of the local sport scene for probably half a dozen years before Austin even attended his first T-ball practice. It wouldn't have been like trying to fill *your* big shoes when they were practically still smokin'." He waved the comparison aside. "In any case, from what I saw today, he's good." A headache sent preliminary scouts to see about the possibility of setting up camp in his temples. "That's no thanks to my influence, either."

Max gave him a level look. "So why did you walk?"

Jake stilled, his heartbeat a solid *thudthudthud* in his chest. "You really interested in knowing?" Who would have thought Max, of all people, would be the one to come right out and ask? No one else had since he'd been back.

"Not really." Max started to turn away, but then stopped and gave his shoulders an impatient roll before meeting Jake's gaze head-on. "No, that's not true. I am."

Girding himself, Jake remained silent for a moment. Then he drew a deep breath and blew it out. "For as long as I can remember, I wanted out of this town." He looked out at the glassy water. "Kari and I made a lot of big plans to move somewhere cosmopolitan, and I spent our entire junior year plotting ways to make it happen that wouldn't end up with me flipping burgers for the rest of my life."

He shoved his hands in his pockets. "Truth is, I had plans long before I met her. I'd been working toward that scholarship since Junior high. When it came through, I thought we were finally on our way."

He looked over at Max. "Then, barely a month into our senior year, the fucking condom broke."

"You stepped up and married her, though. And from what I hear, took a job at the inn."

"Because I didn't want to be another Charlie Bradshaw, y'know?"

"Hell, yes. We've got that in common." Max studied him for a moment. "You must have loved her a lot."

An unamused laugh escaped him. "Like that ever lasts," he said dismissively. "She went almost overnight from the fun head cheerleader I knew to a cranky, complaining shrew who was convinced I'd ruined her life. Not that I was any better. I was miserable working the front desk at The Brothers, and it made me damn moody."

"Then she died."

"Yeah." Digging his fingertips into a headache that now thumped full force, he turned his back on the water, feeling vestiges of the horror he'd experienced at the sight of the blood-soaked sheets when she'd started hemorrhaging. "They send people home from the hospitals too damn fast these days. If she'd still been there they probably could've stopped the bleeding. But they discharged her, and within the space of a few short hours, she was just…gone. And I found myself with sole responsibility for this wrinkly, leaky little creature I had no idea how to parent. When Emmett and Kathy offered to care for him while I got my degree, I jumped at the chance."

And, eaten up with guilt, he'd hated himself for it. He had turned into the very thing he'd sworn he never would: a chip off the old block. Here his wife had died tragically young—yet had he been crushed? Had he stuck around? No, sir. He'd never wished her dead, but his dirty little secret was he'd been beyond relieved not to be stuck in a nowhere position in a nowhere town with a wife he'd fallen out of love with.

At least Charlie had loved him for a while. Jake hadn't felt anything but panic when he'd looked at his son.

Max looked as uncomfortable hearing all this shit as Jake was at telling it. No doubt his brother was on TMI overload, and his gaze slid past Jake's shoulder. Then he stood straighter. "Hey, what do you know?" he said with a casualness that was a little overplayed. "There's a couple of cutters. The Trident's likely not far away."

Grateful beyond measure for the change of subject—for anything that would rescue them from this dangerous talking-about-*feelings* territory—Jake turned to look.

There was nothing to see except a couple of mid-size navy boats cruising a half mile or so from the far shore, but he went over to his car all the same to retrieve his camera from the passenger seat. Back on the beach, he watched with Max as the boats navigated an obviously circumscribed area.

Nothing happened, and perhaps to fill the long silence between them, Max suddenly said, "I'm sorry about your mom. I heard about it when I was in Camp Lejeune."

Jake nodded, his eyes still on the glassy water. "Thanks. Her having a heart attack wasn't something anyone expected. She was only forty-six." He turned to look at Max. "I'm surprised anyone here even knew about it—she moved to California the same time I started college."

Max made a wry face. "Small-town connections, little Bradshaw. She kept in touch with Maureen Gilmore, who was friends with my mother."

"Is your mom still in town?"

"No. She's living in England, of all places."

"Why of all places?"

"My mom is filled with a small-town prejudice against any town bigger than Razor Bay—never mind big cities in a foreign country. But she met a guy from London in the dining room of the inn one night, and that was all she wrote."

The Ohio-class black nuclear submarine suddenly surfaced from the depths and they turned their attention to it. Nearly as long as two football fields, sleek as a shark and quieter than death, it was an impressive, ominous sight. "That doesn't make me want to break into a chorus of 'Yellow Submarine,'" Jake said, raising the Nikon D3 to his eye.

Max laughed. "No shit. But I never get tired of watching it. It's like the Darth Vader of submarines. Strategic deterrence at its best."

He lowered the camera long enough to shoot the other man a sardonic glance. "Spoken like a true soldier boy."

"Wasn't a soldier, sonny. I told you before, I'm a Marine."

"Ex."

Max snorted. "No such thing as an ex-Marine. Former, maybe, if you wanna be picky about it."

"Whatever." Jake shot a couple frames of Max,

who immediately scowled at him. "So, tell me. I know there's more than one of these subs stationed at Bangor—so why are they all called the Trident?"

A bark of laughter exploded out of Max. "For a guy with a bachelor of business from a fancy u—"

"I never actually got that degree," he interrupted. "I interned with *National Explorer* my junior year, got a once-in-a-lifetime opportunity to show my photography skills when their usual photographer was laid low with dysentery, and never went back to school."

Max nodded. "Explains why you're not the brightest bulb, I guess. None of the subs are named that. There's eight of them out of Bangor, and except for the USS *Henry M. Jackson,* in honor of our late, great Senator Scoop Jackson, they're all named after states. Alaska, Alabama, Nebraska—and who cares what all. Tridents are the missiles they're packing."

"Huh. Who knew?"

"Not you, obviously."

A short while later the submarine submerged as quietly as it had come up, and Max abruptly morphed from fairly friendly for a guy who "wasn't ever going to be your bud" to blank-faced deputy. He stepped back. "I've got work to do," he said and pointed to where Jake's SUV was blocking half an access that nobody was using. "Get that off the ramp," he growled. Then without another word, he turned and strode up the slope in question to his rig.

Leaving Jake with an inexplicable smile on his face.

WORRY OVER HIS NONPROGRESS with Austin had replaced the unexpected moment of good humor by
the time he got back to the inn. He headed straight
for Jenny's office.

He heard her voice before he reached it. "...fore-
casting staff needs for next week, and I need to set
up a meeting with you before you leave for the day
to discuss doing one of those Groupon or Living-
Social discounts. Reservations will get the immediate brunt of extra work," she said, then laughed.
"Well, if it does what I'm hoping, at any rate. What's
a good time for you?"

He stopped in the open doorway. Jenny sat facing the door, but twisted slightly to the left as she
glanced back and forth between a weekly planner
and a spreadsheet laid across the desk, the phone re-
ceiver wedged between her ear and a hunched shoulder. Light from the overhead fixtures and the lamp
on her desk detailed the creamy curve of high cheekbones and picked out the sheen of her dark hair on
either side of her center part. She'd tucked the long
layers behind her ears, and they tumbled over the
girly, not-quite-but-damn-near sheer fabric of her
little black blouse, their blunt ends curving slightly
in alternating lengths against the petite thrust of her
breasts. He could almost distinguish the outline of a
black bra beneath the top.

If he didn't mind giving himself eyestrain.

"Five o'clock is perfect," she said. "I'll see you
then." Hanging up the phone, she leaned forward,

made a notation in the planner, then turned her attention to the worksheet.

He could have sworn he didn't make a sound, but her head suddenly jerked up and she looked straight at him, eyes startled and slender fingers spread like starfish on the oversize spreadsheet. And for just an instant their gazes melded with a spark that wasn't solely on his side.

His whole body perked up.

He didn't get it. He'd come away from his relationship with Kari with a carved-in-stone belief that there was no such thing as true commitment and a determination to never again put himself in the position of testing that belief. From the age of eighteen, he'd chosen women who knew the score. They understood they'd have a good time but that any relationship with him had a finite shelf date.

Jenny was so not the cool, casual-sex kind he usually went for. Yet she still had a way of making his hormones come to attention and lock on her like heat-seeking missiles.

Eye on the prize, Bradshaw! Shoving the attraction down where it belonged—in the subterranean depths of his mind—he stepped inside and for a second wasn't sure where to start.

Her brow furrowed. "Are you okay? Can I do something for you?"

He walked over to her desk, spread his hands against its messy surface and leaned into them. His head drooped for a nanosecond before pride put some bone back in his spine. "He wouldn't even talk to me."

"Who wouldn—?" Jenny blinked. "Austin?" The breath she exhaled wasn't one of those exasperated, big sighs that females excelled at, but it wasn't exactly a "poor baby," either. "And you think this is my problem why?" she asked drily. "I gave you an opportunity. What you did with it was up to you."

"I know." Noticing a luscious, amazing whisper of scent rising off her—a female aroma he could've happily gone all day without detecting—he straightened and took a step back. "I do know that. Damn." Using one hand to massage the knot of tension from the back of his neck, he tried to explain. "It's just— they got in the backseat." He could see she didn't have a clue what he was talking about. "Austin and Nolan, they got into the backseat like I was the damn chauffeur!"

The delighted laugh that rolled out of her lit her up like a little girl presented with a princess dress. But even as he was drawn to her unfettered enjoyment, even as he felt a spark of warmth take root low in his gut and high in his chest from the sound of her mirth, he found himself snapping, "It's not funny!"

Amused appreciation for the boy's tactics dropping from her face, Jenny's laughter died even as her warm brown eyes sobered. "Yes," she said quietly, "it actually is. It's rebellious, yet polite, which has a certain creative charm. What *isn't* funny is the fact that you ignored your son for thirteen years but expect him to get with your damn program in one week. Well, guess what, Bradshaw?"

She got up from her desk and circled it to the door. "It's not all about you. So here's an idea—quit expecting me to do your legwork for you, and try figuring out a few things for yourself." She tapped the toe of one sexy high-heeled shoe against the carpet, her arms crossed beneath those cupcake breasts.

It couldn't be any clearer she wanted him to leave, and his first impulse was to apologize for intruding and saunter past her as if her words hadn't drawn blood.

Only…

She wasn't wrong, dammit.

He hated to admit it, but avoiding the truth wouldn't change the facts.

"Look, I don't disagree," he offered, stopping less than half a foot from her. "I've been expecting too much too soon, and relying on your efforts without putting enough of my own into the things I need to do to transition Austin from hating my guts to at least tolerating me. But it must be as painfully clear to you as it is to me that I'm crashing and burning here. So, if I promise to head back to my room—" even though the thought made him feel itchy and confined "—to put some serious thought into the matter, could you see your way clear to steering me in the right direction? Like…" *What, genius?* Then it came to him. *Duh.* "He played great in practice today, for instance, and I'd love to see him in action during his actual games. But I don't know when they are."

"I'll make you a schedule," she said, then hesitated. "And I *suppooooose*—" the word was drawn out with palpable reluctance "—it would be okay if you wanted to sit with Tasha and me at the next game."

He grinned. "That would be *great!* Thank you."

She gave him a little smile in return, free from the lack of enthusiasm she'd just displayed. For a moment he thought they might have an honest-to-God rapport.

Then Jenny stiffened. "Well. I need to get back to work. I'll get you that schedule when I get a minute. Meanwhile—" she shot him an I-mean-business look "—get busy on more ideas. One-trick ponies only get you so far down the road."

"Yes, ma'am," he said. "I'm heading to my room to do that right this minute." He supposed kissing her, even if only in gratitude for her help, probably wasn't appropriate. He stepped back instead. "Thanks again."

Her shoulders twitched. "Sure."

Jake left her office, but only got as far as the hallway outside before he halted. He could not face going back to his room.

So, big deal, head outdoors. Or...

He snapped upright as two thoughts occurred to him. Not one, but two actual productive ideas. That made a total of three in the past few minutes.

He'd been concentrating too hard on the end goal

instead of on the smaller steps that might get him there. Yes, he'd have to accomplish his first idea before he could think about implementing the second, but a faint, relieved smile quirked his mouth.

Because as he headed back toward the inn's small lobby, he finally felt like his usual, competent self.

CHAPTER SIX

"HEY, WOULD YA LOOKIT THAT?"

Jenny glanced over as Austin paused in his Saturday-morning dishwashing chore, which he'd been powering through with his usual slapdash, water splashed everywhere, let's-get-this-done gusto, to lean into the window over the sink. She plucked a plate from the drainer and raised inquiring eyebrows as she dried it. "What am I looking at?"

He rocked back on his heels, turning to her. "Blue skies!" he crowed and grinned, his face alight. "I don't know where it came from, 'cause it was, like, all clouded over two minutes ago. But, *dude!*"

"Dudette!" she retorted.

The teen grimaced. "Sorry, Jenny. I forgot you don't like me calling you that." Then he laughed. "Know what else I'd almost forgotten?" He jerked his chin at the warm light outside the window. "What that looks like."

"It's certainly been a while since we've seen any sunshine." And he was right, it was a huge mood elevator. She gave him a friendly hip bump. "I bet that'll make your game more fun."

"You got that right. This is gonna be righteous!"

The welcome break in the weather made them both a little giddy, and they joked back and forth as they finished cleaning the kitchen. Then as Austin squeezed the excess water from the sponge he'd used to wipe up the mess he'd made cleaning, he suddenly stiffened. "What the—? What is *he* doing in the Sand Dollar?"

"What?" Okay, so she'd heard him perfectly well. But hoping against hope that the "he" the boy referred to wasn't actually the one person good sense reasoned it *had* to be, Jenny edged over to peer out the sink window, her heart beating a furious tattoo.

It only drummed harder when she saw Jake's uptown SUV parked in the lot they shared with the most luxurious cottage on The Brothers' grounds. Then she spied the man himself packing a big cardboard box up onto the covered front porch and through the open doorway into the dwelling.

The next thing she knew, Austin was charging out the back door. "Great," she whispered and, tossing the tea towel aside, drew a couple of calming breaths before heading for the cottage across the way.

She climbed its three porch stairs in time to hear the anger infusing the teen's every word as he yelled, "What are you doing here?" Walking into the Sand Dollar living room, she found him standing nose to nose with his father amid a plethora of boxes.

Found Jake placing his fingertips against his son's chest and stepping back to put some space between them. Austin swiped them away with more force than was warranted, but the older man didn't respond to his aggression. He merely glanced over at her, then directed his attention right back on the boy, his voice quiet when he replied equably, "Moving in."

"Dude, I can see that! Why *this* cottage?"

"Because it's the largest one available and I'm going to be here for a while. I need space to work—I left Indonesia in a hurry, and I've got close to a thousand photographs I need to download and go through so I can winnow out the best hundred. And whether I develop them or keep them digital, they'll all need cleaning up before they're ready for the *National Explorer*'s July issue."

Austin snorted, but to Jenny's relief, the explanation seemed to defuse some of his anger. "Big deal, how long can that take? You've got two friggin' months."

"No, I've got a hair over two weeks. They're due the first week of May so the editors can select the ones they need for the edition. The exact number will change a dozen times while the layout's being put together." He stabbed a finger toward the ceiling. "There's a little bathroom upstairs that I can use as a darkroom. I do less developing these days, but it'll be handy for the ones that I do. And with the addition of some portable tables, the bedroom up there can be converted into a work space."

"Whatever," the boy said. "As long as you stay out of my way."

"Yeah, well, about that." Jake looked his son straight in the eye. "Not gonna happen."

"Say what?" Austin started to bristle again.

Jake was contrastingly calm. "Like it or not, Austin, I'm your father."

"I *don't* like it!"

"Yet it doesn't change the facts, any more than your displeasure would affect our green eyes or your ability as a shortstop, which you got from both me and your uncle Max."

"Who?"

"Deputy Bradshaw." Looking at the confusion on the teen's face, Jake frowned. "*Annnd*...crap. You didn't know he's my half brother."

Austin's expression cleared. "Oh. Him. I know he's your half brother and all, but it's not like I've ever had anything to do with the dude." His lip curled derisively. "Aside from seeing him at my games sometimes, Deputy Bradshaw's been an uncle to me like you've been a dad."

Jake let the dig roll off him. "That's fair. He and I never had any kind of functional relationship, and the one time he tried to pursue one with you, Emmett and Kathy discouraged it. So why would you think of him as an actual relative?"

"Why didn't you?" When Jake gave him an inquiring look, Austin clarified, "Have any kind of a relationship."

It was the first interest his son had shown him, and Jake looked tempted to take a side trip down that alley. But he shook his head. "Look, it's a long, complicated story that I'll be happy to tell you some other time. But first *we* need to get to know each other."

"You've had years to get to know me," Austin snapped. "You didn't and I'm not interested now." Turning away, he said to Jenny, "I'm taking my boat out."

She glanced at Jake, who shrugged. Taking that for a willingness to shelve the conversation, if only for the moment, and figuring that Austin had probably had enough upset for one day anyhow, she didn't argue. "One hour," she said. "Get your head together, then get back here. You've got a game to play this afternoon."

He nodded and headed for the door.

"I know I've been a lousy father," Jake said to his retreating back. "But I'm here now and I'm trying to do better. I'm not going away, Austin."

A slight hesitation slowed the boy's step. Then he muttered, "Great," and picked up his pace.

Marching out the door, he slammed it closed behind him.

Jake turned to her. "That went well."

She just blew out a breath.

He moved closer to her. "Did I hear right? He has a boat?"

"Yes."

"Of his *own?*"

She nodded.

"What are we talking about here? Please tell me it's a kayak or something else reasonably small."

"Sure. If you consider a nineteen-foot Bayliner Bowrider reasonable."

"Are you shi—" He visibly swallowed the obscenity. But his eyes were hot when he said, "He's thirteen! That's ludicrous."

Jenny shrugged, but couldn't say she disagreed. She'd argued and *argued* with Emmett about giving the boat to Austin on his thirteenth birthday. "The Pierces had a tendency to spoil him."

"Tell me about it," he muttered. "They did the same thing with Kari, and I'm here to tell you it didn't help her learn to stand on her own two feet. She was totally unprepared for the first bump in her road." He grimaced. "Not that teenage pregnancy isn't one hell of a bump. Still, I married her and she had her parents' full support—that's more than a lot of girls in that situation end up with."

For a second Jenny simply gaped at him. She'd known he'd been married to the Pierces' daughter, of course. Yet with a jolt, she realized her view of him was colored by Emmett and Kathy's disdain for his quick departure after Kari's death to take the full scholarship he'd earned to Columbia, and the fact that he'd apparently never looked back. She'd never considered that he had stepped up, even if only for a while. Emmett and Kathy had never emphasized that—or the fact that he'd been only a teenager himself.

Then she closed her lips. Because even if there

was more to the story, it certainly didn't make up for his years of neglect toward Austin. But it *was* probably good to remember that neither was he the complete monster she'd spent an eon believing him to be.

Jake gazed at her, his eyes narrowing shrewdly. "What, not quite the story you heard?"

Her back stiffened. "I knew you'd married the Pierces' daughter."

"Did anybody mention that nobody forced me to? It was the right thing to do, so I gave up my dream of Columbia and took a job here at the front desk."

That she hadn't known. It must have been quite a comedown to sacrifice the scholarship he'd obviously worked hard to achieve to accept a job at the inn that had to have been much less rewarding.

"After Kari died, it was Emmett's idea that I accept the scholarship after all."

She hadn't known that, either. Still… "Was it his idea as well that you never come back for your son once you left?"

"No." He shoved his hands in his pockets and looked away. "That's entirely on me."

She wondered at what point he'd changed from the boy who had done the right thing to the one who had vanished from Austin's life. Had it been when his wife died? And how devastated had that left him?

Smart enough to keep her curiosity to herself, she turned to him with her brisk, efficient general-manager face firmly in place. "I'll leave you to unpack."

She couldn't quite keep her puzzlement from showing, however, as she looked at all the boxes and shopping bags that littered the living area. So instead of leaving, she asked, "Where did all this stuff come from? Did you make a trip to Kitsap?"

"No." He picked up a large, heavy-looking box containing tubs and cans and jugs and pouches, all of which shifted and clinked together as he settled it on his shoulder. "Kitsap and Bremerton didn't have what I needed," he said. "I had to go to Tacoma."

Eyeing him as he stood hipshot, one tanned arm lifted to hook his fingers against the top edge of the box, pinning it against the epaulet of the khaki bush-shirt he wore, she could easily picture him in some faraway land of heat and dust. Indicating his load, she said, "Is that photography stuff?"

"Developing solutions," he said and jerked his jaw toward some of the big boxes bearing UPS labels. "Those contain equipment from my home studio that I didn't want to have to run around trying to duplicate—"

On this podunk peninsula, whispered the subtext through Jenny's head.

"—so I had my assistant send it to me."

"Yes, well, I'm sure you're very busy," she said with a careful lack of attitude.

But maybe she wasn't entirely successful at keeping her thoughts to herself, because he filled the small distance she'd put between them. He looked down at her, his dark brows inching toward his nose. "Did I say something to offend you?"

"No, of course not." She stepped back. Then stood taller. Because what was she, a mind reader? "At least—it's nothing. When you talked about not wanting to run around duplicating your equipment, I took the teeny-tiniest tone in your voice and turned it into something you probably didn't even mean." She waved a dismissive hand. "In any case, none of my business. And as I said, I'll leave you to it."

But he came near enough that, between his muscular body, the big box still balanced on his shoulder and the other containers strewn across the floor, she felt hemmed in. Warmth and a barely-there musky scent, rimmed with an edge of salt, pumped off his skin.

"What did you think I meant?"

She made a face, but repeated the words that had drifted through her mind.

He looked down at her with searching eyes and a slight, one-sided smile. But he didn't say a word.

As one second stretched into the next, heat began to crawl up her neck. She took another step back. "I told you, I probably twisted your meaning."

"No," he said slowly, "you've got scarily good instincts."

She stopped with her left heel raised to retreat farther yet. "I've—" She gave her head a little shake to clear it. "What?"

"You're right." His free shoulder twitched. "That pretty much sums up my attitude."

She'd never had much of a poker face, and her expression must have shown her immediate spike of temper, because he said, "Look, it's not an indictment of your choices—only of my own. I spent most of my days in Razor Bay plotting ways to get out of it, so it's not like I suddenly think I'm too cool for this place because I've traveled the world or lived in more cosmopolitan cities. I appreciate that small-town life has a lot to offer. It just never has for me. This town's always made me antsy."

She inhaled through her nose and consciously uncurled her fingers from the fists they'd formed. *Fine.* Not everyone had to like the same things.

Jenny blew out a breath because—oh, hell—they really didn't. She gave him a nod. "I can't say that I get it," she acknowledged, "because for me Razor Bay has always meant acceptance—something I failed to get in the big city where I lived before moving here." She forced a shrug, even though she still felt unaccountably…disappointed.

But that was ridiculous and she shook it off. "So, different strokes, I guess."

He looked down at her. Slicked his tongue across his bottom lip. "Yeah. We'll have to agree to disagree."

Dammit, why did she look at him and think *sex on the hoof?* It wasn't like the guy went around shirtless, which, okay, she wouldn't mind seeing, or performed a blatant tongue thrust-and-wag like some cosmetics-heavy Gene Simmons from the old rock band KISS. But, *man*. He just really tripped her buzzer.

And wasn't that the height of unfairness, all things considered?

She put some snap in her spine and, with a stride that was decisive and in command this time, took a definitive step back.

Right into one of the many boxes crowding the living area.

"Crap!" She windmilled her arms for balance, but the backs of her knees buckled on contact and she knew in an instant she was going to fall on her ass.

And that it wasn't going to be pretty.

Then a strong arm snaked around her waist and jerked, bringing her not only upright again but smack against Jake's chest with an impact that flattened her breasts against his diaphragm, punched half the air from her lungs and set the bottles and jars in the box on his shoulder to rattling. His muscles shifted as he braced himself and readjusted his cargo.

She went still as a mouse sensing a cat, her system on sensory overload.

Because there was just…oh, man.

So. Much. *Heat.*

It was the only thing that registered for a minute—the warmth that radiated through his shirt, the hot rub of his bare forearm dislodging the hem of her baby T-shirt, which had barely been kissing her mid-rise waistband as it was, the slow, blistering slide it took against the newly exposed skin at the small of her back. *Oh, man. Oh man, oh man, oh man.*

He stilled as well, and she held her breath as he tipped his chin in to look down at her.

"I couldn't have set this up better if I'd tried," he said in a low, rough voice. "It's sort of like a skit out of the Three Stooges, isn't it?"

Her face flamed. Oh, God. It wasn't bad enough that she was attracted to the last man in the world she should be tempted by? Oh, no. She'd had to go and compound that lunacy by thinking of hot sex on rumpled sheets with him, while *he'd* clearly looked at her and thought extreme slapstick.

It was all she could do not to deflate like a punctured balloon. Because, how lowering was that?

Carefully extricating herself, she dredged up a halfhearted smile and a light tone. "I'm not sure if that makes me Curly or Moe." Once on her feet, with Jake safely out of heat-throwing distance, she tugged her traitor T-shirt back in place and forced herself to meet his gaze. "Austin's game starts at four," she said. "You might want to get there early if you plan on sitting with Tasha and me."

He nodded. "I'll do that."

Yay. Just...yay. "Well. I guess I'll see you later, then."

And gathering her tattered dignity around her, she let herself out of the cottage, carefully closing the door behind her.

CHAPTER SEVEN

WHEN JAKE WALKED INTO the ballpark that afternoon, it was like funneling through a time warp. He stopped to take it in, a smile tugging up the corners of his mouth. Because, damn. The place hadn't changed at all. He'd put money on his ability to close his eyes and describe, down to the smallest detail, every element of the diamond, the field and the surrounding area.

He wasn't prepared for the immediate spike of contentment that gave him. Some of the happiest moments of his youth had played out on this field. When things at home had been messed up or he'd had a particularly bad run-in with the then-detested Max, he'd always been able to lose himself in every glorious inning of baseball. He loved the game, pure and simple, from the team camaraderie—in what he knew couldn't be but he remembered as perpetual sunshine—to the spurt of speed he demanded from his body after a ball cracked off his bat, to the meaty wallop of fielding a full-grain, leather-covered Rawlings with his mitt, to developing and improving his throw.

The aromas that went with this game like PB went

with J were an express train to the past. The scent of freshly mown lawn that filled the air now, along with the bouquet of grilled hot dogs from the snack shack, and the fainter waft of chalk used to define the base and foul lines, were the smells of his youth.

Both teams were warming up and, seeing the familiar green-and-gold home-team colors on the infield, Jake looked for Austin. He located him in position between second and third base, fielding a thrown ball, then pivoting and throwing it to the first baseman. The stands were beginning to fill as well, and Jake headed for the home seating, looking for Jenny.

He saw her friend first, probably because Tasha was a great deal taller, making her easier to spot. Once he identified her, however, he found Jenny right alongside her.

Which did *not* make his heart skip a beat.

Reaching the bleachers, he saw that the two women had saved a space next to Tasha and, excusing himself as he climbed over seated parents, he picked his way up to near dead-center, where they sat. "Hey," he said, reaching them. "Thanks for keeping a spot for me."

"Not a problem," the strawberry blonde said, patting the seat next to her hip. "I'm Tasha. You can save mine in return. I'm going to grab a dog and hit the ladies'. Not necessarily in that order," she added wryly as she rose to her feet. She looked at Jenny. "You want anything?"

Jenny shook her head. "Nah, I'm good."

Tasha turned her attention to him. "You?"

"I could go for a dog," he said, stowing his camera bag beneath the bench. "And maybe a Coke, if you've got enough hands."

"Note the pockets, Bradshaw. I'm a come-prepared kinda woman. While you—" She gave him the once-over before nodding decisively. "You look like a load-it-up-with-everything kind of guy."

"I guess looks don't lie." He fished his wallet out of his pocket, pulled out a twenty and handed it over. "Get yours out of that, as well."

She gave him a deadpan expression. "Hey, big spender."

"They don't call me Gentleman Jake for nothing."

Tasha looked at Jenny. "You sure you don't want anything, now that Mr. Gotrocks here is footing the bill?"

"What the hell," the little brunette said. "I might as well shoot the moon. Get me a Diet Coke." She met Jake's eyes for the first time since he'd arrived. Granted him a lopsided, closed-lips smile that lifted her right cheekbone into prominence. "We wouldn't want you to have too much change jingling in your pockets."

He nodded. "I know, right? You want a dog to go with that?"

"Nah. I'm saving myself for Tasha's pizza after the game."

He tried to look pitiful. "I haven't had a chance to try that yet."

"Tough luck for you," Jenny said with patent insincerity.

But Tasha said, "Then you should join us," and gave her businesslike watch a glance. "I better go get our stuff if I want to be back before the game starts."

Jake settled in after she left, pleased with the invitation. *Hint heavy-handedly enough and ye shall receive.* He probably oughta care that he'd horned in on their postgame plans, but he refused to feel guilty about it. Hell, he had to try—the team's pizza fest was an additional opportunity to get a little closer to Austin.

Or, more realistically, another opportunity for his son to shut him down yet one more time. But risking a repeat of his previous results be damned. He had to make his openings where he could.

He turned to Jenny, whom he'd been trying real hard, since joining the women on the bleachers, not to look at too closely. Unable to help himself, he studied her now.

She'd changed into a little pale pink and olive-drab wide-striped T-shirt or sweater or whatever the hell a female would call it. All he knew was that it was made of a material thin enough for the casual observer to see the outlines of a pink bra beneath it, and that two bands of the olive-drab fabric crisscrossed from the wide, scooped neckline in front to the wide scoop in back.

And that its hem didn't even pretend to meet the hip band of her jeans.

The latter caught his attention in particular. He still retained a tactile memory of the softness of her skin where his inner forearm had slid across it when the top she'd worn this morning had ridden up.

But he wasn't gonna think about that.

He cleared his throat and turned to her. "Where do the Bulldogs stand so far this season?"

"Two wins, one tie," she replied, looking out over the field. "They're shaping up to be a good team." Pulling her gaze away from whatever had captured it, she turned to him. "Their tie was with the Warriors, who've been the top-ranked team to beat the past two years."

"Yeah, I saw the Dogs at practice. Austin's particularly good."

Her face lit up. "You think so? I mean, I do, as well…but I didn't know if that was simply my prejudice showing."

An unaccountable irritation flashed through him. "And you think I couldn't possibly be prejudiced in his favor as well?"

His demand wiped the smile from her face. "I didn't say that—although why *would* I think you'd be? You haven't exactly been a big presence in his life. But what I meant was that you probably have a better idea of what constitutes a good baseball player than I do." She made a face. "The only time I ever even picked up a bat was at a company picnic game—and that was probably eight years ago. My core experience with the sport has been watching Austin play over the years."

Put like that… He shifted on the bench. "I apologize if I jumped to conclusions."

She essayed a shrug that put him in mind of his teenage son. It was a nonverbal *Whatever.*

They managed to exchange idle chitchat for the next several minutes, but Jake was relieved to see Tasha return with a cardboard carton holding their food and drinks. He widened the space he hadn't even realized he'd narrowed between himself and Jenny.

What was up with that? It had to have something to do with being back at the ballpark. Damn place made him feel like a high school stud looking to score.

Tasha jerked her chin toward her friend as she picked her way up the bleachers. "Scoot back over," she ordered when she was a single riser and several parents to his left. "You'll be one less person I have to climb over."

Bad idea. *Baaad* idea! He could appreciate that her route through the families and friends packed together on the benches was easier the way she was coming. But there was still that pull thing to contend with, and why tempt fate before he could do something about the been-a-whiles?

"How about I step up onto the seat to give you room to get by."

"Nah, just scoot over." She grinned as she edged nearer. "We don't get a lot of good-looking single guys at these games as a rule. It only seems fair that you sit in the middle." She looked past him at her friend. "That works for you, right?"

The petite brunette at his side didn't come right out and say, "No, you can have him." But the sound she made in her throat wasn't exactly a rousing endorsement, either. Reluctantly, he slid down the bench in her direction.

Tasha squeezed through the remaining spectators separating them, inched past the woman who had been sitting next to him until a second ago, and plopped down alongside him. Leaning forward, she handed Jenny her can of soda, then gave him his and extended the molded cardboard container to him. "That one's yours," she said with a dip of her chin, then sat back to unwrap the foil from her own hot dog and open her can of pop.

She dug her elbow in his side. "Move over a little. It's been a while since I've rubbed shoulders with such a wide set, and they've got me practically in Maryanne's lap," she said, indicating the woman whose place she'd taken. "I need some elbow room." When he didn't promptly fall in line with her directive, she gave him a nudge of her own shoulder. "Move, Bradshaw!"

His response to the command was purely reflexive, and he raised his butt up to scootch down the bench. Tasha instantly crowded him, claiming more real estate than he'd intended to relinquish. The next thing he knew, he was pushed up against Jenny from knee to shoulder.

And, swamped with sensation, he could only think hazily, *What is this, goddamn Groundhog Day?*

Dammit, being plastered against this woman was not in his best interests. Only by making a joke this morning had he escaped the nearly overwhelming urge to slide his hands up beneath her top to cop a feel of her warm, bare skin, or down over her jeans to cup that sweetly rounded ass. He'd had to clamp a lid on an unwelcome craving to take a big juicy bite out of her.

Now here he was on the same damn day, breathing in the same scent of her shampoo, conscious of her feminine warmth, her softness pressed against his own harder muscle and bone. He looked down.

Only to have his dick give a mighty twitch at seeing her doing some pressing of her own.

Oh. No. *Erroneous information, pal.*

She was leaning around him. "Tasha, quit hogging all the space," she said. "Maryanne's not the only one who's suddenly got someone practically in her lap—and Jake weighs a lot more than you do."

"Oops." Tasha inched over. "Sorry, babe."

He couldn't believe how grateful he was for the breathing room. And if that wasn't bat-shit crazy, he didn't know what was. As sexual titillation went, a little fully clothed, public press-and-rub of body parts that no one in their right mind would ever term erogenous was strictly bush league—and G-rated bush league at that. Which sort of begged the question, didn't it?

What the hell was he doing sitting here in the wake of said unimportant body press, sporting a dick that had pulsed itself to the early stage of an erection? Not even the been-a-whiles covered a response this juvenile.

He knocked back half of his soda in one long gulp. *Daaaamn.* If it wasn't the lack of recent sex, then it had to be the world of memories, the sensory overload, brought on by finding himself at his son's baseball game on the field where he'd spent every spring of his school years.

Why that should matter, he couldn't say. It had been a long time and a lot of miles since his high school days.

A *lot* of miles. He raised his hot dog to his mouth.

Still. His responses, his mind-set, sure seemed to lean in that direction.

He stilled, the hot dog poised at his open mouth. Christ. Because, a lot of distance or not, that was what he'd felt like. Not the sexually responsible man he'd been for the past thirteen-plus years, but a high school kid getting his rub-on against a girl simply because she smelled good and felt better.

And look how well *that* had worked out for him. Snapping his teeth closed, he tore a vicious bite out ˉthe dog.

Intellectually, he knew one thing had nothing to do with the other. And yet—

Damned if he would ever allow himself to get caught in a trap like that again.

"GOOD GAME. GOOD GAME. Good game." It was all Austin could do not to laugh like a lunatic as he and the rest of the Bulldogs filed in a line past the players on the opposing team, slapping hands and chanting the postgame wrap-up ritual with each man. 'Cause, jeez. It had been good game quadrupled. They'd kicked some serious *ass* today, winding up the final inning with a score of six to two.

He didn't even mind that his old man had come. Okay, maybe he was the *smallest* bit glad that he had.

Because the guy had been crazy enthusiastic. He knew his baseball and totally got it when Austin's team did something good, even if the fielding strategy of the moment didn't result in a base gained or a point scored. He'd yelled his support over every single play the Bulldogs had pulled out of their hats, and whipped the surrounding parents into a cheering frenzy. He got them to chanting, "Hey, batta, batta, batta," with each new batter up. That was probably some old nineties thing, but he had to admit, it was a little cool.

What was maybe cooler, though, was the way Jake had vocalized a singsong "Sling it in there, oh babe, oh babe!" every time *he* had winged a ball toward a baseman, then yelled, "Way to go, Austin!"

And the three times his plays had failed, he'd called, "Good try!"

Then there was the photography. *That* was in a category all its own.

At the bottom of the third inning, his old man had climbed down from the stands with a big deal-looking camera slung around his neck. And, *man,* he'd been all over the place, the camera apparently an extension of his eye, one hand supporting the long lens. Whenever Jake—as Austin had caustically begun referring to him when he was forced to name him at all, since he was damned if he was going to call him Dad—was anywhere near, he was accompanied by a constant *click-whir, click-whir.*

Dude had also all but worn a path parallel to the foul lines, stalking up toward the outfield and back to the infield, with stops in between to take shots, often sinking down to squat on his heels. One time, when Daniels took that dive for third base in the sixth inning, his father had dropped full length on his stomach, only his elbows keeping him from doing a face-plant in the grass.

Austin was surprised he hadn't climbed the damn backstop to take a few bird's-eye-view shots.

His friends thought the whole deal was completely bitchin', saying stuff like they could see how he stalked tigers and shit through the jungles. If someone held a torch to Austin's feet, maybe, *maybe* he'd say that he thought it was pretty bitchin' himself.

Maybe.

JENNY TURNED TO TASHA the minute they climbed into her car to head over to Bella T's. Reaching across the console, she poked her friend in the arm. "What the hell was all that about?"

"Huh?" Tasha blinked. "What was what?"

"That whole let's share the hunk and put him in the middle crap?"

"I thought, that is…" Tasha trailed off, giving Jenny a perplexed look. "You aren't attracted to him, then?"

She blew an incredulous *pfffffftt.* "Of course I am—have you taken a *look* at the guy? He, however, is not attracted to me. Which, trust me, made that whole shoving us together thing awkward as hell."

The strawberry blonde snorted. "Please. I saw him looking at you that night at the Anchor—not to mention the fact he was practically in your lap way before I pushed him there—and he is definitely attracted!"

"No, he really isn't." The last thing she wanted was to go into this morning's Three Stooges reference, so she cut to the meat of the matter. "He thinks I'm *amusing.*"

Indignation dawned on Tasha's face, and Jenny straightened in her seat before it could solidify.

"The truth is," she said with a surprisingly decent imitation of cool disinterest, "the only reason I'm all hot for Bradshaw's body—aside from it being eminently hot-worthy—is this embarrassingly long dry spell I've been in. That and the fact men aren't exactly thick on the ground around here."

"At least until the summer people start trickling in," Tasha agreed gloomily. She crossed her arms over her breasts. "Although there is Max Bradshaw. He's almost as tasty as Jake, if you go for the whole brooding Heathcliff type."

"Which, unfortunately, I never have. He's way too self-controlled. I like 'em a little more—well, not hot-blooded, exactly, because under all that discipline, I'm thinking he has serious potential in that department." She glanced across the console at her friend before turning her attention back to the road. "I guess I just like a little more spontaneity in my men."

"I agree. I get Max's sex appeal as well, but it simply doesn't call to me."

"So who does that leave?"

"Wade Nelson?"

Jenny shook her head. "Nah. He's still waiting for Mindy Neff to come back to him."

"Seriously, he's got to get over that. She and Curt just celebrated their seventh anniversary."

"I know, right?" Jenny shook her head. "Guy Wilson is another rebound guy. The ink's barely dry on his divorce."

Tasha drummed her fingers on her thigh for a moment. "How about David Brill?"

"Are you kidding me?" Jenny said hotly. "Mr. Globe-trotter Bradshaw might be a little out of my league, but at the *very* least I deserve a guy with all his teeth!"

"Crap, you're right. We're scraping bottom here. There's only one thing for it. You know that, right?"

I do." She gave her friend a solemn nod. "The next chance we get, you and I are heading into Kitsap."

"Damn straight. And find us some new blood."

EVERYONE GATHERED at Bella T's after the game. When Tasha deserted her for the kitchen, Jenny gravitated toward some of the other parents, making sure to grab a seat as far away from Jake as she could.

Not that he noticed or would care if he did. He was too busy just charming the hell out of everyone left, right and sideways.

"You guys played an *ex*cellent game," she heard him say now, then went on to discuss points of the various plays.

Points that totally went over her head.

That wasn't the case with Austin or his friends or several of the fathers and Coach Harstead. She could almost hear the sucking sound of them being pulled into a spirited discussion.

Sneaking a peek while simultaneously carrying on a conversation with Rebecca Damoth, she watched as Jake homed in on his son.

"You're a really good shortstop," he said unreservedly.

Austin was obviously trying to play it cool, but she could tell he was pleased. "Yeah?"

"Definitely. I do have a few suggestions for improving on what you've already got," Jake continued. "Maybe we could talk about them one of these days."

The boy's shoulders lifted and dropped. "Maybe."

God. Jake was doing so much better than she'd expected. He had been way more engaged in Austin's game than she ever would have given him credit for, his uninhibited enthusiasm for the team and the game firing everyone else to a near frenzy.

Which was saying something, considering how crazy this town already was about its team sports.

She should be glad that Bradshaw was more dedicated to getting to know his son than she'd anticipated… and she was.

Mostly. Because the only way a momentous change, like Jake taking Austin to New York, could be less traumatic was if the teen was fully invested in the relationship when the time came.

But knowing the boy she'd come to love like a little brother would soon be living on the other side of the continent—

Damn. That was a cold dread in her stomach, an honest-to-God ache in her heart that just felt way too permanent.

The unwanted sexual pull Bradshaw exerted on her wasn't helping, either. It sucked that, at the best of times, it was damn hard not to notice the man. And today had been far from the best of times. Between this morning's fiasco, that lightning-fast, electric shock of a body mash in the bleachers, and Jake's engaging gusto both then and now…

She sighed. It was hard not to be attracted.

Her shoulders squared. Well, she'd just have to motor past it. She was a big girl, and big girls—no, grown *women*—minimized their exposure to things that weren't good for them. Especially if those things hammered their egos into paste.

She'd found out the hard way that nothing pulverized an ego faster than being all hot for someone who not only felt zip attraction in return but found you amusing.

So, it was settled, then. Minimizing her exposure to him was exactly what she would do.

Unfortunately, that merely left room for her to think about the letter from her father that had come just before she'd left for the game. In it he'd said he had good news to share and wanted her to visit him sooner than she'd originally planned.

A familiar apprehension tugged at her. Because she knew from experience that what was good for him wasn't necessarily good for anyone else.

No. She sat a little straighter. She wasn't that sixteen-year-old kid who'd been ripped from the life she'd known—and hadn't been for a long time.

Out of the corner of her eye, she saw Jake lean into the table.

"Hey, Austin," he said to his son, who sat a few seats away. "Jenny tells me the boat you took out this morning is a Bayliner Bowrider?"

"Coolest ride ever, dude!" Austin's friend Nolan decreed.

The boys bumped fists before Austin turned his attention to his father. "Yeah, it is."

"And you got it for your birthday?"

"Uh-huh."

"I'd like you to take me out on it."

The teen's mouth dropped open. "Say what?"

"That's a lot of boat for a thirteen-year-old. Now, I'm sure, having grown up on the water, that you're more than up to the task of controlling it. I'm also sure that you must be a responsible boater."

Austin's face went stony. "But?"

Jake gave him a level look. "But I wouldn't be a responsible parent if I allowed you free rein before checking you out. So, when's good for you?"

"How 'bout nev—"

"Jenny, of course, will accompany us."

Say what? She jerked upright, grateful she hadn't chided Austin when he'd said the same thing, because she totally got it now.

Jake flashed her a guilty grimace, to which she responded with a *What the hell?* look of her own— until she noticed Austin turning in her direction. Quickly rearranging her expression, she turned her lips up into what she sincerely hoped was a composed smile. She feared it was probably more a sickly contortion than the calm and collected Madonna-like serenity she was shooting for—but it was the best she could come up with on short notice.

Speaking of shooting, though, when it came to Jake that sounded downright appealing, and for a nanosecond she indulged the fantasy. Sans the blood-and-death thing.

"Jenny?" Austin demanded.

Her mind cleared. Because the truth was, aside from the part where he'd dragged her into it, she didn't need to see a couple of parents' looks of approval to know Jake's decree had merit. Her smile turned genuine.

"You have to admit it's a reasonable request. Unreasonable would be Jake becoming your legal guardian and not caring if you know what you're doing on the water. So what's the harm of giving him a demonstration?"

"Jeeez." All the same, Austin gave Jake a terse nod. "Fine."

His father flashed him a white, white smile. "Excellent. When's good for you?"

Looking hunted, Austin shot her a beseeching look.

"Why don't we look at your practice and my work schedules when we get home?" she suggested smoothly. "We can decide from there."

And you, she thought darkly, shooting death rays Jake's way when Austin turned back to his friends, *had better prepare yourself for an earful. Because you and I are gonna have us a little talk about boundaries.*

CHAPTER EIGHT

"CAN WE GET THIS *OVER* WITH, already?"

Jenny looked at Austin where he stood on the dock next to his boat, the sun slowly sinking toward the Olympic peaks at his back. With his arms crossed militantly over his narrow chest and his eyebrows meeting above the thrust of his nose, he broadcast in high def just how bored and put out he was about having to prove his boating abilities.

She swallowed a sigh because, truth to tell, she was still less than thrilled with Jake for sucking her into his arrangements without so much as a *would-you-mind?* But in unspoken agreement, the two of them were acting like the adults they were and studiously ignoring the teen's pique. Instead, as they'd walked over to the dock, they'd discussed the Bulldogs' practice, which Jake had watched this afternoon, although she'd had to miss it due to her work schedule.

Apparently, however, they'd exhausted Austin's already limited patience.

She drew in a quiet breath, then eased it out. They needed to work on his manners.

She had to give Jake his due: he merely gave his

son a nod and said, "Sure," with no discernible dissatisfaction over Austin's attitude. "Run me through your pre-takeoff safety check."

"Dude, this isn't an airplane." But Austin waved them aboard his boat and squatted to untie the stern line from the cleat attached to the dock. He coiled the nylon rope with quick efficiency and leaned to tuck the line into a tiny side cubby in the boat before crab-walking to the forward cleat. Unlooping that line, he slid into the open bow of the Bayliner and stooped to stow it away, as well.

"Still," he conceded as he straightened, "you gotta put on a life vest. I guess that qualifies as a safety thing. 'No vest, no ride' is a hard and fast rule of boating." He shot Jake a defiant look as he entered the hull through the folded-back split windshield. "My grandpa taught me that."

"It's an excellent rule," Jake said mildly.

"Yeah. It is." The boy's tense shoulders relaxed slightly. "You'll find some under the seats back here." After leaning over the driver's seat to insert the key into the ignition, he edged past Jake and Jenny where they stood in the space between the captain seats and the back bench. Austin hauled his own vest out of the compartment beneath the bench cushions. Shrugging it on, he glanced at his father as the older man came to stand alongside him, then waved a hand at the other flotation devices in the storage he'd opened.

And displayed the first flash of his usual humor

since Jake had arrived at the cottage this afternoon. "The orange-and-yellow youth-sized one is Jenny's."

The two males exchanged grins and Jenny flicked Austin's forehead with her finger. "Brat."

He laughed, clicked closed the triple belts on his vest and snugged up the straps, as Jake tossed Jenny her vest and donned his own. "You know it's true, short stuff. Everybody buckled up?"

They finished fastening their vests, and Jenny waved Jake into the passenger seat as the teen slid into the driver's chair and started the inboard-outboard. She went into the open bow, closed the windshield behind her and, zipping up her fleece hoodie, sat on the padded bench with her feet stretched out in front of her.

Easing the throttle out of Neutral, Austin slowly backed the craft from its berth.

Emmett truly had taught him responsible boating, and the teen kept the speed of the craft down until he reached deeper water. Then he steadily pressed the throttle forward until they were flying across the canal at top speed.

Jenny grinned and gathered her blowing hair at her nape to tie it into a knot before pulling her hood up. When she hadn't been out for a while, she always seemed to forget how much she enjoyed boating and how thrilling it was to race across the canal on days like today, when the water was mirror flat and other boats were few and far between.

As they approached the far side of the fjord, Austin turned the boat in a long arc to the south. Foothills folded into more foothills, which ultimately gave way to craggy, snow-covered mountain peaks. The nuanced layers appeared close enough to trace with her fingertips.

They cruised the western shoreline, and as Austin piloted the boat behind a finger of land, he eased back on the throttle. A moment later, as they neared the opening to Tranquil Harbor, he decelerated even more. Water slapped the hull as the boat's wake caught up with the now slow-moving craft, and they rode the gentle swell into the mouth of the long, narrow inlet.

Thick stands of evergreens, interspersed with the brighter lime and emerald of newly leafed alder and maple trees, surrounded the harbor on three sides. Generous moorage stretched down the west side, connected to the shore by narrow, arched pedestrian bridges.

The marina's permanent tenant slips were occupied, but the majority of its short-term moorage was empty this time of year. Due to the popular year-round Friday- and Saturday-night barbecues, many of those berths would fill up on the weekends. And of course, as the weather improved the numbers would increase.

Until, come summertime, much like The Brothers, it would have so much business there would be waiting lists for a cancellation.

"This is one of Jenny's favorite places," Austin

informed Jake as they motored through the marina under the posted five-mile-an-hour limit. Briefly, he met his father's gaze.

"Grab the stern line," he instructed as he let the boat drift up to one of the docks and put it in Reverse for a moment to halt its forward momentum.

Jenny retrieved the line at the bow, and she and Jake were winding figure eights around the dock cleats, fore and aft, when someone hailed Austin. She looked over her shoulder in time to see her honorary brother's face light up.

"Hey, that's Mr. D's Chris-Craft! Looks like Nolan and Squirt and their folks and..." He rose to peer over the windshield, then shrugged at Jenny. "I don't know who the girl is."

The boat pulled alongside them. "Ahoy," Mark Damoth said, using the same technique as Austin to stop his fishing-style boat before stretching out a leg to brace his foot against the Bayliner, keeping the two boats parallel without allowing their sides to bang together. He gave them all a cheerful smile before saying to Austin, "Nolan thought that was your boat."

Austin blinked at his friend. "I didn't know you guys were coming out today."

"Me neither," Nolan said. "But we wanted to show Bailey around and I remembered you sayin' you were bringing Jenny and your da—um, him—" he tipped his head at Jake "—here." Obviously wanting to change the subject, he grabbed the hand of a girl who looked to be about his and Austin's age. "This is Bailey."

"She's our cousin," Nolan's little brother Josh interrupted.

"Right," Nolan said drily. "I think I told you about her, didn't I, A? The girl who rocks baseball?"

"Sure, who could forget that?" Sliding his fingertips in his front pants pockets, he looked at the girl. "How ya doin'?"

"Okay," she murmured.

"My aunt Debbie's been sick," Nolan said. "So Bails is gonna live with us through the summer."

Jenny saw a shadow cross Bailey's blue eyes. It came and went so fast, she couldn't swear she hadn't imagined it—or that it hadn't been caused by one of the puffy clouds drifting across the sky or the brim of the girl's blue-and-brown plaid newsboy cap, which she wore pulled down to the delicate arch of her dark eyebrows.

She suspected, however, that it was neither of those things. Not if the girl's mother was sick enough to send her daughter to a new school this close to the end of the school year.

The brief look she exchanged with Rebecca Damoth didn't lessen her suspicion.

"This is Jenny and Jake, Bailey," Austin informed the girl, jerking his chin to indicate them. "I don't think you've met Jake either, have you, Squirt?" he asked Josh, then turned to the boy's father. "How 'bout you, Mr. D? You met him?"

A muscle in Jake's jaw ticked, no doubt due to Austin's continued insistence on calling him by his first name rather than acknowledge their relationship. But if so, he smoothed out his expression so quickly, she wasn't sure what she'd seen.

"Your dad might not remember," Mark Damoth said with easy friendliness, leaning out of his boat to offer his hand, "but I student coached Jake's Little League team with my dad one summer."

"Wow." Jake shook the other man's hand across the foot of water separating the two boats. "I didn't put you together with that kid from back when. I thought you were so cool when I was twelve." He shot the other man a sly smile. "But you're old, dude."

Mark threw back his head and laughed. "Not to mention a few pounds heavier," he agreed amiably, giving his paunch an affectionate slap. "I'd hoped to meet you again at the kids' pizza party, but I got held up at work."

"We thought we'd hike up to the café and get the kids a cone," Rebecca said. "Why don't you join us?"

The suggestion clearly appealed to Austin, and Jake nodded. "Sounds like an excellent plan."

"I'll go moor the boat," Mark said and pushed his craft farther away from the Bayliner.

"Woo-hoo!" Austin was all smiles as he climbed out of his boat and strode down to where Mark docked behind them. He caught the line Nolan tossed him, and the two boys secured the boat.

Jenny watched Jake hesitate for a moment before

he reached for the flat, plain brown paper-wrapped package she'd noticed him carrying earlier. Then he turned and held out his free hand to her. Lacking the length of the Bradshaw men's legs, she knew better than to turn up her nose at the gesture. Scrabbling out of the boat like a two-year-old, only without the charm, held no appeal. Sliding her fingers into his palm, she allowed him to hand her onto the dock.

He followed behind her, making the single steep step from the deck of the boat to the float look effortless.

Austin and the Damoths met them moments later, and they all crossed a nearby footbridge and hiked to the top of a switchback trail. A café, general store and coffee shop/ice-cream parlor nestled in a sunny clearing among the trees at its top. They headed for the latter and a bell *ting-a-linged* over the door of the shop as they entered.

The kids promptly claimed a white wrought-iron table that was barely big enough for the four of them once Austin had pulled over two additional chairs from a neighboring table. The message was clear that no adults were allowed.

Mark laughed and claimed a slightly larger table on the other side of the room. The shop wasn't spacious enough to support a reasonable expectation of privacy, but the teens seemed satisfied with the bit of independence the separation provided them.

Josh was clearly happy just being able to hang with the bigger kids.

Jenny discovered the adult table wasn't all that roomy either when her feet tangled with Jake's much larger ones beneath it. The second time it happened she tucked hers between her chair's legs.

The Damoths were open and friendly, and they all chatted easily as a young woman distributed laminated lists of ice cream flavors to both tables. Mark, big and easygoing, waved a beefy hand in the kids' direction. "Put whatever they're having on my tab."

Jake had set his small package on the table, but had to move it to the floor when their coffee and ice cream arrived a short while later.

"What've you got there?" Mark asked, as Jake rested it with patent care against the leg of his chair.

"Just something I made for Austin."

Jenny watched the teen snap his head up to stare at his father. He'd obviously heard and was torn between a natural teenage curiosity and his need to hang on to the distance he'd stringently been trying to maintain. The green eyes so similar to Jake's lit up when Mark demanded for him, "That right? What is it?"

Seeing that Jake was about to answer, Jenny didn't have a clue why she jumped in before he could. "You ever do much fishing when you were a kid?" she asked him.

He looked puzzled, undoubtedly as much by the rudeness of her interruption as the out-of-the-blue question. But he said politely, "Not so much. My dad took me once or twice, but he left my mom and me when I was still pretty young. Why?"

"Because one of the hard-and-fast rules when you get a fish on the line is to let it run with the bait a bit to set the hook before you haul him in." As if she'd know. Still, she'd certainly heard enough fishermen over the years to talk a decent game.

His dark brows furrowed. "O-kay."

Mark, who faced the kids from Jenny's side of the table, caught on much faster. "It's true," he said. "Trying to reel a fish in too quickly rarely pays in the end." His gaze rested on the kids' table for a second before he gave Jake a meaningful look. "You get a much more satisfying result if you play 'em a little, then haul them in slowly."

Enlightenment dawned. "Aw," Jake murmured. "Sure. You probably have a point."

"Okay, I don't have a clue what you all are talking about," Rebecca said mildly. "But this sure is good ice cream."

They laughed and turned the conversation in another direction.

Suddenly Austin blurted, "Aw, man, how'd you get so lucky?" Nolan said something in return, and Austin pushed out of his chair and came over to the adults' table. "Nolan and Bailey getta watch the new Transformers movie tonight on Mr. D's Blu-ray."

"Me, too!" Josh said.

"Yeah, even Squirt gets to see it," Austin agreed. "You remember that show, Jenny? The one I didn't get to see when it played in Silverdale because I caught the stinking flu from the guy in room 118? The one who—"

"—ran around spreading germs instead of having the decency to stay home when he was sick?" she completed the lament in unison with the boy.

Yes, she remembered. It was hard to forget when he'd been so vocal about the way he'd been robbed of the movie that he had waited *forever* to see.

Nolan and Bailey joined him at the table, Josh scrambling in their wake. "I told him he could watch it with us, Mom," Nolan said. "Bailey'd like that, too, wouldn't you?"

The girl nodded politely and he promptly turned back to his mother. "See? And I think he should probably ride home with us to save time. That'd be okay, wouldn't it?"

No, Jenny thought. She wasn't going to get stuck alone with Jake.

"Well, it would be," Rebecca said, "except for the part where it's a whole lot of unfair to Jenny and Jake. They were on an outing before we came tootling along to horn in on it."

You tell him, sister, she thought. "Not to mention it's a school night," she added with faux regret.

"No, it's not." Austin said. "Tomorrow's teacher prep, remember?"

Crap. She'd forgotten.

"Teacher prep?" Jake said.

"Or something." The boy grinned. "Who cares what, exactly, as long as it means a day off for us?"

"Not me!" Nolan whooped.

"Not me," Josh echoed, his eyes alight and a glaze of chocolate ice cream ringing his mouth.

"So how about it?" Austin asked Jenny.

"Don't look at me. It's up to your father." Sitting back, she refrained from patting herself on the back for her slick passing of the buck. But, really. If Jake wanted to be a parent so bad, then let him drive the last nail in the coffin. She'd been the biggest disciplinarian in Austin's life for quite some time now. It would be nice not to be the one saying no for a change.

"Okay," Jake said.

She whipped around to stare at him. "*Excuse* me?"

"Just sticking to the spirit of hook, line and running with the bait," he said with the facial equivalent of a shrug. Then he turned to Rebecca. "So it's okay with me, but you're the one who should have the final say. The boys worked the angles pretty hard to railroad you into doing what they wanted. If you're not in the mood for another kid tonight, just say the word. We can always rent the video this weekend."

"Dude!" Austin protested. "We don't have a Blu-ray."

"And yet I'm pretty sure we'd somehow muddle along." The level gaze Jake used to pin his son in place stayed steady until Austin looked away.

"I guess," he muttered to the floor.

"Austin's welcome to join us," Rebecca said. "We're just going to set them up in the family room with the video and a bowl of popcorn—nothing fancy."

The boys cheered, and Bailey, who had been fairly quiet—at least where the adults were concerned—smiled.

"Speaking of which, we should probably get going," Mark said. "I'll go settle the bill."

Jake crooked a finger at his son and, when Austin cocked his head, he held out his hand. "I need the key to the boat."

The teen dug it and its small rubbery key ring out of his pocket, but gave him a suspicious stare. "You ever even driven a boat?"

"Not often, but enough to know what I'm doing. If you'd rather come home with us, though—"

Austin handed the flotation key ring over.

Jake grabbed the plain package. "Here." He held it out. "This is for you." Turning to Rebecca he said, "Let me give you my card. My cell number is on it. Have Austin call after the show and I'll come pick him up."

"He can stay overnight," Nolan said, but zipped his lips when Jake turned his gaze on him. "Uh, that is…we'll do that, okay?"

Rebecca watched her flustered son turn away, and her lips curled up at the corners. "I need to get me that look," she said under her breath as she accepted the card Jake fished out of his wallet. "Because that was *very* nicely played."

Jenny had to admit it was. He'd acted like a real father for perhaps the first time since coming back into Austin's life. He hadn't tried to be the boy's friend. He had let it be known, not only that he understood they were being played, but that going with the Damoths tonight was a privilege—not a right—and had laid down the conditions under which his son could reap the benefit.

"Oh. Man."

The awe in Austin's voice had her turning in his direction. He held a framed photograph in his hands, its brown paper discarded on the table, and he was staring at it with dazzled eyes.

Even as she watched, however, he marshaled an expression of boredom.

The other kids didn't share his reserve. "Dude!" Nolan exclaimed, while Bailey said with breathless appreciation, "That. Is. So. *Cool!*"

Truly curious now, she joined them. "May I see?"

Wordlessly, Austin held out the frame. Taking it from his hands, she looked down.

And blurted, "Oh! My." Glancing over at Jake, she noted a hint of color on his cheekbones, but the black-and-white photograph he'd taken tugged at her like a toddler for her mother's attention, and Jenny turned back to study it.

It was an action shot of Austin just after he'd hurled the ball toward first base. It showed his body

English and the blur of the baseball in midair not far from his fingers, showed, too, the determination and concentration on his face.

"That's incredible," Mark said from over her shoulder.

Rebecca wriggled her way between them. "Don't leave me in suspense—let me see!" The same look that appeared on everyone else's face suffused her expression when Jenny handed it over. "Wow." She looked up at Jake. "*Wow.* This is amazing."

"It turned out pretty good," he said in a low-key way. "That's always a good feeling." His shoulders gave a subtle hitch. "I thought Austin might get a kick out of it."

"Yeah, it's okay." The teen was clearly trying to adopt his father's casual cool. "Uh…thanks."

"No problem. You want me to take it back to Jenny's for you?"

"No, that's all right," Austin said a hair too quickly.

Jake, however, didn't indicate by so much as a muscle twitch that he'd caught on to the fact that Austin wasn't ready to let it out of his sight. "Well, I guess Jenny and I should take off. I want to check over the boat before I drive it. Give me a call when you're ready to come home."

"'Kay."

They thanked Mark for the ice cream and said their goodbyes, then left the clearing and walked single file down the switchbacks to the docks. Jake didn't talk and, once on the boat, sat in the driver's seat to study the boat's instruments.

Jenny got out their life vests and began to relax. Heck, it didn't matter that it was just the two of them. It was a short ride to The Brothers' dock on the other side of the canal, Jake was clearly preoccupied, and all she had to do was sit tight for fifteen minutes max, and she'd be snug as a bug in a rug back in her own space. She passed Jake his safety vest, untied the back of the boat and stood prepared in the bow to un-loop the front line as well when he was ready to go.

With an economy of motion, he donned the flotation device and started the boat's engine. As soon as she freed the boat from the last cleat, he put the craft in gear and slowly pulled away from the dock, then headed for the mouth of the harbor.

Jenny returned to her seat, expecting him to give the boat a burst of speed as soon as they hit open water.

Instead he looked at her across the short space separating the two seats and continued putting along at a snail's pace. "So this is your favorite place, huh?"

She made a face. "Actually, it's Austin's favorite place, but he likes to attribute it to me."

"You got any hot plans for the night?"

"What? No." *Dammit!* Wrong answer. But caught flat-footed by the change of subject, she could only stare at him, too slow to lie through her teeth and say, "Yes, indeed. Big plans. *Biiig* plans. Gotta hurry."

She'd always stunk at on-the-fly lying.

"Excellent," he said easily. "I'm too wired and it's too nice a night to head straight home. Let's go explore a little bit."

Oh, let's not. But she didn't want to make a bigger deal of this than it warranted. She'd give him ten minutes or so, then plead a long day today and a bigger day at work tomorrow.

She tried to ignore the kick in her stomach as their eyes met. "Ducky."

CHAPTER NINE

OKAY, SO JENNY WASN'T THRILLED. Jake's initial inclination was to ignore the fact and just enjoy a little freedom on the water. Hell, his hand was on the throttle and he was ready to give it the forward momentum that would send them blasting down the canal.

But he couldn't in all good conscience do it. Pulling the throttle into neutral, he turned to look at her. "You're pissed at me." Although she'd been nothing but outwardly polite this evening, he'd felt her underlying reserve.

She raised her brows. "Am I?" The shiny dark hair he'd watched her tie in an honest-to-God knot earlier had listed to the left until it now nestled just behind her ear. Silky pieces had escaped the knot to float about her face or slither down her nape.

He ignored the sudden itch in his fingers. "I know I said I'd quit depending on you to smooth my way with Austin—and, swear to God, I intended to. But my timing's been off all over the place, because— damn, Jenny—I also knew better than to bring up the boat business in front of his friends, where it had a high potential to embarrass him or put him on the defensive right from the get. But I'd been worrying about the idea of him being out in a powerful boat without supervision, and the words just slipped right out of my mouth." He gave her a stern look. "Trust me, blurting things out that way? That's not me."

"Is that a fact?" she said in a tone dry as dust. "How fortunate for you."

He thrust a hand through his hair. "Look, I'm not bragging. I'm just usually very careful about that sort of thing. So the fact that I didn't even come close to thinking before I opened my mouth threw me in a panic, and I fell back on what I knew would work. Because where I can't seem to do a damn thing right with Austin, *you* never make a misstep."

"Are you kidding? Of course I do." But the corners of her lips crooked up. "Still—flattery works."

For a moment they simply looked at each other in silence. Then Jenny said, "You wanna see my real favorite place?"

He had no particular reason to feel so pleased, but he did all the same. "Sure."

"Do you know where Oak Head is?"

"Isn't that the beach over by Dabob Bay?"

"Yes. Take us there and I'll tell you something flattering about your parenting skills in return."

"Deal." He hit the throttle, sending the boat jetting across the water, and grinned when he heard her laugh. He'd always liked boating, although he hadn't actually done any since he'd left Razor Bay. Up until then, however, his summers had been filled with taking turns driving when water-skiing and bellyboarding with his crowd. With exploring every inlet and shoreline along their part of the canal.

They approached Oak Head a short while later. A few feet from the shore Jake cut the engine and raised the propellers. The Bayliner's bow scraped against the pebbly shore as it drifted up to the beach.

Jenny had climbed to straddle the point of the bow, the rope and anchor in hand, and he watched the knot in her hair slide another half inch down her neck. Then she jumped onto the beach and held the rope taut to keep the boat in place and, hauling his mind back to the business at hand, he climbed out.

He relieved her of the line and dragged the boat up until half the bow rested on dry land. Stretching the anchor line tight, he dug the points of the anchor into the sand and shale to prevent the craft from floating away on the still-rising tide. Once the chore was complete, he trailed her up the beach, glancing away when his gaze threatened to linger longer than it should on the hypnotic twitch of her hips.

Stopping at a stand of driftwood separating the beach from the cliffs, they settled on one weather-bleached, silvery log. Twilight was coming on fast, the sun hovering on the mountaintops. Feet planted in the finer sand fronting the log, they sat in silence for a moment, simply admiring the golden light and high clouds that were uplit like a Maxfield Parrish painting.

Then he turned to her. For a few additional seconds he studied her profile, admiring the flush that boating had raised in her smooth olive-skinned cheeks.

He drew a quiet breath and slowly exhaled. "Okay, lay it on me. I could use a compliment on my parenting skills right about now. Because from where I'm sitting, I really suck at it."

"I doubt you appreciate how much I'd love to agree," she said in a low voice, scooping up a handful of sand and staring straight ahead while the grains drifted through her fingers, until she was left with a couple pebbles that she flicked toward the waterline. "Maybe then I could talk you into leaving Austin here when you go back to your life in Manhattan. God knows I wouldn't feel nearly as crappy as I do at the prospect of you taking him away," she said to the sand between her feet. She turned her head to look at him. "But you know what, Bradshaw? You really don't."

"No?" It was pathetic how hopeful her words made him.

"No. You did the right thing making Austin demonstrate his ability to safely pilot a boat."

"It turns out he's a responsible driver."

"He truly is—and I credit Emmett for that. He was an ardent promoter of boating safety." She made a shooing gesture. "But that aside, you also handled Austin and Nolan's manipulation of the whole Transformer video thing the way a real dad would do."

He snorted. "I let them get their way."

She grinned at him. "Yes, you did. But you didn't let them have it all their way, and sometimes that's all parenting is—picking your battles. Watching a video on a non-school night when the other kids' parents have told you to your face they don't mind having an extra kid isn't worth fighting over."

"Thanks." He swayed in her direction to bump shoulders, then wished he hadn't. There was just something about *touching* this woman—something he'd be smart to avoid. He moved away, inching down the log.

And felt her eyes on him.

Then the weight of her gaze was gone and she sat quietly for a moment before she said, "Can I ask you something?"

"Sure." *Anything to take my mind off...what I don't want it on.*

"What are your plans for The Brothers?"

"Huh?" Swinging a leg over the log, he straddled it to face her. "What do you mean, what are my plans?"

"For when you go back to New York. Did you plan to sell it?" She was clearly trying not to show her tension, but her shoulders looked stiffer than a preacher's neck at a hooker convention.

"No! Jesus. Why would you think so?"

"You'll be living on one side of the country while the resort is on the other."

He hitched a shoulder. "Maybe so, but it's clear you've been running it just fine without any input from me. And it's Austin's legacy." He gave her a level look. "Right?"

"Yes. Emmett left me a quarter share in it, but the rest is in trust to Austin."

"And you're the trustee."

Her chin went up. "Yes."

Her bristling tugged a smile from the corners of his lips. "Believe me, I have no problem with that. Better you than me."

Her eyebrows rose. "That's an…interesting comment. Coming from someone with a business degree."

"Like I already told Max, I never actually got my degree." His own brows drew together. "And how the hell does everybody know what my major was, anyway?"

"Please." Elbows tucked in, arms angled out and hands held palms up, she turned from side to side indicating their surroundings like a game show hostess exhibiting the grand prize. "Small pond," she said, then swung back to flourish those same hands at him. "Big fish."

"You know, that everybody-knowing-everyone-else's-business shit was right up there on the list of things that bugged me most about Razor Bay when I was a kid." He shook his head. "Still, as Austin's trustee, you must already know that you have nothing to worry about as far as the resort goes. Emmett put you in charge of Austin's finances—that means you can legally do whatever the hell you want."

She jackknifed upright. "I would *never*—!"

"You think I don't realize that? My point is, you don't need my permission to do the job you've been doing. But if you want it, you've got it. Take care of Austin's investment, that works for me. Anyone with eyes in their head can see you're crazy about him, and I do know you'd never do anything that wasn't in his best interests. Hell, I didn't come here to mess with whatever arrangements you've got going. I just want to get to know my kid."

"Okay." Evidently mollified, she faced front again, staring at the show playing above the mountaintops as the sun sank behind them, turning the thin clouds above them a deeper, richer gold. "Thanks."

He'd seen the view a thousand times and opted to watch her instead. She steadfastly ignored him—if she was even aware that he was staring—and, drawing a deep breath of the salt-tinged air, he looked around the deserted beach.

And admitted slowly, "For all my problems with Razor Bay—and I own up to more than a few—this is really nice."

"I know." Her own issues with him apparently forgotten, she turned to face him, swinging her leg over the log to mimic his pose. Hands braced against the sand-and-wind-weathered wood between them, she leaned in, her dark eyes shining with enthusiasm. "I love this spot. I love that you can see civilization just across the canal, yet this end of the peninsula is still largely undeveloped. I hear there are a few places up on the bluff, but down here it's just pretty and quiet and...nice."

He found himself edging forward. Despite the in-grained survival instincts he'd developed as a teen, which were semaphoring frantic *don't-go-there* flags in his mind, he couldn't come up with a reason compelling enough to back off.

Planting his own hands until his fingertips were half an inch from touching her pink-tipped nails, he picked up his feet and raised his butt off the log, balancing his entire body weight on his palms. When he lowered his torso again, his knees brushed hers. "Pretty, quiet and nice," he said softly. "Kind of like you."

"Yeah, right." She made a rude noise. "You've clearly never heard me when I get away from the resort. I'm not particularly quiet on my own time."

"But you cop to the pretty and nice?"

"Hell, yeah." She gave him a cocky smile. "Surely you've heard I'm Razor Bay's reigning beauty? It's common knowledge. And I'm so nice, goodness sheds from me like stardust. There's often a stampede to collect the glittery wake I leave everywhere I go."

He nodded solemnly. "I have heard you're quite the paragon."

"Oh, yes." Then she threw back her head and let loose a deep belly laugh like the one he'd heard that night in the Anchor, her white teeth flashing while peals of contagious laughter poured from her throat.

Little by little she subsided, until she finally pressed a fist between her breasts and inhaled a deep breath. She gave him a little one-sided, close-lipped smile that was sexy beyond belief. And sighed contentedly. "Aw, man, I needed that. Is there *anything* that feels better than a good laugh?"

"Yes," he said, his heart beginning to thump, thump, thump against the wall of his chest. "This." And closing the distance separating them, he lowered his head and kissed her.

He wasn't prepared for the jolt that a mere touch of the lips gave him and didn't know whether pressing his to hers was the smartest thing he'd ever done— or a big mistake. It felt contrarily like both.

What he did know was that he'd meant to keep it brief. Well, probably, anyhow.

No. He likely had.

Okay, the truth was, he didn't know what the hell he'd intended—actual thought didn't seem to be playing a major part in his actions. Anything even resembling cognition had apparently drained from his generally facile brain and disappeared like water poured into the sand. So although he felt Jenny's start of surprise, the lion's share of his attention was focused firmly on her lips.

God. Such soft, soft lips.

They were smooth and so incredibly *supple* as they cushioned his own. And Christ on a crutch, they were sweet. As if she'd just bitten into a Rainier cherry and a hint of its juice lingered still.

It made him greedy for more and, lifting his head, he came at her from another angle. He opened his mouth over hers, then dragged it closed again to apply persuasive suction against the pliable fullness of hers. He tickled the seam of her lips with the tip of his tongue, wordlessly encouraging her to open to him.

She made a soft sound deep in her throat. Slipped her hands between the open lapels of his jacket to press against his chest beneath his worn, soft Columbia U. hooded sweatshirt.

And shoved him back, ripping their mouths apart.

Fuck. *Fuck!*

They stared at each other, only the lap of the tide against the shore and their ragged breaths sawing in and out of their lungs breaking the quiet of the evening.

"What the… You can't just—" She snapped her lips shut against the fragmented sentences issuing from them. Shot him some *you've-got-some-'splainin'-to-do* eye contact. Cleared her throat. "What was *that* all about?" Her eyes a little wild, she licked those soft, soft lips.

Which, Jake noticed, slicking his tongue over his own, were reddened from his kiss. "It was—" *What, genius?* He scratched the back of his head. "Hell if I know. I wanted to kiss you and couldn't talk myself out of it." His shoulder hitched. "Trust me, I gave it the old college try, but there's just something about you. It makes me crazy."

"Oh. Good. The diminished capacity defense." Then, deepening her voice, she said in a truly bad imitation of guy-speak, "'It's not my fault, judge. She made me do it.'"

Jake couldn't help it; he laughed. "Yeah. Something like that." Her way of refusing to take crap from anyone—or maybe it was only him?—shouldn't give him such perverse pleasure. Yet for some reason it did just that. To avoid examining *that* too closely, he changed the subject. "I bet you've heard a hundred times you taste like cherries."

"What?" She looked at him as if he'd gone insane. "No, of course I haven't."

"You're kidding me. How could you not? You've got lips just. Like. Cherries. Hand to God. I've never experienced anything like them."

She blinked at him. Then… "Ohmigawd, that's a line, isn't it?" she demanded, narrowing her eyes at him. "Oh! You are *smooth*. I bet you say that to all the—"

"Jesus, you're a hard sell. You honestly think anyone in their right mind would go around spouting that trash on *purpose?* Hell, I'm embarrassed to hear it coming from my mouth. But you can take this to the bank," he said irritably. "I said it because it's true and I can't believe no one else has ever told you so. You taste just like fucking cherries!"

"Silver-tongued devil, thy name is Jake." She crooked an amused smile at him. "But I'm sure I don't have to tell *you* that. I bet women tell you all the time, hey?"

"I'll give you silver-tongued." Disgruntled, he let his gaze wander back to her mouth. But that was clearly a mistake, for all it resulted in was his once again licking his lips and tasting a trace of those cherries.

Her smile faded. "Dammit," she whispered. "This is just *asking* for a big dose of regret." Raising her hands, which had somehow remained on his chest, she grabbed two fistfuls of the hoodie covering it and yanked him to her as she half rose off the log to kiss him.

Yes! He opened his lips beneath hers and sucked in a breath when her tongue slicked over his lower lip. His vision developing a distinctly red tinge, he wrapped his fingers around the backs of her legs, pulled her forward, then lifted her effortlessly to straddle the spread of his thighs. Resisting the urge to jerk her atop his burgeoning hard-on, he instead raised his hands to carefully frame her face, his fingers sliding behind her ears while he framed them with his thumbs.

His fingertips bumped the precarious knot of slippery hair behind her left ear, and it lost its fight with gravity, unraveling down her neck. Its cool, smooth weight as it waterfalled over her shoulders and partway down her back buried his fingers to the second knuckle, and streamers of it draped over the backs of his hands and wrists.

That was all it took—that and her renewed flavor as it spread across his tongue—to turn him inside out. From his mouth, his fingers, his thighs, sensation ricocheted to his brain—only to be immediately sent out again as fractured, kaleidoscopic impressions.

A beckoning woman scent that owed nothing to perfumes or soaps. Smooth skin. *Warm* skin. No, not warm, *hot*. That faint taste of Rainier cherries.

More than delicious. Damn near addictive.

He smoothed his hands down her neck beneath the loose hair, outlined her shoulders with his fingertips. She was such a little thing—a fact he couldn't seem to retain with any kind of permanency, considering how it managed to surprise him anew every time he saw her.

But as his hands explored the smooth flesh on her shoulders, then stroked the length of her back, he decided to cut himself some slack. He saw not only with his eyes but what she projected. And evidently *she* viewed herself as an Amazon.

Jenny did something talented with her tongue, and all thoughts fled as the blood in Jake's head aimed for more southern climes. Wrapping his hands around her hips, he picked her up once more and this time set her exactly where he wanted her.

Then sucked in a breath at the *feel* of the soft notch between her legs unerringly pressed against his cock.

She ripped her mouth free. *"Gawwd,"* she exhaled, her eyes heavy lidded and darker than midnight as they gazed into his. For a few hot seconds she oscillated her hips, riding him like a wet-dream cowgirl on a slo-mo mechanical bull, setting up a friction between their sexes that all but crossed his eyes.

Then out of the blue she stilled, and the sensual haze in her eyes began to evaporate while something that looked perilously like panic flashed in their depths. A second later, she scrambled from his lap and shoved to her feet.

"My God." She hitched her leg over the log to stand militarily erect in the little patch of sand. Her breasts rising and falling with her quickened breathing, she gazed at him in consternation. "What the hell have you started?"

"Hey, don't put this all on me," he snapped, his cock throbbing in unrelieved misery. "I might have started it, but nobody forced you to keep it going." Not that he'd had any complaints while she'd done so.

Her shoulders snapped back and her arms crossed over her breasts. "So much for Mr. Smooth."

He felt heat suffuse his face. Usually he could be counted on to be smoother than silk; he didn't know why with her he had all the finesse of a pimply faced boy stealing his first kiss then pulling the girl's hair to let her know she hadn't affected *him*.

"Still," she continued coolly, "you're right. I was a full participant." She glanced at the sky. "It's starting to get dark. Shall we head back?"

Yeah. They should. He wasn't even sure how the hell they'd come to be in this position.

When Kari died he'd been too shell-shocked to even look at another female. University was harder than high school by miles and, in order to keep his grades up, he'd had to bust his butt. By the time his interest in women—or at least in the prospect of sex—resurfaced, he'd had time to consider what he was looking for in a relationship.

And what he'd decided was nothing long-term. After all, he wasn't the best bet in that arena, was he? At first, his need to keep his eye on the prize interfered; he couldn't afford to let anything get in the way of his studies. Then he'd nabbed the opportunity at *National Explorer* during his internship. And that meant he was out of country too often and sometimes for too long to build a relationship even if he'd been interested.

Whatever the reason at any given time, his decision had rendered him some seriously good, if temporary, times with a number of the world's most beautiful women. Women who, like him, desired nothing more than what he had to offer.

Jenny wasn't like them. As Max had said, she wasn't the casual kind. And although seriously cute, she was nowhere close to drop-dead beautiful.

So why the hell did she pull at him like a tide at full moon?

Hell. He rolled his shoulders. *Because it's been*

a while since you got laid, bro. That had to be the reason.

Whatever it was, as he handed her into the boat, coiled the anchor rope and shoved the Bayliner's bow off the beach, hopping aboard as it floated free of the shore, he determined one thing for sure.

This strange attraction he felt for her had too damn much potential for disaster—so from here on out, he was going to treat her like a downed live wire.

And give her a wide, big-ass berth.

CHAPTER TEN

AUSTIN'S FRIEND NOLAN was almost late for practice the following Tuesday and he had Bailey with him when he finally did arrive. They jumped off their bikes, letting them drop to the grass next to those of other team members, then loped over to the dugout.

Austin found himself watching Bailey just as he'd watched her the other night at the Damoths', but shrugged off his interest. Hell, even though she was almost as tall as he was, she was really cute with her blue eyes and pink lips. Plus she had those pretty white teeth, the top middle ones not only longer than the rest but with a tiny gap between them. There was just something so girly about that.

Hell, what guy wouldn't look at her?

"Hey, coach," Nolan called out as the two of them reached the diamond. "This is my cousin Bailey. Can she practice with us today?"

"You kiddin' me, Damoth?" Sam Jenkins jerked upright from where he'd been tying the cleats he'd propped against the dugout bench. "She's a freakin' girl!"

"Dude, chill," Austin heard himself say. "It's practice. And you've heard Nolan talk about her enough to know he thinks she's good." Okay, so she probably wasn't as good as a guy. But, like he'd said, it was just a practice game, not the real deal.

Coach Harstead ignored everything but the original question. "Sure." He gave Bailey a nod. "Let's see what you can do in left field."

She shot him a grin, whipped a smooshed baseball cap out of her hip pocket and pulled it on, threading her long, dark ponytail through the donut hole in the back. She caught the mitt Nolan tossed her from his gym bag, then trotted to the outfield.

Austin was assigned to the field team as well and took his position between second and third base. A few minutes later practice started in earnest.

About ten minutes into it, Oliver Kidd hit a ball that flew over Austin's head and Austin whipped around to see how Bailey handled herself. The ball was a long fly and she backpedaled like a pro to get under it. The thing was sailing high, though—a home run in the making if he'd ever seen one—and he could tell that by the time it reached the end of its arc and started to drop it'd probably be in the trees.

Then Bailey took a few running steps toward the woods and, watching the ball over her shoulder, leaped into the air.

It was as if she levitated straight up, her feet together and toes pointed, one arm stretched overhead with the mitt extended toward the sky, her long-limbed body in its white T-shirt and washed-out jeans a pale parenthesis against the evergreens.

The team went so silent you could hear the ball smack into her mitt.

Then they all went apeshit, with Nolan screaming loudest of all, "I toldja so, I *toldja!*" As she landed lightly on her feet, the team surged toward her.

Austin was one of the first to reach her. "That. Was. Epic! How did you *do* that?"

Pink tinged her cheeks, but she shrugged as if it was no big deal. "Eight years of ballet."

"If that's the result, I should sign my guys up for classes," Coach said as he joined them on the field. He clapped his hands. "All right, let's get back to it, boys. Bailey, grab a bat. Let's see what you can do on the infield."

Turned out she was a solid hitter, as well. She could stand more speed running bases, but even then, she stole second base with a sweet slide. All told, she pretty much owned the game, and was actually better than a couple of their weaker players and maybe even a couple of their more solid ones. Austin had never seen anything like it.

"Man," he enthused as he and Nolan and Bailey pedaled their bikes back to town after practice. "You were great!"

She gave him a quiet smile. "Thanks. So were you."

"Yeah, but I'm a guy. Who knew a girl could be that good?"

The warm blue eyes she'd turned on him grew cool. "'*Scuse* me? Do you have any idea how sexist and insulting that is? It's attitudes like that that passed Title Nine into law."

"Huh?"

"I'm great…for a girl?" She coasted alongside him on her bike. "You don't see how I might—no, how I *do*—take that as a very backhanded compliment? I'm good, period."

He felt his face grow red and opened his mouth to cut her down to size. But then he thought about the way she'd played in practice, surrounded by all the guys. And he had to swallow his pride and admit…

"You're right. I'm sorry. You played damn near as good as everyone on the team. And better than Mikey and Dan."

"And me, some days," Nolan said cheerfully, "although I rocked today."

Bailey grinned at her cousin.

After Nolan and Bailey turned off for the road to the Damoths' house, Austin pedaled full-out toward The Brothers. Jenny was still at work when he let himself into the cottage a short while later. He was happy to see that his dad's Mercedes SUV was gone from the lot, too.

Although…

Retrieving the baseball photo Jake had taken of him from his backpack, he stared at it for several long seconds before putting it back on the dresser, where he'd been keeping it ever since last Thursday when Jake had given it to him. Even when it was out of his hands, he had a hard time looking away.

And he had to admit he hadn't been quite as pissed at his father since receiving it. Neither had he felt as annoyed when he couldn't avoid spending time with the guy. Jake was more persistent than he'd expected.

He ran his fingertip over the action shot. That had to be the dopest picture *ever,* and he'd even taken it to practice today to show everyone. But Bailey's arrival and inclusion in practice had shuffled it to the back of his mind, and he'd forgotten he had it with him until he was almost home.

Not that it was a big deal or anything. Still. He might take it to this Thursday's practice or, if not then, maybe to the game on Saturday.

But, hey, that was a lifetime from now. Right this minute he had better things to do. He pulled open the fridge door and started hauling out food. Lots better things.

Like making himself a sandwich or two so he didn't drop dead of hunger before dinner.

"I'M TAKING OFF, JENNY."

She looked up from her rocker on the cottage's darkened front porch. She sat sipping a cup of tea and watching Friday-night guests unload their car behind the Starfish, a rental situated two small cabins away and staggered a touch nearer the shoreline than her own. Raising her eyebrow at Austin, who had poked his head out the door, she said in surprise, "Don't you want a ride?"

"Nah, I'll take my bike."

"It's going to be a busy night at the Anchor. Be sure to wear your jacket with the reflective tape."

He rolled his eyes. "Yes, Mother."

"Okay, sorry, I know you will—and that your bike is equipped with that blinking light under the seat. What I *meant* to say was 'have fun.' And tell Nolan he can spend the night here next time."

"That's all right," he assured her quickly. "The Damoths've got way more room than we do."

Funny, that had never stopped him from inviting his best friend here before. And was that *cologne* wafting her way? Telling herself not to be silly— something must be in bloom—she focused on what really had her eyebrows drawing together: the thing she feared he was *not* saying. "Do you miss your house, Austin?"

He shrugged. "Sometimes."

"Do you...want to move back there?" She had known the day would come that he would, but she'd been happy to delay it for as long as possible. She loved living in her own place, a home she was earning with hard work. The big Craftsman was a lovely place, but it was Emmett and Kathy's. She couldn't help but feel it wouldn't seem right living there without them.

"Not really." He leaned against the doorjamb. "I mean, I miss the media room and there was a lot more space. But..." What looked like a shudder shivered his torso. "I don't want to live there. Not without grandpa."

"You know you can tell me if you ever change your mind, right?" She was immediately slammed with guilt as she remembered he likely wouldn't even be here come summer.

"Sure." He pushed upright. "I gotta go. Nolan and Bailey got a new video game we're gonna try out."

And before she could tell him once again to have a good time, he disappeared back into the house. Seconds later, she heard him close the kitchen door behind him, the faint sound of him wrestling his bike out of the mudroom, then that door banging closed, as well.

So. Nolan and *Bailey,* huh? That explained a few things.

Since she didn't have to drive tonight, she went into the house to trade her tea for a glass of wine. When she came back out, she set the goblet on the little porch table and wrapped herself in the blanket she'd grabbed from the back of the couch, then sat in the rocker again, comforted by the creak of its ancient wicker seat beneath her weight. She'd left the porch light off and watched as the path lights, which had flickered to life throughout the grounds earlier, glowed a bit brighter as the sky steadily darkened.

It was another clear evening and stars clustered the heavens.

The couple at the Starfish slammed the trunk of their car and went into the one-bedroom cabin. Two

tween girls wearing oversize guest robes and flip-
flops giggled down the path on their way—she'd
hazard a guess from the towels hugged to their
chests—to the indoor pool.

Jenny liked nights like this, when she could sit in
the dark surveying everything that went on around
her without being on display herself.

Not to mention the built-in bonus of removing
herself from the temptation of that damn kitchen
window overlooking the Sand Dollar.

Just beyond the Starfish, the resort's hot tub nestled beneath a rustic roof in an oasis of plantings
at the back of the inn, to the left of the pool-house
door. Her peripheral vision caught the motion-sensor
light above it when it came on. She sighed, hoping
it wasn't the gigglers, since children under thirteen
were not allowed in the hot tub unattended and she so
didn't want to be the one to bust up their good time.

The discount deals she'd made with the Groupon and LivingSocial deal-of-the-day websites were
paying off even better than she'd dared hope. What
they'd lost by cutting their usual room rates in half
was more than compensated by the inn's apprecia-
bly higher occupancy numbers for the rest of April
and the early part of May than generally was the case
this time of year. She was tickled not only by what
the bar and restaurant were taking in and the side
benefit of being able to keep more staff on, but by
the number of full-price reservations they'd garnered

as well from participants who'd wanted to give The Brothers a try, but not during the restricted dates.

The downside, of course, was that having more guests put her on perpetual duty. So raising her glass to her lips and hoping she wouldn't have to chase the girls out of the tub, she started to stand, thinking it was best to get it over with.

But the gigglers disappeared through the door to the pool before she was even fully on her feet and, blinking, she turned her attention to the spa.

Only to choke on her wine at the sight of Jake, naked from the waist up, in the hot tub. Holy Krakow, what was *he* doing there? Well, okay, that part was self-evident. It was just—

She'd had zero luck, since last Thursday, forgetting the kisses they'd shared over on Oak Head. God knew she'd done everything she could not to remember, but the recollection persisted in popping up no matter how often she shoved it down. Like a manic carnival barker, it bid for her attention with promises of a front-row seat and all the popcorn she could eat.

Practically living in each other's pockets didn't help. She'd swear every time she'd looked out her kitchen window this week, Jake had been right there in her line of vision.

And her damn stubborn eyes hadn't improved matters. They'd refused to look away every time they'd caught him in the cross hairs. Hadn't done so before tonight, and definitely weren't cooperating now.

In her defense, though, was there a woman *alive* who'd have the willpower to look away from the spectacle of water glistening on those hard brown shoulders? The man was built. And she didn't need the evidence currently in front of her eyes to know he had long, lean muscles that rippled beneath his skin when he stretched his arms along the back of the hot tub the way he was doing now. Didn't need to see his corrugated abs nor the visual reminder of that sculpted chest. She'd been up close and personal with both.

Hell, she'd been plastered against them about as close as a woman could get.

Her head went back, pressing into the high back of the rocking chair. Whoa. What was she thinking?

Well, lemme think, her sardonic inner woman whispered in her head. *That the man is* h-a-w-t *hot, and you wouldn't mind being body to body again with all that hotness sometime in the future?*

"No," she whispered. It didn't matter how sexually appealing he was. He could dance naked for all she cared—she wasn't going there again. He'd be back in New York soon, she would be here and, even though Austin didn't yet know it, the teen stood squarely between them with a foot in each camp.

But dammit, in spite of her sarcasm when she'd called Jake a silver-tongued devil, she secretly believed him to be exactly that—and not merely with words. Because if his tongue was silver when he spoke, it was downright platinum when he kissed.

Annnd—I'm not going to recall that. Not gonna-not gonna-not gonna.

Suddenly his lips shaped a swear word and he surged to his feet. Water cascaded the length of his torso, from his wide shoulders to the fan of hair on his chest and down his midsection. Most of it at that point trickled a river along the narrowing line of body hair that bisected his diaphragm and six-pack to disappear into the navy-and-white hibiscus-printed board shorts riding his hip bones.

Even as Jenny watched, he turned and planted a knee on the underwater seat, then leaned over the back of the hot tub. She swallowed drily as his shorts plastered against his butt as if vacuum-packed. They clung with equal faithfulness to the muscular backs of his thighs.

Tongue sticking to the roof of her mouth, she could only stare.

Then he yelled, "Shit. Shit-shit-shit!" and it broke her reverie.

She surged to her feet. *For God's sake, girl,* she silently chastised herself. Gawking at his fine bum was *not* helping her put his kisses out of her head. Jerking the two sides of her blanket together, she anchored it in one fist between her breasts, then slid her free hand through the separation below to gather up her still half-full wineglass.

She didn't know what his drama was, but he looked pretty damn fit to her. So, unless there was blood involved—and she'd seen no evidence of that—he was on his own. Letting herself into the house, she left the living room lights off and made her way to the kitchen by the dim illumination from the microwave light over the stove.

She'd lost her taste for the Riesling and was rinsing her goblet when there was a knock on the door. She froze, then simply stood there, barely breathing, thinking in the subterranean depths of her mind that if she stayed very still, perhaps Jake—as she didn't have a doubt in the world who stood on the other side—would go away.

Instead, she heard the door open. "Jenny? You're here, right? I saw your car in the lot."

Crap. "Close the door, Bradshaw—and be sure that you're on the other side. I'm not in the mood for company tonight."

"Neither am I," he snapped. "I've got a shitload of work to get done. But I have need of your managerial skills."

Damn! She blew out an aggrieved breath. "Fine. Give me a second." She took a few calming breaths, smoothed her hands over her hair and concentrated on not leading with her chin when she walked into the living room. "What can I do for you?"

"You can lend me a flashlight and the use of your dainty little hands."

She gaped at him. "Excuse me?"

"Well, it's either that or call maintenance for me. I knocked my keys behind the hot tub, and my arms are too big for the space between it and the wall.

My room card is on the ring, so I'm locked out. And in case you haven't noticed, it's on the chilly side here." His lips crooked up on one side. "At least when you're wet."

She had to give herself a stern, silent talking-to in order not to check out all that wetness more than she already had. She was just grateful that he'd at least wrapped a towel around his hips. "Tell me you didn't have them sitting on the rim of the tub," she demanded as she went back into the kitchen for her flashlight.

"Well, I could do that," he agreed from the living room. "If you don't have a problem with lying."

She exhaled a disgusted breath. "Doesn't anybody read the signs? It's not like we don't have them posted all over the place." Then she shook off her pique and slapped on her professional face as she re-entered the living room with her flashlight in hand. "Let's go see what I can do."

When they reached the hot tub, she crouched down at one of the corners nearest the wall of the pool house. She freely admitted this spa was an odd design. Of poured concrete and beachy blue-and-green tiles, it was half sunk into the ground, but not entirely so—a foot and a half of it stood above the patio. It also should have been situated either flush against the inn wall or a decent space away from it.

"You're not the first person to have this problem," she allowed as she trained the beam of her flashlight into the gap. "I'm just not the one who's usually called in to deal with it. Okay, there's the key ring. Oh, crap. I don't think you could have put it more squarely in the middle if you'd tried. I shouldn't have a problem getting my arm in there, but it's not going to be long enough to reach the thing from either side. Let me see if there's something in the pool house I can use."

"There's not," Jake said. "I already looked."

"Shit." She shot him a guilty look. "I'm sorry, that's not very professional—"

He made a rude noise. "And yet it fits the situation."

Since she'd heard him say it several times since his keys had taken a dive, she nodded acknowledgment and turned back to study the tub.

And sighed. "Turn around."

He turned his head to look at her. "What?"

"Turn around. If we want to get this taken care of sometime tonight, I'm going to have to get in the tub. I'm not getting my jeans wet and I'm not stripping in front of you, so turn around."

He did, presenting her with his wide bare shoulders and long bare back, and Jenny kicked off her shoes and socks and stripped out of her jeans. She climbed into the tub, shivering as luxuriously hot water lapped above her knees when she descended to the second step. Having no desire to turn her nicely opaque hipster boy shorts translucent with water, she swung around the hand railing that followed the steps into the spa and made her way along the seats until she reached the midpoint at the back of the tub. She flashed her light down into the gap and bent over to slide her arm into it.

It was an awkward stance. The position left her butt jutting out. It also left her with her head turned to one side, and she could only see in bits and pieces.

But at last her fingers brushed the metal ring. It took her two additional tries but she finally hooked it with a couple of fingers. "Gotcha!"

"Great," Jake said. "Like I told you, I've got to get back to work, so I really— Whoa, *mama.*"

She whipped around, the sheer appreciation in his voice sending scalding heat into all four cheeks. She watched him watch her, and even as embarrassment crawled through her veins, she had the oddest urge to thrust her pitifully small breasts out, to…God, preen. And realizing it was all she could do to keep her own gaze on his face, she snapped, "I didn't tell you to turn around!"

"Sorry. I thought you were done. But damn, Jenny. Purple. Those are seriously hot panties."

"You're supposed to look away when you see I'm still in my undies!"

"Yeah, that's gonna happen." Amusement laced his tone. "Hey, I turned around just like you asked. But I'm a guy and you've got a great ass. It's like a rule of the brotherhood or something—given the opportunity, even if accidental, we're honor bound to take full advantage."

"Honor bound. Now, there's an interesting choice

of words, considering." She tossed his key ring at him, hoping to take a little divot out of that hard hide.

He snatched them out of the air before they could do any damage, then had the temerity to grin at her when she growled. Reaching out, he half assisted, half hauled her out of the tub.

Whipping off his towel, he extended it to her. "Here. It's damp but it's better than nothing."

She accepted the offering with an insincerely muttered thanks. He seemed to be watching her every move, so after a quick swipe that sopped up the worst of the wetness, she stepped into her jeans and pulled them up her legs.

And felt better at being covered.

He gave her a knowing look and said, "Thanks for your help, Jenny." He jerked his chin at the tub. "You really should get a little shelf installed to fill in that space." Then without another word, he turned and headed for his cabin, six feet of mostly bare man cockily whistling in apparent satisfaction at having the last word.

As she watched him stride into the night, she decided she'd talk to maintenance tomorrow and see that they installed a shelf, exactly as he suggested.

If only to avoid another night like this one.

CHAPTER ELEVEN

LATE THAT NIGHT JAKE PUSHED through the doors of the Anchor Bar and Grill. Spotting Max lounging on his tailbone in the same booth Jake had seen him in the last time he was here, he made a beeline across the room, weaving between tightly packed tables. He dropped down onto the wooden seating across from his half brother moments later. "So, what's the deal?" he said. "This your personal booth or something?"

"Yes. Go away."

"I can't. I need guy time."

"Try Greg over there at the first table this side of the dart-throwing space. I'm sure he'd appreciate your kisses."

"Yeah, kissing a guy—that's what I need. Because I'm not traumatized enough as it is."

"What's the matter, little Bradshaw? Couldn't get in for a manicure?"

"Don't be an ass. Oh, wait. That's pretty much your full-time job description. I don't know why I thought tonight would be any different." He started to push out of the booth.

"Oh, sit down." Max shook his head. "Jesus, you're a drama queen."

"Says the guy who picked on a nine-year-old on a daily basis to make his own problems seem more manageable."

Even in the dim light, he could see the rush of blood beneath Max's skin. But Jake had to hand it to the guy, he didn't detonate the way he used to.

Instead, he shrugged. "Maybe so. You gonna tell me why you're traumatized or not? The kid giving you grief?"

"That's actually improved a fraction. No, I saw Jenny's panties tonight. Purple panties, Max. With Jenny in them. And the fucking image is seared into my retinas—I can't get it out of my head."

Max came half out of his seat. "I told you to stay the hell away from her."

"I wasn't making a move on her." *Not* then, *anyway.* Letting his breath out with a sigh, he explained the situation.

Max's heavy brows remained gathered over his nose. "You told her you'd turn around."

"And I *did!* But then she said 'gotcha!' and I thought she was all done." He frowned. "According to her, once I saw she was still in the tub in her underwear, I should've turned back around and pretended I didn't see."

His half brother snorted. "Like that's gonna happen. I'm pretty sure there's a code or something. We can't break the code." He shook his head as if amazed anyone would even suggest such a thing.

With a quick slap of his palms, Jake jerked one

hand back and pointed the other at Max. "Exactly! That's what *I* said. But she all but told me I was full of shit."

"And she'd be right. But she was wrong about expecting any red-blooded man to turn his back again once he'd clapped eyes on the panties. So, purple, huh?"

"Deep purple. Those stretchy little boy kind that hug the ass like a lover. And you can take this to the bank—her ass is *fine*."

"Don't want to hear that part. Still, purple panties. And you said she climbed in the tub? Tell me they were wet."

He shook his head regretfully. "I wish. She managed to keep them dry. The girl's damn tricky."

"Yeah, she's a smart one." Max knocked back his beer, rubbed foam from his lips with the back of his hand and shook his head. "Women like that are a serious disadvantage for our gender."

"Tell me about it," he muttered.

Max set down his beer and appeared to dedicate an inordinate amount of attention to his own big-knuckled hand as the tip of his blunt forefinger circled the mug's rim. Then, blowing out a breath, he sat back in the booth, crossed his brawny arms across his brawnier chest and eyed Jake.

Who had gone on alert even before his half brother cleared his throat.

"So," Max said. "I've got me four tickets to a Mariners game Friday. I was supposed to go with friends, but you know how it goes—plans have a way of falling through. If you're interested, you, the kid and maybe a friend of the kid's can join me instead." He gave Jake a hard-edged stare that warned him not *even* to get any ideas. Then, underestimating Jake's ability to read signals, he added, "I can think of a helluva lot better things to do than spend several hours in your company. But I wouldn't mind getting to know my nephew a little."

Yeah? Jake wondered. Because if the expression flashing across the big man's face was anything to go by, just acknowledging his relationship with Austin had Max unnerved.

Which tickled the hell out of Jake. God knew he could relate. And having developed a definite fondness for messing with his half brother, he said, "C'mon, admit it." He shot Max a lopsided smile. "Austin's just an excuse. You love me. Ya wanna spend time with me."

Max's response was a rude, anatomically impossible suggestion.

Jake answered in kind even as he acknowledged, if only to himself, the kernel of warmth unfurling in his own chest from the invitation. So he added, in dead earnestness, "I'd like that. Thanks."

Max looked uncomfortable. "Yeah, well, I thought it might give you a hand up with the kid."

"Austin."

"Yeah." One big shoulder twitched and that unsettled look came and went again. "Austin."

"For what it's worth, I think you're probably right. Tickets to the Mariners should earn me some points with him. And asking his friend Nolan is brilliant. Austin'll dig scoring a few points of his own." He planted his elbow on the scarred wooden table and his chin in his palm and gazed across the table. "Man. Who knew you'd turn out to be so smart?"

Max flashed an unexpected grin, and as Jake took note of his brother's white, white teeth, it hit him that smiling was something the guy didn't do nearly enough.

And wasn't that all kinds of ironic? Here Jake had thought *he* had control issues. But compared to Max he was effing Little Lord Fauntleroy.

Humor lingered in the other man's dark eyes even after his smile had slowly faded. "Yeah," he agreed with a wry twist of his lips as he picked up his beer again. "Who the hell knew?"

AUSTIN PLAYED IT COOL when Jake dropped by the cottage and invited him and Nolan to the Mariners game. But moments after his father left to return to the Sand Dollar, he grabbed his bike and pedaled like the wind to Nolan's house.

Reaching the Damoths' front yard, he jumped from his ride and was halfway up their steps before he even heard the bike clatter to the lawn. He gave his friend's door an impatient *rat-a-tat-tat* with his knuckles.

Mrs. D opened the door, but when he went to step

over the threshold, she unexpectedly blocked him. "I'm sorry, hon," she said. "You can't come in. Nolan has chicken pox."

"Huh?" He blinked at her as he assimilated the information. "Chicken—? Didn't that used to be a baby disease?"

"Not necessarily. It did mostly strike the young, but back before vaccinations, it wasn't unheard of to get it later in life. And now we've got ourselves a mini-breakout, because old Dr. Howser apparently stored the vaccination improperly, which made it ineffective." She gave him a significant look. "You went to Dr. Howser. And chicken pox is highly contagious."

"Aw, man!" He stepped back. "I was gonna invite Nolan to a Mariners game my dad and uncle are taking me to Friday night." It seemed weird to call the men that, seeing how he didn't know either of them worth spit. But still. That's who they were, if only in a legal way.

He gave his best bud's mom a hopeful look. "Friday's almost a whole week away. Maybe Nolan'll be better by then." *He has to be. I don't wanna be all by myself with those guys!*

She shook her head. "I really am sorry, Austin, because I know he'd love to go and is going to be even more disappointed than you that he can't. But he only just broke out in a half dozen bumps, and Dr. Janus tells me that means he'll have more tomorrow and likely even more the day after that, since the farther away from babyhood you get, the nastier the disease tends to be. Once he's finished breaking out, it'll take about a week before they quit being contagious. Until then, he's in quarantine."

He kicked his toe into the floor of the porch. "Crap."

"Yeah, I know. It stinks." Then her face brightened. "You could take Bailey, though. She was vaccinated by a different doctor."

A voice in Austin's head chanted, *Yes Yes Yes!* and his heartbeat broke into an energetic B-boy routine. He essayed a shrug of his shoulders, however, and managed to sound bored when he said, "I suppose that'd be okay. If she wantsta, that is."

"Well, let's ask." Turning into the foyer, she called, "Bailey! Come here a second, will you, hon?"

Almost in concert with the question, Bailey materialized in the living room end of the entrance hall, looking pretty and fresh in blue jeans and a multicolored T-shirt, her dark hair spilling in a shiny curtain below her shoulders.

Mrs. D smiled at her. "How would you like to go with Austin to a Mariners game next Friday?"

Bailey gave him an uncertain look, then turned her attention back on her aunt. "Could I talk to Austin alone for a minute?"

The older woman blinked, but then gave a nod. "Sure. Why don't you two go sit out on the stoop. When you make up your mind, hon, come let me know." Mrs. D gave Bailey a fond smile and headed toward the living room.

Bailey gave her aunt a quick kiss as they passed each other, then came out onto the small porch and pulled the door closed behind her.

For a moment he and the pretty thirteen-year-old simply looked at each other, then in unspoken agreement they took their seats on the top step just as Mrs. D had suggested. Gripping her knees, Bailey turned to him. "Tell me the truth. Did Aunt Rebecca guilt you into inviting me?"

"What? No!" For a second he struggled with an ingrained need to keep the crazy feelings roaring through his veins to himself. Especially any that could be construed as even the faintest bit girly.

Yet in the end, he wanted her to accept the invitation more than he worried he might come across as less manly than, oh, say, his father or uncle would in the same situation.

"She suggested you," he admitted, "but I jumped all over it. Jake said Deputy Bradshaw—that is, my… uncle—invited him, me and a friend of my choice to CenturyLink stadium this coming Friday. And I barely know either one of them, ya know? So as much as I'm all over seeing the Mariners play live, what the eff am I supposed to talk to them about for—man—what could be four, six, even *eight* hours?"

The delicate wings of her eyebrows drew together. "It'll go that long?"

"It takes an hour and a half, minimum, to get to Seattle from here—and that's if the boats are on time or the traffic isn't all bollixed up if they decide to drive around instead of taking the ferry. So, multiply that by two and add it to the game itself, which can go middling fast or really slow." *Annnnd,* crap. *Way to go, ass-cap.* Now she *really* wouldn't want to go.

But she only murmured dreamily, "I love the ferries."

Okay, maybe things weren't in the crapper yet. He sat straighter. "I'll ask if we can go that way. Either way, though, Bailey, it would sure be easier if I had someone my own age there. Mrs. D says Nolan can't leave the house. I'd like it if you'd say yes."

He didn't add that, even if it hadn't occurred to him to ask her until Mrs. D had suggested it, if Nolan *had* been available it would've been a tough choice between taking him or her. Because Nolan had been his best friend forever.

But *she*…well, she was just so…he didn't even know what.

No, untrue. He sure as hell knew she was pretty.

And he knew that if he should ever work up the nerve to touch her, she would be…

Just.

So.

Effing.

Soft.

The fact that she was also one dope baseball player was just the sprinkles on his cupcake.

She swiveled toward him. "If they're your dad and uncle, how come you don't know them? And why do you call them Jake and Deputy Bradshaw?"

He shrugged. "Jake went off to college when I was like a newborn and didn't bother coming back until a few weeks ago. Deputy Bradshaw—*Max*—is his half brother. He's been in town practically my whole life, but he and Jake were like enemies and shit all through school, so he never acknowledged me as a relative. I got no idea why they think now is a good time to try to fix their relationship, let alone drag me into it. Maybe they think they can make up for all the times they weren't there when I might've actually liked them to be." Gazing out at the currently deserted road, he shook his head. "They can't."

She looked at him for a moment, then slowly said, "My mom has cancer. She sent me here so I could—" crooking her index and forefingers, she sketched quotation marks in the air "'—live a normal life' while she concentrates on getting well." Her hands dropped to her lap and, staring down at them, she said in a low voice, "The truth is, though, I don't know if she will. Get well, that is." Tears welled in her eyes.

Oh shit, oh shit! Crying girls scared the bejesus out of him, because he never knew what to do to make things better. But he reached for her nearest hand anyway and gave it a squeeze. "Are you that convinced she won't?"

She went very still, her only movement that of her

sweetly curved boobies as she drew in a shuddery breath. "No," she said in a tiny voice.

"Look," he said to the curtain of hair that spilled between them, masking her face, "my grandma and grandpa died this year, so I know what it's like to lose family. I can't promise you that everything will turn out fine, 'cause the truth is it doesn't always. But Jenny says that it's just as easy to keep a positive outlook as a negative one—and that sometimes doing so sends positive energy out into the universe and generates positive results in return." He shrugged. "I don't know if that's too woo-woo for you, but I found when things turned to shit, thinking that way kind of helped."

The eyes she suddenly raised to lock onto his own were so sad and yet filled with such resolve that they just devastated him.

"Yeah?" she demanded quietly. "So, why aren't you taking your own advice?"

"Huh?"

"If you're all about the positive, why *not* take your dad and uncle up on their offer to get to know them better?"

His first thought was to summarily blow her off. But before he could so much as open his mouth to tell her that *she* hadn't been there when he was growing up, so she didn't have the first idea what she was talking about, she was already going on.

"It sucks that they weren't around until now, and I can't pretend to know how that must have felt, because my dad died in Afghanistan before I was born—which was crappy but at least didn't feel like he'd deserted me. But don't you see? Just the fact that they're alive and at least wanna get to know you is good news. *Isn't* it?" Her blue-eyed gaze bored into his. "Because what if it turns out you like them? You might have years and *years* to do all kinds of great stuff with them."

It had never occurred to him that Jake or Max could die. Not that he knew them well enough to get all torn apart about it if they did—not like he had when Grandpa died.

Not like the way he knew he would if something happened to Jenny.

Still it gave him an awful feeling in his gut. As if something scaly were slithering around in there.

"Did you ever miss him?" he asked. "Your father?"

"Sometimes, like on father/daughter days at school." She rolled her shoulders. "But mostly I never knew him—so I didn't have anything I could point at *to* miss."

"That should have been me, too, 'cause fuck knows I never knew my old man, either. But when I was little, I kept thinking he'd show up for some of my stuff."

"Like what?"

"Just…events, you know? My graduation from preschool and open-house nights at my grade and Junior high schools. Baseball games. Which, okay,

Jake's been at since he came back. But he wasn't at the Thanksgiving pageant to see me be a turkey or at the Christmas one the year I was the blue satin We Three Kings of Orient Are. My grandma made me that robe and the matching head towel thing."

Shaking off the stab of loneliness that speared through him at the mention of his grandmother, he turned to Bailey, and his forehead furrowed as a thought struck him. "If you didn't have a dad, who taught you to play baseball so good?"

"I had coaches, just like you. But it was my mom who spent nights and weekends throwing or catching the ball with me." She flashed a smile radiant with adoration. "She doesn't even like sports. But she spent hours helping me, encouraging me to improve because *I* like baseball. And until she got sick, she never missed a game."

She drew in an unstable breath. "Man. This is so hard."

"Yeah, I'm sorry, it sucks. I know, 'cause I went through it with my grandparents, who were like my mom and dad, since my real mom died giving birth to me and—like I already said—Jake wasn't around."

She straightened. "But we're going to go to the game with them anyway, right? And you'll put yourself out there with them for at least that night?"

He could see that, for whatever reason, it was important to her that he try. So he gave her a game smile.

"Sure. Whatever milady wants."

Oh, crap. Had that actually come out of his mouth? Stupid! *Stupid, stupid, stupid!*

He shoved to his feet. "Well, I'd better get home before Jenny sends out the troops. But I'm mad glad you're coming with." Realizing she'd never actually accepted, he said, "You are, aren'tcha?"

She rose, too. Slid her narrow hands into her jeans back pockets. "Yes. I've never been to a professional game, so I'm totally stoked."

"Sweet. I'll give you a call later this week when I find out what time we're gonna leave." Grabbing the back of his neck, he simply looked at her for a moment. "Well, hmmm. So, I guess I'll see ya soon, right?"

"Absolutely."

"All right, then." He backed down the stairs, then finally turned. And picking up his bike, he threw a leg over and shoved off.

"See you, Austin," she called. He waved, kept peddling and didn't look back.

But he smiled the entire way home.

CHAPTER TWELVE

"YOU'RE KIDDING ME! He was in the hot tub? And you didn't climb in with him?"

Jenny, sprawled back on the mushroom-beige chaise lounge that thrust out from one end of Tasha's comfy couch, looked up at her friend and sighed. It had been more than a week since they'd touched base. Thanks to the continuing flood of reservations from the online discount sites, she and her staff had been crazy busy. She could have sworn it was Friday just yesterday—yet here they were again, smack in the middle of another one.

Jake and Max had headed out with the kids not long after school got out. Their reasoning was better to be too early for the seven o'clock Mariners game than late, and this way they could get fish-and-chips at Spuds' on Alki before heading to the Sodo district.

She and Tasha were in full take-advantage mode. Tash had even turned Bella T's over to Tiffany just so they could catch up—although they did plan on going back to the pizzeria for the dinner rush.

Impatiently tapping the toe of her shoe against the hardwood floor, her friend gave her a stern look. "I'm waiting, Salazar."

"Yeah, yeah." But she explained the situation more comprehensively than she'd done the first time, starting with her initial sighting of Jake in the spa, clear through to her decision to fix the gap problem as he had more or less dictated.

When she fell silent, Tasha skipped right past nearly everything she'd said to lock onto a single fact. "Man, I bet that man is seriously pretty in a nearly naked state. He's so easy on the eyes fully dressed that I'm boggled simply imagining the stripped-down version."

"*Partly* stripped down."

Tash gave her a puzzled look. "Who are you and what have you done with my friend? You say 'partly' as if the man not being full Monty naked is a *plus*."

"Oh, for God's sake."

Tasha effortlessly ignored that, as well. "Thank heaven you at least had the good sense to be wearing your good undies instead of those raggy beige ones you had on the day we went jeans shopping."

"Hey! I got rid of those that day, remember? Well, okay, maybe it didn't register on your radar, but it'll be a wicked long time before *I* forget shelling out enough cash to pay off the national debt for a handful of underwear."

"And worth every penny."

"Yeah, I gotta admit, they're beautiful. Sometimes I open up the drawer just to admire them."

Tasha shot her a smile that might scare a woman less accustomed to the strawberry blonde's one-track mind. "Speaking of which," she said, ruthlessly corralling the conversation back into the pen where she wanted it. "Hello! built, almost nekkid guy." She raised an auburn eyebrow. "And you *hid* from him in your cottage?"

"I know." Jenny sighed and hugged a chocolate-and-tan zebra-print throw pillow to her breast. "Not my finest hour. But it wasn't entirely my fault. It was those damn kisses the week before."

"*Which,* as I've told you more than once, you should be looking to repeat at every opportunity. I mean, what the hell, Jenny. You've plainly got the hots for him."

"For all the good that's gonna do me."

"Okay, a full-blown relationship might not go anywhere, seeing as how he's leaving in a little over a month."

"With *Austin* in tow!"

Tasha's pale brow furrowed. "I know, sweetie. That's going to be rough on you. But it's gonna happen regardless—and as much as I hate to admit it, at this stage in Austin's life, he could probably stand a little male influence. Preferably from a man who won't spoil him rotten the way Emmett did."

"I can't deny that," Jenny admitted. "And I might even believe it'd be good for Austin, *if* I felt confident Jake won't revert to his old habits and disappear from his life for huge blocks of time. Because what happens when the newness wears off, Tash? It's just so damn hard to tell at this stage if he's in it for the long haul. He hasn't been around long enough for me to make an informed decision."

"Kissing him a few more times would likely help."

The sound that burst from her was half laugh, half snort. "God, you're single-minded."

Tasha nodded. "What can I say—it's been a long dry spell for both of us." Her lush mouth twisted into the droll equivalent of a shrug. "Don't you think it's about time one of us got lucky?"

"I have to admit, I wouldn't mind that."

"Me, either. And if it has to be you, let me at least live vicariously."

"I do miss kissing," Jenny said wistfully. "Maybe that's why Jake's hit me so hard."

"Sure, kissing's good," Tasha said. "But I miss *sex*. That's the downside of living in a small town. There are only X number of men you'd even consider getting busy with. And if you've been there, done that with the ones you're interested in—or some of those just aren't that into you…" She hitched a shoulder, then pinned Jenny in place with her overcast-sky eyes. "Well, that's the reason a Razor Bay girl grabs her opportunity at a man like Jake Bradshaw when she gets one. She doesn't *ignore* it."

Jenny was abruptly tired of the subject. "Look, if you find him so damn hot, why don't *you* take a shot at him?"

"Maybe I will. If you're just gonna let him go to waste."

Over my dead body, sister! The immediate, visceral rejection sent heat blistering through her veins.

But she didn't say it aloud. God. At least she didn't do that.

Not that it mattered. Tasha knew her too well, and the corner of her best friend's lips promptly curved up in a knowing smile.

"Uh-huh." She gave Jenny a who-do-you-think-you're-fooling look. "That's what I thought."

JENNY AWOKE TO THE MUFFLED sound of shuffling footsteps in the living room. Blinking owlishly at the red numerals on her bedside clock, she saw it was one-eighteen. Oh, God, was Austin sick?

Throwing back the covers, she stumbled drowsily across the room and opened the door.

At first she didn't understand what she saw. Why was Jake opening Austin's bedroom door and slinging an arm around the boy's shoulders? Then her mind cleared a little.

Of course. The game. They must have just gotten back. It was obvious Austin had been asleep—he had that near catatonic look he got whenever he was awakened before he was ready, which was basically anytime before noon.

"There you go," Jake said in a low, encouraging voice as he guided the teen across the threshold. "You want help getting ready for bed?"

That elicited the first sign of life from the teen. "Do I look like some stupid preschooler to you?"

Clearly it was a rhetorical question, for he stepped deeper into his room and slammed the door in Jake's face.

But faintly, through the wooden panels, came a belatedly mumbled, "Thanks for taking me and Bailey to the game." His bed creaked a protest as he likely fell face-first upon his mattress.

Jake's hand raised as if to knock, yet he settled his unfurled fingers and palm lightly against the door. The longing in the gesture and in the little she could see of his expression squeezed Jenny's heart.

As if he felt the weight of her stare, he suddenly turned, pinning her in his sights.

Making her aware of the lace-trimmed baby doll she had on—and the nearly full moon illuminating the little bungalow.

Well, hell.

Not that her nightie was of the transparent variety— she lived, after all, with a teenage boy. And Jake didn't possess X-ray vision, so no way could he see the tiny matching panties beneath it.

But its silky orange, pink and white-flowered fabric that flowed down her torso to culminate at the top of her thighs, with a second tier that ended just a few inches below that, plus its narrow straps and the white lace trimming its skimpy, not-much-more-than-two-triangles bodice screamed *lingerie.*

Worse, coupled with her crazily mussed hair, it whispered *bed.* Why the hell hadn't she put on her robe?

"Whoa," he said…and wasn't shy about checking her out from head to toe.

Instead of running for her room as any sane woman would do, she found herself squaring her shoulders to make the best of her less than impressive breasts.

Jeez, girl, are you crazy? her saner self demanded. But her lusty, curious side saw an envelope and gave it an experimental push.

Which truly was crazy, and she eased out of her let's-thrust-my-boobs-in-his-face pose and cleared her throat. "Did the kids have a good time at the game?"

"Yeah, the kids were a kick—they really got into it. It was fun for Max and me to see it through their eyes, though I doubt big bro would ever admit that out loud. Damn thing went into extra innings, though. And if that wasn't bad enough, we were stuck in the parking garage for more than an hour. Next time we'll take the Bremerton ferry instead of the Southworth so we can walk on. Driving into town pushed getting back at a reasonable hour way past good sense." His gaze continued to roam, then abruptly returned to her face. "Nice nightie."

She hummed something incomprehensible and once again cleared her throat. "Yes, well…hmmm." She flapped one hand vaguely toward her bedroom. "I'll just go grab my robe."

"Hey, you don't have to go to any trouble on my account."

Damn him, he wasn't supposed to be wry and charming. It was ridiculous enough that she'd been unwillingly impressed with the way he'd handled this outing with Austin and the plan that he apparently had for the two of them to see additional Mariners games in the future. Did he have to have her checking him out every bit as blatantly as he had her and getting all sorts of ideas on top of it?

Dammit, this was all Tasha's fault. Why, out of a billion and one subjects they could have discussed tonight, had her friend had to focus on the potential of Jenny having sex with Jake? She wouldn't have all these inappropriate thoughts agitating for her attention if not for her so-called BFF.

She twitched her posture a fraction more erect. Just because she had them didn't mean she was obligated to act on them. She gave Jake a repressive look. "That's very big of you."

"You don't know the half of it," he muttered and, oh, God, she couldn't help it, her eyes went straight to his crotch.

Where she saw that, while he might not have been sporting a full-fledged erection, he certainly wasn't disinterested. Heat crawled up her cheeks.

But she didn't look away.

"Shit," he whispered as his sex continued to enlarge beneath her fascinated gaze. "You wanna quit looking at my dick?"

Guiltily, she pulled her gaze away.

"Thanks," he said, and Jenny watched from the

corner of her eye as he reached down and adjusted himself. "If I'd seen you wearing that the first time we met, no way I would have mistaken you for a kid," he said drily.

Then he shook his head. "Look, I need to get my head in a place that doesn't involve coming over there and nailing you against the wall. So if you've got any suggestions, now would be a good time to throw them out there."

"A nice predawn swim in the canal maybe?"

"It's definitely cold enough, but I'd probably generate so much steam I'd end up destroying the ecosystem."

Oooh. She kind of liked that. "How about a long jog?"

Jake snorted. "With a third leg? That ain't likely to happen."

"Hey, I'm trying here. I don't hear you coming up with any brilliant ideas."

"Right. Sorry." He straightened. "Okay, I've got one. I'll just concentrate for a minute on being stuck in Razor Bay for the rest of my life. Wait, *waaaait* for it—

"Damn." A strange expression passed over his face. But before Jenny could interpret what it was, he merely said, "Even *that's* not doing the job. Okay, you gotta admit I tried. But I give."

And in a flash he closed the distance between Austin's door and hers. Curving his hands around her upper arms, he backed her against the wall that separated the living room from her bedroom and rocked his gorgeous mouth over hers with take-no-prisoners purpose.

This kiss exploded through Jenny even more quickly than the previous ones they'd shared. Jake's hands slipped up over the curve of her shoulders to her throat, then glided up her neck to cradle her head with a tenderness she felt to the soles of her feet. His calloused fingertips, which held her firmly in place as he devoured her mouth, lightly scratched her skin.

It never entered her mind to waste time on the "should we, shouldn't we be doing this" question. She simply rose onto her toes to kiss him back.

He made a rough sound deep in his throat, then pulled back to look down at her for a moment. Slicking his tongue over his lower lip, he demanded in a low, raspy voice, "What is it with you and the taste of cherries?" Then he eliminated the distance between their lips to kiss her even deeper.

For endless moments, Jenny was caught in a montage of sensations. Jake's beard abraded her skin; his aggressive tongue, hot and firm, pursued, then tangled with hers, unequivocally taking the lead in this sensual dance they performed. His hard-muscled body pumped heat through his clothing to permeate her own until her skin burned nearly as scorching hot.

Eventually, he loosened his gentle grip on her head and smoothed his hands firmly down her back, his slightly roughened fingertips riding the long, narrow groove of her spine. An instant later he palmed her bottom, his fingers curling to secure his grip. Then he picked her up and jerked her close to his body, even as he took the step back that cost her the support of the wall at her back.

Despite his steady hold, she found herself clinging to his neck and wrapping her legs around his waist for added stability as he opened the door to her bedroom.

Jake carried her to the bed and, with her still wrapped around him like a treed cat, knee-walked partway across the mattress before lowering her onto it. He pushed up on planted palms and bent his head to give her a fierce kiss, then slid down her prone body to press languid, open-mouthed kisses to her jaw, to the sides of her throat, to her shoulders. Sliding farther south, he strung love nips along the skin bordering her baby doll's lace bodice trim to its V's lowest point, where the slight swells of her breasts formed a shallow cleavage.

Without tearing his gaze from it, he raised his head slightly. "Aw, sweet," he said roughly and hooked a finger into one lingerie strap and tugged it off her shoulder. Glancing up at her, he reached for the other. "I've been wanting to get a look at these babies for some time now."

Shooting him a crooked smile, she warned, "Prepare to be disappointed." Yet the appreciation in his eyes burned away even the smallest semblance of her usual self-consciousness when it came to her much privately lamented, not so womanly breasts.

"That's not going to happen." He lowered the other strap and slowly peeled the skimpy cups away. His breath hissed through his teeth as he exposed the pale golden globes.

It was the look on his face, more than the cool air in her bedroom, that caused Jenny's burnt-sugar-colored nipples to twist into little diamond points atop their small aureoles. And when he reached out to circle one with a fingertip, she inhaled a sharp breath of her own and her head kicked back into the mattress.

"*That's* right," he breathed. "Jesus, these are pretty." He lightly pinched a nipple and her back arched to thrust it closer yet. He groaned. "You like that, don't you?" He squeezed it again, apparently just to replicate her reaction.

She obliged him and he licked his lips. "Damn. You're so responsive."

Austin's door on the other side of the bathroom separating the two bedrooms suddenly opened and Jenny went from burning up to colder than ice, stilling like a rabbit caught in a coyote's sights. Jake pushed up on one side, looking down at her as she stared at him in return, holding her breath as she waited for the teen to finish whatever had pulled him from his bed.

The toilet flushed and a moment later Austin's door closed.

Jake started to roll back into the position he'd relinquished, but she slapped a hand to his chest to hold him away. "You've got to go," she said in a low voice.

"What?"

"Look," she said, using her free hand to pull the baby doll's top back up over her breasts and slide at least that strap back into place, "I was wrong to have started this with you with him in the house. It was irresponsible of both of us, and you need to leave."

He rolled onto his side and propped his head in his hand. "Come with me."

"No, you and me—" she waved a hand between them "—we're just a bad idea all the way around. I know it's probably hard to believe, given the way I always seem to behave with you, but I don't generally do this sort of thing. I don't just hop into bed with guys I barely know."

"It's not hard to believe at all."

Instead of being relieved she felt irrationally irritated. "Why, because I'm so unsophisticated?"

He looked at her in surprise. "No, because…" He hesitated, then said, "You're so sweet."

The breath that escaped her was rife with incredulity and so, she assumed, was her expression.

"It's not an insult, Jenny," he said and laughed.

"Oh, yay, and to top things off, I'm a figure of fun."

"The hell you are. I just meant you're not a sexual pushover, ya know?"

"Great. Well, listen, you should run along. I've

got to get up early in the morning." *And if I hope to sleep I need to scrape my ego up off the floor.*

He rolled over on top of her. "We might be done for tonight, but you and I aren't finished."

"Oh, I think we are." *Says the woman who just heated up twenty degrees. God, Jenny. You are in so much trouble.*

"You want me just as much as I want you," he said without a discernible shred of doubt.

"Yes, I imagine I probably do. Yet by your own admission, I'm no sexual pushover, and I've decided to take that as a compliment after all. Because we nonpushovers don't have to act on our desires when doing so just borrows trouble. You're in town to take away the boy I've considered a brother since he was barely out of diapers. And even if I were able to put that aside, we have different goals. So this is a relationship going nowhere. And I'm really, really not looking for one of those."

For a moment, he looked as if he wanted to argue. Then he pushed off her and rolled to his feet. He looked down at her. "You're right, of course," he said with cool courtesy. "I'll try not to put you in this position again." Without another word, he turned on his heel and walked out of her room. Jenny heard the outer door open and close a moment later.

While she lay there trying to convince herself that what she felt was relief.

CHAPTER THIRTEEN

"Nolan's all pissed off at me."

Austin lowered his joystick and looked at Bailey, who sat beside him on the couch where they'd been whiling away Sunday afternoon playing "Grand Theft Auto." She'd been subdued since she'd arrived on his doorstep and apparently this was the reason why. "How come?"

"Because I get to go out when he doesn't? Because I get to see you? Got to go to the Mariners game?" Her chin wobbled. "Because I *breathe?*"

Oh, shit. Please, God, don't let her cry!

He didn't know if his prayer was heard or she was simply a warrior, but whatever the reason, she firmed up her chin, drew a deep breath and turned her head to look at him. "Aunt Rebecca says it's because he has cabin fever and he's jealous that we're having fun without him. That he can't help feeling that way and to be patient with him. But he's always been my favorite cousin and I hate it that he's mad at me!"

"Aw, *man!*" A clammy concrete-gray load of guilt dumped down on him. "This is my fault, not yours. I haven't exactly knocked myself out to make him feel better since his mom told me about his chicken pox. I mean, I've texted him and all, but except for one online game of 'Call of Duty,' I sure haven't gone out of my way." *Because I've been too busy enjoying having you all to myself.* "I'm a crappy friend."

"No, you're not. Heck, I don't know if it would've made a difference if you had knocked yourself out. I've played cards and video games with him, but he's dumping on me anyway."

"It's probably like his mom said, though—I know I'd go nuts if I was stuck inside all the time." Then he brightened. "But you know what? It's not too late to do something. Let's go!"

"Where?" she asked even as she rose to her feet and followed him to his room.

She really was the best, because she didn't do the usual talk, talk, talk thing like so many girls. Instead, she stood silently in the doorway while he rooted through the mess on his little desk and on the floor. He shot her a glance over his shoulder. "Grab my small pack off the back of the door."

She did and he waved her over to the bed where he'd unloaded his booty. She brought the pack over and held the top open.

"Okay, we've got a couple rockin' DVDs, a few comic books, the newest Pendragon book that I'm pretty sure he hasn't seen yet and my—wait for it…" He held up the board he'd mounted with different size and shape echinoderms. "Awesome dried starfish collection."

"You're kidding me. You collect dead sea critters?"

"Hell, yeah. And Nolan's been trying to get his hands on them since we were, like, in fifth grade. There was no way. But now—" He stopped and shrugged. "Now is sort of an emergency. Getting them there might be an issue, though—these babies are fragile. Huh. While I think about that, why don't you see if Epic Fail, Damn You, Auto Correct, and I Can has Cheezeburger? are all their-name-dot-com. If those don't make him laugh, nothing will. Well, okay, maybe my copy of Dave Barry's *Science Fair: A Story of Mystery, Danger, International Suspense, and A Very Nervous Frog.* That's gotta be around here somewhere."

Bailey shook her head. "You're a dork, you know that?"

"Maybe, but I'm a manly one." He flexed biceps at her and grinned when she laughed. "So what do you read?" He gave her a look of faux concern. "You *can* read, right?"

"Funny guy." She punched him on the arm. "I like Harry Potter."

"Me, too!"

"And the Meg Cabot Mediator books."

"I don't know those, but it sounds like you're a dork, too."

"Nah. It's acceptable when girls like to read."

"No fooling. I don't tell just any Sam, Dick or Harry that I kinda like it, too."

"Tom."

"Huh?"

"It's every *Tom,* Dick or Harry."

"See what I'm talking about?" He pointed at her. "Dork squared."

Ten minutes later they climbed the stairs to the Sand Dollar's porch and knocked on the door. There was no response, so Austin knocked louder, then pressed his ear against the panel. Faintly, from what sounded like upstairs, he heard a noise. Almost on top of it, he heard footsteps coming down the stairs and took a swift step back.

Jake opened the door, smelling of chemicals and looking more raggedy than Austin had ever seen him, in an old faded T-shirt and stained jeans. But his face lit up. "Hey, there. What's up?"

"Can you give us a ride to Nolan's house? I've got some stuff to cheer him up, but one of them's too big to take on my bike."

"I'm sorry, buddy. I can't leave right now—I got a wild hair to actually develop some photos and I'm hip deep in solution and timing. Tell you what, though, if you can find something to cheer him up in the meantime, I'll run you over this evening. That way he'll get two separate surprises out of it. Will that work for you?"

Austin's first reaction was to say, "No—and thanks for nothing." But the nice time they'd had at the game the other night flashed through his mind and, looking beyond his original disappointment, he realized it wasn't an unreasonable alternative. He nodded. "Okay." After a small hesitation, he ventured, "In fact, if you want to come over for dinner, I'll make my famous tomato soup and grilled cheese sandwiches."

"Deal. I'll bring the cold milk."

Austin grinned. "Deal."

"Six o'clock work for you?"

"Long as you're on time. Jenny says I'm not fit to be around if I eat much later than that."

On their way back to Austin's house, Bailey unexpectedly reached for his hand. "That was cool—the way you handled that, I mean."

"Yeah?" His breath caught in his throat a little at the delicacy of her fingers compared to his, but he did his best to sound offhand. He didn't want to totally give in to dorkdom. "I've thought a lot about what you said about getting to know him and Max. I…liked being with them Friday. They were easier to talk to than I thought they'd be." He'd particularly enjoyed watching the way they were with Bailey. They hadn't been stupid obvious about it, but observing them opening doors for her, blocking her from the worst of the crowds and not swearing and shit—well, it had given him a new understanding of the way he should probably be treating girls himself.

The swearing part was gonna take a little effort. Everyone swore—it made them sound more like they were in high school instead of sucky Junior high. Still, he had to admit, Jake and Max were kind of dope. So if they tried to watch their language around girls, he supposed he could. too.

"So what do you think? Should we take the stuff in your backpack to Nolan now?"

"Yeah, probably. Or…how good are you on your bike?"

"I'm okay. I don't know any tricks or anything." She studied him. "Why?"

"You know any tricks off your bike?"

"Like what?"

"Like—I don't know—you ever take gymnastics or learn anything else cool in your ballet class?"

"I did! I'm actually not bad at gymnastics. But again—*why?*"

"Good." He pulled her to a stop and bent his head close to hers. "'Cause, here's the deal."

AN HOUR LATER, they'd conferred with Nolan's dad and turned on the ancient boom box Mr. D had set up outside Nolan's window. Old-fashioned circus-type music blared out of it.

"Holy crap," Austin yelled over it. "Doesn't it make you kinda wonder about your uncle that he'd actually have this kind of music just lying around?"

Bailey laughed, then said, "There he is!"

He turned to see Nolan standing in his window, his face a nightmare of eruptions, his hair flattened here, standing on end there. Austin hit his best friend's auto number in his Droid, and Nolan disappeared from the window for a moment before coming back with his own cell phone in his hand.

Bailey cut the music and Austin held his phone so both of them could hear. "I can kind of see why you haven't wanted to Skype," he said when Nolan answered.

"Ya think? Jeezus, can you imagine my chances with Stefani Baldwin if she ever caught sight of this?" He grimaced, then asked, "What's with the crap music?"

Bailey snatched the phone from Austin's hand and bawled, "Laaadies and Gentlemen! The moment you've been waiting for is finally here! Pull up a seat, grab your popcorn—" Mrs. D came into sight with a bowl that she passed to Nolan as his little brother jumped in excitement next to him "—and welcome the Amazing Austinini!" Snapping the cell closed, she tossed it back to him, turned on the music once again and performed a cheerleader-like jump while he shoved the phone in his pocket. Then she took three running steps and did a flip.

He picked his old BMX up off the grass and mounted it. He hadn't ridden the low-slung bike since last year, when he'd graduated to a more grown-up model. But he hadn't been able to let go of it entirely and now he was glad. While Bailey did ballet-type leaps and gymnastic flips and Mr. D grinned over by the garage, he broke out the tricks he and Nolan had spent a good part of their childhood practicing: balancing on the back tire, balancing on the front while twisting the rest of the bike from side to side, bouncing across the lawn on the front tire, riding around the lawn hands-free.

Okay, that last one was weak and he flubbed the others a time or two. He was also forced to repeat himself more than once, since he only had the three real tricks. But he took theatrical bows after each one as if he was the hottest performer this side of Las Vegas. And in the end, his screwups didn't really matter, because the payoff was huge. He could see Nolan stuffing popcorn in his mouth and grinning his ass off.

He was still pumped when Jenny arrived home from work, as afternoon faded into evening and found him grilling sandwiches.

"What's this?" she asked with a smile. "You're cooking? What a treat!"

"Yeah, I invited Jake for dinner. Would you grab me a can of tomato soup outta the cupboard? Maybe you'd better make that two. You and I usually kill off one."

She was silent and he turned to look at her. "Jenny?"

"What? Oh, sorry. Maybe I'd better get three. *You* usually kill off one by yourself, and your father's probably the same." She went out to the cupboard in the mudroom that they used as their pantry. "So, uh, Jake's coming for dinner, huh?"

"Yeah." Her voice sounded kind of funny, and he said uncertainly, "That's okay, isn't it? I mean, you don't usually care if I ask, like, Nolan or whoever without checking with you first."

"Sure, sure. That's…fine. The more the merrier."

He grinned. "That's what you always say."

And usually I even mean it. In the other room, Jenny ground her forehead against the cupboard door she'd just closed and concentrated on drawing in and exhaling deep, calming breaths.

Inaudible deep, calming breaths, since she didn't want to ruin Austin's great mood. And really, she assured herself, this was fine. It was good, in fact. It was important that Austin forge a relationship with his dad. Jake was going to be taking him with him when he left—so the sooner they bonded, the better shape the teen would be in to deal with all the changes that were about to turn his life upside down.

But, oh, crap. It had been less than forty-eight hours since she'd rolled around on her bed with Jake, and she would really, really rather not have to face him just yet.

Or, say, ever.

Okay, that was childish. She pushed away from the cupboard. But she couldn't pretend she was thrilled at the prospect of being thrown together with him again. How was she going to look him in the eye, knowing he had seen her bare breasts? How was she supposed to *not* think about the way he'd touched them? Hell, easy for him to sit across a table from her—*he* had nothing to worry about. He hadn't even unbuttoned his shirt!

Her boobs had been out there and she was going to have to act all cool, as if it were no skin off her nipples, so to speak, should she see anything in his eyes that indicated he might be visualizing them.

The sudden knock at the mudroom door made her jump and emit an embarrassing almost-scream. Austin laughed in the other room.

"That must be him," he said. "Toss me the soups before you let him in."

Leaning through the open doorway to the kitchen, she lobbed them to him one after the other. Then, blowing out a final quiet breath, she turned back to the door, shook out her hands and reached for the knob. Damn. It would've been nice if she'd at least had a chance to refresh her lipstick. Not that she had any burning desire to impress Jake Bradshaw. But ask any woman and she would testify to the confidence-boosting armor of a dash of lipstick.

Plastering a smile on her face, she opened the door.

IT WAS STUPID, JAKE KNEW, but he hadn't expected Jenny to be here. He'd jumped to the conclusion that Austin had invited him for the sole reason that she was working tonight—maybe because the kid was cooking and an unconscious corner of Jake's mind had made the assumption that the teen probably only did that when she wasn't around to make his dinner.

Well, he knew what they said about *assume* making an ass of *U* and *me*. And seeing her, in a trim

camel-colored straight skirt, one of those filmy, ul-
trafeminine blouses—this one in black and tan—
and the skyscraper needle-heeled shoes she favored
for business attire, stopped him dead in his tracks
for a moment.

Acrimonious encounters with Max had taught him
never to give anyone the advantage of seeing him off
guard. He flashed her an insouciant smile and deliberately dropped his gaze for a moment to peruse
those sweet little cupcakes beneath her blouse.

If he thought it would rattle her, he'd seriously
underestimated her. The girl was clearly made of
titanium alloy. Her cheeks turned a little pink, but
she met his gaze coolly and raised her eyebrows at
him, as if to say, "Well, aren't *you* a tacky lowlife
scumball."

"You guys planning on standing around out here
all night?" Braced against the doorjamb, Austin
leaned into the small enclosed porch. His gaze went
to the container in Jake's hand. "Oh, good. You remembered the milk." Releasing the jamb, he came
over to relieve him of the gallon he'd picked up at
the General Store. "I'll throw this in the freezer to
get it real cold, then I gotta get back to my cooking."
He cocked his brows. "If you wanna give yourselves
a treat, you're welcome to come watch the master
at work."

Jake's grin had no agenda this time as he looked
at Jenny. "He always so modest?"

She rolled her eyes. "Pretty much."

"Hey!" Austin protested. "I don't think I'm half as good as I really am. But wait until you taste my grilled cheese—never mind my Campbell's soup. The Food Network begs me—*begs* me!—to ditch Junior high and host one of their shows. You think *you* two are gonna be able to resist demanding my recipe?" His laugh scoffed at the very idea.

It was the first time Jake had ever seen him completely at ease in his company. They'd had a good time Friday night, but Austin hadn't been anywhere as easy in his own skin as he was this evening.

He had to admit he was charmed. He'd already harbored a fierce desire to get to know his son better. But *this* kid—

Man, he *really* wanted to get close to the boy in front of him tonight.

And he'd never regretted more deeply all the years he'd let slip by without bothering to do so.

He discovered during dinner that Austin was riding high on the performance he and Bailey had put on for Nolan after they'd left his place this afternoon. The thirteen-year-old had Jake in stitches as he re-enacted not only his own tricks—complete with the ones he'd messed up—but Bailey's ringmaster announcement and flips and leaps, as well. He even attempted to duplicate the circus music in a falsetto.

"Have you ever *heard* music so lame?" he demanded in conclusion and took another huge bite of his second grilled cheese sandwich.

Jake glanced over at Jenny, who was beaming at

the teen as proudly as any mother. Her expression made his heart give a funny quickstep, *tha-thud*. And something deep in his gut hitched tight.

But he shook it off as Austin pushed back his empty plate and belched.

"'Scuse me," the teen said and shot the adults a pleased-with-himself smile. "I cooked. That means you guys gotta clean up."

Jenny groaned. "Great," she groused, turning to Jake. "He might make the best grilled cheese sandwich in Washington state—"

"Or maybe even the continental United States," he interjected.

"Try the universe," Austin said.

"In any case, that's the upside. The downside is that when he cooks, he manages to use every plate and pot and pan in the house."

"A gifted chef is only as good as his tools," Austin sassed and pushed back from the table. "And while you tools clean the kitchen, I'll go get the stuff we're taking over to Nolan's."

Her delicate brows drew together in confusion. "What are you taking over to Nolan's? You can't have contact with him yet. You're getting your new vaccination on Tuesday, and we'll have to see what Dr. Janus has to say about the timeline after that."

"That's right, you don't know." He looked at her. "I'm not going in. I've just got some books and things to give Mrs. D to help him pass the time while he's still in quarantine. I would've taken it in my backpack this afternoon, but I'm going to lend him my starfish collection, too. And there's no way that'll fit."

Her expression went all sentimental-soft. "You're going to lend him your prized starfish collection to cheer him up? That's really nice, Austin."

"I know." He shot her a cocky smile. "I asked Jake to take me over this afternoon, but he was developing photos and stuff and couldn't leave right then. But he said he'd drive me over after dinner. So you guys go clean, and I'll put the stuff in his car." He turned to Jake. "I assume it's open?"

"Hell, no." He dug the keys out of his pocket and tossed them to Austin. "Nobody in their right mind would ever leave their car unlocked in Manhattan."

"You're not in Manhattan anymore, Toto." Austin shook his head. "I don't know how you live like that."

Jake's heart dropped a little at the sentiment, but he managed to say lightly, "Oh, now you're just trying to piss me off by talking like Max."

"He's got good taste, too, huh?"

"Go get your stuff, Austin," Jenny directed, climbing to her feet and reaching for the boy's abandoned plate to stack atop hers. "You," she said, pointing at Jake. "Come with me."

He gathered up what she didn't and followed her over to the sink. "You want me to wash or dry?"

"I'll have you dry," she said. "You're taller—it'll be easier for you to put the stuff away."

He grinned. "A little height challenged, are you?" he asked. "I hadn't noticed."

"You're such a card," she said in a voice that suggested he was anything but—even as the corners of her mouth curved up. "Dishes go in the cupboard here and the glasses in that one," she directed, turning on the faucet and squirting dish soap into the sink. "The pans go in the drawer under the stove."

"Got it," he said crisply and tossed the towel she handed him over his shoulder. "You want me to put the milk in the fridge?"

"Yeah, that would be good." Plunging a hand into the water she swished it around to increase the soap suds.

They conversed easily as they cleaned up the kitchen, and Jake let his guard down all the way with her for the first time since she'd opened the door. Keeping it up had probably been overkill, but he'd been caught by surprise and that tended to slam his defenses in place. Chances were he'd gotten a little carried away exaggerating the attraction between them.

Then he reached across her to stow the final dried glass in the overhead cupboard. He'd done the same thing with the last two glasses, but this time Jenny simultaneously leaned to wipe down the counter and he found himself snugged up to the resulting thrust of her round little ass.

And even as they both froze, he quit fooling himself. Because he wanted her. He wanted her bad.

Then she straightened and he eased his own hips back. But he was still stretched over her and he inhaled a slow, deep breath through his nose, drawing in the scents of dish soap, herbal-smelling shampoo—and woman.

Damn. She always smelled so good. He didn't think it was perfume, either. He thought it was just... Jenny.

His testicles drew up, and he shoved the glass in the cupboard and took a granddaddy-size step back, slinging the towel onto the counter. "Well, hey," he said, damning the husky note in his voice as she slowly turned her head to look over her shoulder at him. "I'd better go see if Austin's ready to take his stuff over to Nolan's. Thanks for dinner."

And calling out his son's name, he blew out of the kitchen so fast he was surprised he didn't leave friction marks.

CHAPTER FOURTEEN

MONDAY MORNING, JENNY STOPPED by Tasha's on her way out of town. She raced up the outside stairs to the apartment over Bella T's and gave the door an impatient rap. "What's so important it couldn't wait?" she demanded the moment Tash opened the door. "I don't have much time."

"Get in here." The strawberry blonde stepped back to make room for Jenny to pass. "I checked the ferry schedules—you have fifteen minutes to spare."

She blew out a breath but knew better than to argue with her friend. With ill grace, she stomped past her. "Look, I'm in no mood—"

"I know, sweetie. You never are when you're going to see your father. And you never feed yourself properly, either." She led her over to the breakfast bar. "Sit. Eat."

On the counter sat a cobalt Fiesta-ware plate that held a heap of steaming scrambled eggs, two sausage links and several beautiful strawberries. "Oh. Tash." Jenny's lower eyelids welled with quick tears.

She hated these trips to the penitentiary but knew that Tasha understood she couldn't be talked out of them. Instead, her friend had found a way to make it a little bit easier. Jenny watched Tash round the breakfast bar and pick up the coffeepot. "You know I love you, right?"

"I do—just like you know I love you back. Here." Tasha handed her a tissue. "Blot your eyes, blow your nose, then eat your breakfast." She filled an orange Fiesta-ware mug, which she set on the had-seen-better-days-twenty-years-ago countertop by Jenny's plate. "You've got less than fifteen minutes now, so eat. Drink. If you're going to stew all the way to the pen, you might as well do it on a full stomach."

Jenny picked up her fork and dug in.

Tasha returned to claim the chair next to her. Swiveling to watch Jenny, she sipped at her own coffee. "I don't know why the hell you put yourself through this."

Jenny couldn't honestly say either, so she gave her friend the only answer she had. "It's only twice a year. And he's my father."

"Who didn't give a good goddamn that he was destroying your life when he—" She cut herself off. Shook her head, which made her vibrant curls quiver. "I'm sorry. I know that doesn't help."

Jenny hooked her inner elbow around the back of Tasha's neck and nearly hauled her off her stool, meeting her halfway to plant a noisy smooch squarely on her friend's lips before turning her loose. "This breakfast does, though. And I love that you care enough to be concerned."

Tasha made a rude noise. "Yeah, like *that* makes

your life any easier. *I* love that at least you're cranky about the whole ordeal." She gave her a smart-ass smile. "And people think you're such a sweetheart."

It was Jenny's turn to emit a rude noise of her own. "I know. How did that get started? When I told Jake I didn't just jump into bed with guys I barely knew, he said he didn't find that hard to believe at all. Because I'm so *sweet*. And this despite the fact I'd nearly jumped into bed with him."

Tash, who had heard the story of their encounter the morning after it happened—and was all for it— nodded. "Men can be such idiots sometimes. Even the so-called smart ones."

"Amen to that, sister."

"Although you gotta admit, your default nature is pretty damn sweet." She gave her an elbow in the side and a repeat of the smart-ass smile. "More often than not."

"Yay for me. But would it kill a guy to see me as the last of the red-hot mamas occasionally instead of Polly-fucking-anna?"

Tasha tipped her chin in a judicious nod. "A valid point."

Jenny finished her meal a few minutes later, climbed off her stool and, when Tasha did the same, gave her BFF a fierce hug. Pulling back, she looked into her face. "*Thank* you. Most helpful fifteen minutes ever."

"Good. Here." Tasha reached for a brown paper lunch bag on the counter and shoved it into her hands. "I packed you a couple snacks. Drive careful, you hear me?"

"Yes, Mom."

Tasha smacked her on the butt. "Get out of here, you fool kid."

Jenny appreciated her friend's thoughtfulness even more than usual as she hit the road the second time and realized she didn't feel nearly as pissy as she had when she'd started the day. It was a long trip from the peninsula to Monroe, however, and by the time she'd taken a ferry, driven several hours, gone through processing at the penitentiary and been escorted to the visitors' room by an armed guard, she was right back where she'd started. Tense as a hungover bomb-disposal specialist.

And that was before her father was ushered into the room.

She'd come by her lack of stature honestly. Lawrence Salazar was barely five and a half feet tall, but he strode into the visitors' room as if he were six-six. His dark hair had turned a distinguished silvery salt-and-pepper, his cheeks gleamed with the closeness of his shave and one could be forgiven for wondering if his prison jumpsuit was fashioned by Armani, such was the confidence with which he wore it. He strutted over to the table as she rose to her feet.

"Hello, Jennifer." He gave her the allowed hug and took a seat across from her.

"Dad." It had been twelve years since his arrest

and conviction, but staring at his still-handsome face she was overwhelmed by ancient sentiments.

Once upon a time she had idolized him. He'd been Santa Claus and the Easter Bunny combined—a glitter man who, even though they lived in the same big mansion, seemed to pop in and out of her life like magic. He'd showered her with gifts, if not a lot of one-on-one attention. But he was so charming and charismatic that the attention he *had* given her made her feel like a Disney princess. She'd thought he was the most brilliant man in the world.

When she'd discovered at sixteen that not only did he have feet of clay but was a *crook* whose largesse had been financed through the financial destruction of a horrifying number of people, it had threatened to tear her apart. Crushingly disillusioned, she'd longed to indulge in the drama of ranting and railing and committing rash acts to display her rage and mind-numbing fear.

But since her mother had suffered a so-called nervous breakdown and opted out of her parental responsibilities at the same time, Jenny had been too damn busy just trying to keep them afloat to indulge her emotions.

Maybe it was not being able to afford a good, solid teen meltdown that had left her with these painful love-hate feelings for her father. Or the guilt born out of the five years he'd been incarcerated before she'd finally saved enough money for an old but reliable car to come visit. Whatever the reason, she found herself going through the same emotional turmoil every time she visited. And while she hated what he'd done and the arrogance that not even prison life could eradicate, he was still her father. For that fact alone and because she couldn't seem to forget those rare moments when he'd seemed to be aware of only her, she loved him.

"What did you bring me?" he demanded.

Even if I don't always particularly like him, she thought and swallowed a sigh. "The usual."

"Excellent." He flashed her the smile that had separated millionaires from their discretionary income and little old ladies from their pensions. Then he sat forward, reaching a hand across the table. As if catching himself just in the nick of time, however, he stopped short of actually touching her.

It would have warmed the cockles of her heart if they weren't sitting in a minimum security facility where the rules were much more lax than, oh, say, the maximum security building, where the gesture would earn him a swift reprimand from one of the guards.

Well, that and the knowledge that even there it likely would have been a gesture geared to soften her up.

"My parole hearing is coming up," he said.

"Dad!" She gave him her first genuine smile. "That's wonderful!" *Okay, not cool that you're mostly thrilled you may never have to visit a state penitentiary again.*

"I've been an exemplary prisoner, so I should be released, no problem. But I'll need you to attend the hearing to tell them I have a job waiting at your little inn."

"Oh." She sagged back in her plastic chair, awash in yet more conflicting emotions. The dutiful daughter wanted to give him anything he wanted.

But her instincts were screaming, screaming, screaming. And she'd learned the hard way that she ignored them at her own peril. She slowly straightened. Blew out a quiet breath. And said, "No."

"Excuse me?" His already flawless posture somehow managed to snap even more militarily erect. And if his voice were a visible entity, it would have been formed of ice crystals. "What do you mean, no?"

Did I say no, Daddy? I didn't mean it!

The thing was, though: she did. Gathering her composure, she met his gaze with a level one of her own. "I can't in all good conscience do that."

"Of course you can. I'm going to need a job."

"And you would be happy being, say, part of the grounds crew at The Brothers?"

The look he gave her was Lawrence Salazar at his arrogant best. "Don't be ridiculous. The first rule of business is to place employees where they can be most effective. In my case, that would be in accounting. Or sales. I'm brilliant at both."

"And yet the last time you did both, people lost their life savings."

His voice chilled even further. "I'm being released because I've paid my debt to society for that, Jennifer."

"And that's wonderful, Dad, it really is. But are you the least bit *sorry* about all the people whose lives you destroyed?" She studied him closely.

And knew damn well that he was lying through his pearly white teeth when he replied smoothly, "Of course. I'm profoundly ashamed of all the harm I have caused."

"Well, good for you," she said. "But as I said, I can't in all conscience hire you at The Brothers."

He slapped a hand down on the tabletop so hard the sullen teen visiting at the next table jumped. "I'm your father!"

"Oh, trust me, I'm well aware of that. That's all anyone remembered—that I was your daughter—when you were jailed as a crook and left me to fend for myself." She kept her voice low, but years of repressed rage abruptly crowded her throat. "Your *sixteen-year-old* daughter! You and Mom were both too self-absorbed to even notice I was the only one doing anything to keep the wolf from the door. And let me tell you, having your reputation hanging over my head like my own personal rain cloud didn't help!"

Whoa. She dragged in a deep breath. She'd thought she was long past the pain—and shame—of those days of sideways glances, distrustful stares and kids unafraid to use her father's reputation to beat her over the head. Apparently not.

"I was hardly in a position to do anything for you from prison, Jennifer."

"Maybe not, but you were in a position to use your talents to make an honest living so you didn't end up in prison in the first place.

"But you know what?" She waved an impatient hand. "Screw that, it's water under the bridge." She leaned forward with a little arrogance of her own. "Because I *did* fend for myself and for my mother as well, since she couldn't seem to get off her butt to do a little fending of her own. But I'll tell you something, *Daddy,* it wasn't easy and it certainly wasn't thanks to either of you that I didn't sink like a rock beneath the weight of my responsibilities. The *Pierces* taught me how real families function, and gave me the skills to make a decent living. Damned if I intend to allow you to come waltzing into the inn they built and do God-knows-what to it while you work your own agenda. And *double* damned if you'll ruin the excellent rep I spent years of hard work building.

"I love you, Dad, and I always will." She shoved to her feet. "And I wish you luck. If you'd like to come visit me when you get out, I'd be happy to comp you a room for a couple days anytime you care to visit. But other than that, you're on your own."

He shook his head. "You've become so hard. What on earth happened to my little princess?"

"She had to scrub toilets and pick up other people's messes. She had to overcome a reputation as a felon's daughter."

"Which you have. So what's the big deal about helping your dear old dad out?"

"Was I not clear? Did you miss the part where I said I have no intention of jeopardizing what I've built?" She signaled the guard, then turned back to her father as the uniformed man wove through the tables.

"Stop by if you'd like to have a more equitable relationship with me. I know I'd enjoy that. But find a way to take care of yourself—preferably a *legal* way. Because I'm done providing for people who should have made it their job to care for me."

Good girl, she kept telling herself as she went through the sign-out process and made her way to her car. *Good girl.* She'd been strong, and she was *right,* dammit. It was too late, of course, to have a mother who'd take up the heavy lifting when things fell apart. And God knew it was past time to stop hoping her father might show interest in anyone but himself. So she'd finally done what she should have years ago: demonstrated once and for all that she no longer expected it. *Go, me.*

Reaching her car, she unlocked it, climbed in and tossed her purse on the passenger seat. She buckled her seat belt.

Then looked at her shaking hands and burst into tears.

TRAFFIC WAS A NIGHTMARE—silly her to have expected any different when everything else had gone so goddamn swell today. She was exhausted and running on empty by the time she reached Razor Bay and oh, so grateful moments later when she finally pulled into the small parking area behind her bungalow. Collecting her purse, she climbed out of the car and let herself into the mudroom. All she desired at this point was a tall, cold glass of water, a couple aspirin and maybe an hour in the prone position in a dark room.

As she let herself into the kitchen, she heard Austin's shoot-the-hell-out-of-everyone "Halo" Xbox game playing in the living room.

Heard Austin himself crow, "You're going *down!*"

Fool that she was, she assumed he was talking to Bailey and headed for the living room doorway to greet them.

But it was Jake's voice that rumbled, "In your dreams, oh vanquishable one. This is no kiddie tournament. You're playing with the master now."

Jenny stopped dead. *Well, crap. Isn't* this *just fucking perfect.* Jake was the last person she wanted to see. But she'd asked him to spend some time with Austin while she was gone, so what was she supposed to say—*get the hell out of my house, I'm in no mood to deal with you?*

Suddenly her purse seemed to weigh a hundred pounds and, as if it had multiplied tenfold, she'd swear she could *feel* the earth's gravitational pull.

Sliding the purse strap off her shoulder, she trudged into the living room.

"Hey," she said, trying to sound upbeat but fearing she fell woefully shy of the mark. "I'm home."

"Hey," Austin replied without taking his gaze off the television screen. He did something that made guns blaze and a character die and he laughed in triumph. "Yes! You're toast, ancient one! Who's the master now, huh?"

But Jake wasn't paying attention. He was staring at her, his dark brows furrowed. "You don't look very rested for someone who just spent her day shopping in the city or at a spa, or whatever. In fact, you look like crap."

Austin turned to stare at him, openmouthed. "Seriously, dude? That's cold. She's been at the state pen all day."

Head whipping around, Jake gaped at the teen. "What?"

"She spent the day in Monroe, man." Austin's tone suggested he was speaking to the mentally impaired. "Seeing her dad. Jeez." He gave Jake a hard look, glanced at his watch, then up at her. "Look, I was supposed to meet the guys—a few of us are having a mini pinball tournament at Bella T's. But if you'd rather I stay—"

"No." She shook her head. She'd kill for some alone time.

"Are you sure? I can hang around."

"No. Go. Knock 'em dead."

"Okay, if you're sure. My homework's done." He jerked his chin toward Jake. "The grinch here made me do it before we could play 'Halo.'"

He took a few steps toward the kitchen. "I'll be home by nine, 'kay?" And between one second and the next, he'd disappeared into the kitchen and from there to the mudroom. The exterior door slammed a moment later.

She turned wearily to Jake. "Thanks for staying with him. And for the homework thing." That was more than she'd expected, and she was so grateful she didn't need to ride herd tonight.

He crossed over to her. "Why didn't you tell me where you were going?"

When she'd asked for his help, she'd merely told him she had a long day planned off the peninsula. She just looked at him now.

"Of course, why would you?" he muttered. "But you look like you've been through the wringer. You hungry? I could make you something to eat."

The idea of food made her stomach pitch. "I'm really not."

"How about a nice relaxing glass of wine?"

The suggestion piqued the first interest she'd felt in putting anything in her mouth since leaving Tasha's apartment. "That I could go for."

"Uh, you have any?"

The sheepish question elicited a faint smile. "In the cupboard over the broom closet."

He went into the kitchen, and she kicked off her

shoes and collapsed on the sofa. Picking up the remote from the coffee table, she powered off the television Austin had left on, sighing as the blue screen disappeared.

Jake was back in a moment with one of the extralarge wineglasses she hardly ever used generously filled to the rim with chardonnay. He extended it to her.

She took a grateful gulp and felt warmth spread a trail from her throat to her stomach. She took another, even bigger swallow, then looked at Jake over the wineglass rim. "Thank you."

"How long has it been since you've eaten? You sure you don't want something?"

She ignored the first part of the question in favor of quaffing more wine. Her blood developed a pleasant buzz beneath her skin, and the tension she'd been packing all day began to dissipate from her muscles. "Maybe in a bit."

He shrugged and took a seat on the opposite end of the couch. "Your day was pretty bad, I take it."

A harsh laugh escaped her. "You could say that." She lifted the glass. A small voice in her head suggested maybe she should slow down, but she ignored it. After all, she was in her own home, on her own couch, and it wasn't as if the world would rock to a halt if, for one hour of one day, she was the tiniest bit reckless.

"Is it always like this?" When she merely looked

at him, he demanded, "Are you always this upset when you get home?"

"It's never really fun," she admitted. "But today I had a come-to-Jesus talk with my father."

"So that's probably a step in the right direction, right?"

She shrugged. "It was long overdue, anyhow." She looked at him and noticed he was growing a little fuzzy around the edges. Oops. Maybe being reckless wasn't her best idea.

Even so, that didn't stop her from draining the glass. Because, what the hey. It had been a day filled with less than brilliant ideas.

All the same, she could hardly believe it when she heard herself admit, "There was a second there that I was tempted to cave in to my dad's demands to give him a job at the inn. But this place is Austin's birthright, I have a responsibility to him—and my dad is an unrepentant thief. So I did the right thing."

"Damn straight," Jake said with none of her own misgivings and second-guessing. "I don't believe I want my son around him."

"Me, either." She squinted at him. "So why the hell don't I feel better?"

"Oh, baby, you're asking the wrong man. My father was what you might call serially monogamous. He left Max and his mother for mine. I mean, he poured *all* of his attention into us and cut them off as if they didn't exist. Then he left me and my mom for some other woman who had a kid that may or may not have been his. I'm kind of fuzzy on the paternity details, and my mother died before I was interested enough to ask her about it." His shoulder hitched and he met her gaze squarely. "You already know that *I'm* no shining beacon of fatherhood."

"That's true," she agreed amiably. But, Lord, he was attractive. She set her empty glass on the coffee table. Well, she attempted to. It took her two tries.

"Shit." He looked at her more closely. "You're hammered."

"I am," she agreed and, smiling happily, scooted down to his end of the couch. She climbed onto her knees facing his right side. "I'm feeling way better than I did when I got home." She angled a friendly arm across his chest, curling her fingers over his shoulder. He was so warm and hard-bodied. "Let's get it on."

"What? No!" He lunged to the edge of the couch, knocking her loose.

She fell into the space he opened up and barely avoided a face-plant by thrusting out a hand to catch herself. Shoving back to sit on her heels, she pushed her hair out of her eyes with her forearm. "Why not?" she demanded reasonably. "You know you want to."

"Yeah, I do. But low as your opinion is of me, I draw the line at taking advantage of drunk women."

She blew a pithy raspberry. "Spoilsport."

He laughed and climbed to his feet.

She reached out to stroke one hard thigh and gave

him a loose smile when he took a hasty step back. "Sure you don't wanna change your mind?"

"Hell, no, I'm not sure. That's why I'm getting out of here." He looked down at her and a crooked smile slashed a shallow groove in his cheek. "Man, you're going to hate yourself in the morning."

She shrugged. "'Que Sera, Sera.'"

"Be interesting to see if you're singing that tune in a few hours. And, hey." Reaching out, he ran a rough hand over her hair. "If your offer still stands once you've sobered up, you know where to find me."

CHAPTER FIFTEEN

"JUST SHOOT ME NOW." Carefully avoiding looking at herself in the bathroom mirror, Jenny picked up the aspirin bottle, shook a couple tablets into her palm and washed them down with a glass of water.

Not that her headache was all that unbearable—its cause more from tension than a hangover. After all, wasn't she flipping Pollyanna? She'd only had that one measly glass of wine. Sure, it had been a big sucker and she'd downed the thing on an empty stomach. But if she'd known it was going to turn her into *that* woman—the one who occasionally hung out at the Anchor and made drunken passes at all the guys—she'd have gone ahead and knocked back a couple more. Maybe then at least last night would be a nice comfortable blur in her head.

Blurry would be a definite improvement.

But she wasn't getting off that easy. Because God forbid her memory should extend her the courtesy of failing for just one stinking night.

No, she remembered every embarrassing moment.

Not that all of it had been awful. After all, she recalled exactly how hard and warm Jake had felt. How yummy he'd smelled.

But sweet baby Jesus—she could have gone forever without remembering the horrified look on his face when she'd hit him with that truly *suave* proposition. And she didn't even want to think about the way she'd draped herself all over him.

She didn't get it. That so wasn't her. She was no Mother Teresa, but she didn't sleep around casually, either, let alone make sloppy passes at men.

But there was something about Jake that…drew her. Oh, sure, there were his looks and that body. But if it were just about the physical, she wouldn't feel so unnerved. She could dismiss the desire to get closer to him horizontally as a mere matter of chemistry and attraction; biology, pure and simple.

But the layers he'd managed to burrow beneath— that was something else. Something more.

At first she'd attributed the emotional tug she felt around him—a tug that, to her unease, was *growing*— to his budding relationship with Austin. The more things he did right, the more effort he put into his son, well, it just made her heart expand, that was all.

Not in a that-thing-called-love way, though! No sir, no how. Because where would that get her? Jake was leaving and taking Austin with him. It would be exceedingly stupid to allow herself to feel anything deeper than simple lust.

She had firsthand experience with loving people and having them choose other things. Her dad had chosen wealth and power over her; her mother image and status. Damned if she'd go down that road again.

Just thinking about it had her head pounding harder than before. Leaning into the sink, she pressed her forehead against the mirror's cool glass. "Please," she whispered. "If no one's gonna shoot me, then a lightning bolt would do the trick. Something. *Anything*. I'm begging you."

The phone rang.

"Okay, not what I had in mind," she muttered, pushing back from the counter. *Still, it's better than reliving my stellar stupidity.*

Well, depending on who was calling.

Unearthing her cell phone from her purse, which she had to first locate beneath the jumble of last night's discarded clothing, she gave the screen an apprehensive glance.

And exhaled a breath she hadn't realized she'd been holding when she saw it was the inn's head of maintenance. She opened the connection. "Hi, Dan, what can I do for you?"

"Hey, Jenny," he boomed and, pulling the phone away from her ear an inch, she easily envisioned him in her mind's eye: a short, stocky, perpetually sun-and-wind-burned man who, five would get you ten, had a faded brown John Deere baseball cap pushed to the back of his head, its bent bill pointed north.

"I'm out at the storage sheds," he said, "and the damn salt air has eaten clean through two-thirds of the hinges. I swear they go along just fine—then corrode overnight. Anyhow, I'm gonna go ahead and replace all of them to save me from having to turn around and do the rest next week."

"O-kay." It wasn't like Dan to ask permission to do his job. Generally, he simply fixed things before they became a problem.

He laughed. "I know, I'm babbling. The problem is I don't have enough in my existing supply. And I wasn't sure if you want me to put them on the inn tab at the General, or if you'd rather pick some up for me yourself."

"You do it. And figure how many you can handle in your supply closet so you can get those at the same time. Caleb's good about the volume discount."

"You got it."

They discussed which cabins Dan's paint crew planned to spiff up for a couple more minutes, then disconnected. Jenny tossed her purse on top of the clothing pile and raised her eyes to meet her gaze in the mirror.

"Okay," she told it firmly. Time to stop obsessing over her idiocy and get to work. She needed to call in additional staff for both housekeeping and the restaurant for the coming weekend. Needed to touch base with the head gardener to ask about his staffing needs as well, since it was that time of year, and discuss his budget. She also needed to check with Maria to see how Abby was working out at the front desk, as it was important the younger woman be at full speed when things began accelerating in the coming weeks. What she *didn't* need was to waste any more time thinking about Jake Bradshaw.

It didn't pain her to admit, however, that she wouldn't bitch if they managed not to run into each other for a while.

A nice *long* while.

STANDING IN THE KITCHEN in his boxers, lazily scratching his stomach above the low-slung band, Jake wondered if he'd run into Jenny today. Maybe he oughta drop by her place 'round about three-thirty and see how Austin's pinball tournament had gone. She usually made it a point to be at her cottage for at least part of the afternoon when the kid came home from school.

"Damn, Bradshaw." His hand stilled, then dropped to his side. He shook his head in disgust. "That's pathetic." Scowling at the coffeepot, he willed it to get a move on and produce the damn joe. Obviously he needed to clear his head.

Except...

If he thought that was pathetic, what was he supposed to make of the fact that he'd had a lush, desirable woman throw herself at him last night and he'd played the goddamn hero? Where had that come from? Wasn't he the guy who had walked out on his kid? The man who cold-bloodedly chose women who were a slightly upscale, sophisticated version of a good-time girl expressly because they wouldn't expect a damn *relationship* from him?

So why choose *now* to be honorable? He grabbed the coffeemaker's glass carafe, ignoring the splatter and hiss on the hot plate as the last drops of water dripped through the grounds and hit it. Gratefully, he poured himself a soup-bowl-size mug.

Gut in an unaccustomed uproar, he took a big gulp and burned his tongue. Jerked in reaction to the scald and splashed some coffee from the cup onto the back of his hand.

"Ouch! Shit!" He fumbled the mug onto the counter, gave his hand a fierce shake, then slapped the faucet on, producing a voluminous gush of water.

"Christ." He thrust his hand beneath the cold flood.

And wouldn't have been the least bit comforted if he'd known he was mimicking Jenny—who was in his head too damn deep as it was—when he said, "Somebody just shoot me now."

"I'M SORRY YOU CAN'T see Nolan right away," Jenny said that afternoon as they climbed in the car.

Austin shrugged and focused his attention on his hands as they slowly fit the male end of his seat belt into the female and clicked it home.

Anything not to have to look at her. Jenny already seemed to possess this spooky ability to see into his head and read his thoughts.

They'd just walked out of Dr. Janus's office, where he'd gotten his shot to replace the messed-up vaccination Dr. Howser had given him and Nolan and a bunch of other kids back when they were little.

It turned out he was gonna need a second one as well in about a month. Plus, Dr. J had said Austin's body needed time to generate its own antibodies, so he had to keep on keeping his distance from Nolan.

It really sucked that he was sort of happy about that. What kind of shitty friend was he?

"It won't be for long," Jenny continued reassuringly, and he really wished she would quit talking.

Oblivious, she reached across the console to pat his knee. "Rebecca tells me Nolan's eruptions are starting to crust. He won't be infectious very much longer."

"Yeah," he agreed glumly.

"Hey, I know!" She took her eyes off the road long enough to shoot him a glance. "Why don't we swing by and pick up Bailey? She'd probably appreciate the opportunity to get out of the house, too."

"I've got to get to practice. But Bailey talked about being there."

"Oh. I totally forgot about that. Still, I'm glad she's going. You two are good together. And I think she can probably use all the friends she can get right now. Rebecca said she's having a tough time in school."

"It's those damn snobby girls!" Okay, maybe that came out sounding a little too angry, because Jenny shot him an odd look. But it pissed him off that none of the girls at school would give Bailey a break.

And Jenny merely said, "It's not easy coming in at the end of the year—especially in a school where everybody knows everyone else. Trust me, I've been there. You want to give her a call to see if she needs a ride?"

"Yeah, I guess," he said, pulling his Droid from his pocket.

"Hey," he said when Bailey answered. "Me and Jenny are on our way to practice. Want us to swing by to pick you up? You can tell Mrs. D if you want that I'll walk you home when it's over, so she doesn't have to come pick you up."

"That would be great," Bailey said, and the pleasure in her voice sent an embarrassing heat through him.

"Sweet. See you in a few."

"That works for her, I take it," Jenny said and detoured to the Damoths' house at the next turn.

"Yeah." He kept his gaze firmly on the scenery outside. Because he was pumped knowing he'd have Bailey all to himself after practice. And he really wouldn't mind if Nolan's contagion took a bit longer to go away.

Which, as he'd already established, made him the shittiest of shitty friends.

JAKE WAS RESTLESS. He'd turned in the last of his *National Explorer* assignment a few days ago and had been enjoying a little R and R. But today being unproductive chafed him. Pacing the rental house ate up a little time, but not nearly enough. He was bored.

The thought stopped him in his tracks. "What are you, eight?" His *kid* acted more mature than this. Exasperated with himself, he grabbed his camera, threw a couple of extra lenses in the bag and slammed out of the house. It had been a nice day, weather-wise, and was gearing up to be a decent evening, as well. Getting out and enjoying the weather beat the hell out of rambling around the cottage.

He killed some time stretched out on his stomach on the edge of the inn's lawn to get shots of the sun-dappled water through the sea grasses. But landscapes weren't exactly the creative outlet he was looking for. He liked photographing people best, yet did he take the boardwalk into town where he was likely to find a subject or two? No, ma'am. He found himself stalking down the beach away from it. Because as much as he'd enjoy shooting some portrait studies, he really wasn't in the mood to talk to anyone.

Until he spotted his brother—*half* brother— through the sparse screen of trees and waterfront properties that separated this section of the beach from the shore road. Max was cruising tortoise slow in his department SUV and—his frame of mind inexplicably lightening—Jake found himself cutting across the lot of one of the summer people's buttoned-up cabin and heading toward the road to see where Deputy Dawg was going.

The action was about as dumb as everything else he'd done today, but what the hell. For the first time since he'd awakened this morning with little Ms. Salazar burrowed firmly in his head, his mind was engaged in something other than her.

The million-dollar question, of course, was what made him think he had a snowball's chance of keeping pace with a man in a car. But, hey, it was something to do and it wasn't as if he didn't have plenty of time on his hands. If—or, more realistically, *when*—he lost the trail, he'd at least have burned some time in this interminable day.

But—whataya know—he caught a break. As he rounded the slight bend in the road, he saw the back end of Max's cruiser disappearing down the public boat launch where they'd watched the nuclear submarine. Red taillights blinked, then disappeared into the trees that bordered either side of the drive and parking area.

Cutting back toward the sun-dappled water, he lengthened his strides down the high, intermittently sandy sections of the pebble-and-rock beach.

The tide was in, and the shoreline mimicked the curve to the east that the road had taken, so the boat ramp was out of sight until Jake navigated the bend. The first thing he saw when he cleared it was Max sitting in a patch of sand with his back propped against a log, staring out over the canal. Jake stopped in his tracks and groped for his camera.

His brother looked so…lonely. Or, hell, maybe just

alone. All Jake knew for sure was that the guy was all big, brooding angles, from his austere mouth and sharp cheekbones to the rawboned massiveness of his shoulders and wrists and his big-knuckled hands. His long legs were drawn up, his muscular arms crossed over his knees, and he'd planted his angular chin on one wrist.

Max's dark hair, dark brows and thick fan of lashes, not to mention the black, almost military-style uniform sweater he wore with his jeans, were a study in contrasts against the bleached-out log he leaned against and the pale sand he'd dug his bare feet into.

Sand that had to be cold as hell this time of year. High-end running shoes with a sock stuffed in each were planted neatly on the log at his back.

Jake snapped off several shots.

The quiet *click-whir, click-whir* sent Max's head whipping in Jake's direction, and the deputy's right hand had his pistol almost clear of its holster before Jake's identity apparently registered.

"Christ." Jake's own hands snapped to shoulder height in an instinctive *see, no weapon, no threat here* demonstration, sending his camera swinging from its strap around his neck. Embarrassed by his reaction, he snapped, "What the fuck? They issue *guns* to guys with PTSD?"

"We prefer to call it razor-honed instincts," Max said coolly, reseating his weapon. "Something I don't expect a guy who takes pretty pictures for a living to understand." But the dig was nowhere up to his usual standards, and something in his dark eyes suggested that maybe Jake's crack had some basis in fact—if not currently, then in the not too distant past.

Something clenched low in Jake's gut, because he didn't like to think about what his half brother must have seen overseas to cause such a thing.

If it even were a fact and not just a figment of his imagination. He didn't think his imagination was that good, though, and knowing instinctively that Max would hate anything he'd construe as pity, Jake sank into the sand next to the bigger man and lounged back against the same log. Turning his head to look at him, he said lightly, "So, you ever actually work? I mean, every time I see you, you're either here or drinking beer at the tavern."

The corner of Max's mouth ticked up. "I just finished a nine-hour shift. I like to come here sometimes to watch the water and the mountains and maybe catch the show on the access."

"What show?"

His half brother turned to pin him in his head-on gaze for the first time since Jake had sat down next to him. "You're kidding, right? Didn't you ever come down here in high school to watch people put their boats in and take 'em out of the water?"

"Can't say that I did. I rode in friends' boats sometimes, but they usually had private docks. I guess I never considered how they got them in and out of the canal."

"That's right. You ran with the rich crowd."

He shrugged. "I started going out with Kari around my sixteenth birthday. Most of her friends came from the wealthier families in the area."

"My friends were more the beer-blast and burger type. Sometimes a parent would have a nice little runabout or a beater boat that you could fish or crab from, but mostly we just came down here to party and watch the yahoos launch their boats. Probably eighty-five percent know what they're doing, but that still leaves a shitload who don't have a clue."

An old Wahoo, running on fuel that emitted a smoky stench suggesting it was too rich in oil, pulled into shore. A passenger jumped onto the beach, then turned to push the boat back out before striding toward the parking lot. The boat took off, but circled around to idle twenty feet offshore.

Max grinned. "Speaking of which—"

Jake looked at him. "You know these guys?"

"Nah. But I've seen them before. Watch and marvel."

Except for the soft slap of the small waves generated by the boat's wake unfurling against the beach, it was quiet for a moment. Then a panel van backed a boat trailer down the ramp. As they watched, the trailer was maneuvered deeper and deeper into the water, until it covered first the trailer's wheels, then its fenders. Even then the van continued to back up.

Jake jackknifed upright. "Are you kidding me?" He turned to stare at his brother. "He's got the whole back end in there. Doesn't the idiot know what salt water does to metal?" He turned back to watch the van on the access and snorted an incredulous laugh. "Seriously, man? The fucking tailpipe's blowing bubbles!"

"Gotta love it, right?" Max demanded drily and cracked a rare smile.

"You see this kind of thing often?"

"All the time. Here's a tip for you, little Bradshaw. Never buy a vehicle with Kitsap plates and a trailer hitch."

"Ya think?" He laughed and settled back against the log.

Max was right—he watched and marveled. But it wasn't so much the yahoo on the Wahoo's lack of technique that held him in awe as the fact that this— this being with his brother and actually laughing over the idiocy of people together—had done what nothing else had managed to do: drained the edgy restlessness that had plagued him all day right out of him. Who would have predicted that?

With an odd little twist in his stomach, he realized that sometime in the past few weeks, Max had ceased being the bully from his past and become a...friend.

But he wasn't stupid enough to say so out loud. "I can't believe, with all the years I lived here, that I missed out on this. Look, here comes someone else." He glanced at Max and grinned. "Give me a heads-up next time, yeah? I'll bring the beer and popcorn."

CHAPTER SIXTEEN

"NO TEAM PICTURES!" AUSTIN groused for the ump-teenth time as he took the plate Jenny had just rinsed and extended to him. "We're going to be the first team in Bulldogs *history* not to have our pictures taken! And forget about the special annual or the write-up about you and the inn."

She wouldn't particularly miss the big ad she always bought to accompany the write-up, as it was more to support the team than bring in customers. Although to be fair, they had gotten occasional bookings from it.

But that wasn't the point. She looked at the misery etched on Austin's face and felt helpless. It didn't stop her from trying to soothe him. "Honey, I'm sure—"

The teen banged both fists down on the kitchen counter, making her bobble the pan, in which he'd made their boxed mac-and-cheese dinner, back into the soapy water.

Unclenching his fingers, he braced his palms against the tiles and stiff-armed himself away, his head drooping disconsolately between hunched-up shoulders. "Sorry," he said to the countertop. "You can't help this time, though, Jenny. *No*body can—"

Then his head abruptly snapped up and he thrust a finger at the Sand Dollar across the small parking area. "That's not true. *He* can!"

And before she could say a word, he'd ripped open the door to the mudroom and banged through the outer one. "Austin, wait!"

He didn't, and jamming her feet back into the heels she'd kicked off for the aborted cleanup, she hobbled as fast as she could behind him. She finally stopped at the bottom of Jake's porch and stood on one foot while hooking a finger under the leather she'd bent trying to jam her foot too quickly into the back of her other shoe. *Damn cheap designer knockoffs.*

She smoothed out the abused leather as best she could and, seating the heel of her foot properly this time, straightened, twitched her dress in order and took a deep breath before she climbed the stairs.

Maybe Jake wouldn't be home. That would be a shame for Austin, of course, but not such a bad deal for her. Was it truly all that wrong to think of herself first in just this one itty-bitty instance?

She winced at the sound of the boy pounding on the door.

Because if Jake *was* home, this would be the first time she'd come face-to-face with him since that embarrassing pass she'd made the other night. Twisting, she brushed nonexistent lint from the retro kick-pleats of her dress skirt.

"Good! You're here. You gotta help me!"

Damn! She slowly faced front again.

Jake stood in the doorway, dressed more casually than usual in his ancient Columbia University sweatshirt, threadbare baby-wale cords and white athletic socks. Dark stubble framed those beautifully cut lips and strong jaw, and his hair was attractively rumpled.

"O-kay," he said amiably. "I'll do my best. What do you need?" Then his voice deepened a notch and managed to sound like hot sex on cool sheets when he added, "Jenny."

She gave him a brisk nod. "Jake."

"Yeah, yeah, everyone knows everyone's name," Austin snarled impatiently.

She'd love to just let it slide, but couldn't. "Snapping at everyone is not the way to make friends and influence people, Austin Jacob."

He opened his mouth, undoubtedly to impart something snarky, but snapped it closed. Gave her a nod. "Sorry," he muttered with zero sincerity. Still, he'd apologized instead of singing the ubiquitous teenage *"Whatever"* anthem, so Jenny gave him a pass on the tone.

Taking an audible breath, Austin turned to his father, then exhaled it with a whoosh. "Dude. Because of Dr. Howser's stupid screwup with the chicken pox vaccination, we've got no photographer for the team pictures. The guy who always does it came down with a case of the pox, too, and they're telling us, like this *helps* at all, that adult cases are usually ten times worse."

"So, can't he simply do it when he's feeling better?" Jake inquired reasonably.

"No! He's booked right up until the end of June, when he's taking some big-deal family vacation to Europe!" The teen's voice rose with each word until he was one decibel shy of yelling.

Then to Jenny's eternal pride, he composed himself. His voice was still passionate, however, when he said, "These pics are a big damn deal. Not only do we get our individual and team photos, but there's this dope bound book with everyone's picture in it, kinda like a high school yearbook, ya know? And there are stories and photographs of the people and businesses that support us through the year. Like Jenny here!" He grabbed her by the shoulders and pulled her to stand in front of him, displaying her like Exhibit A.

"Really?" she demanded incredulously, craning her head to look over her shoulder at the teen.

"Work with me here," he muttered. Then looking past her to Jake, he slapped on a better-grab-the-tissue-'cause-this-story's-gonna-be-*sad* face. "Jenny waits all year for the publicity her write-up brings to the inn."

"Sure," Jake said with a straight face. "Because tons of local people must stampede for the chance to shell out their hard-earned bucks on a hotel a mile from home."

Exactly!

Austin growled like a cat faced with a raccoon.

"Hey, the coupon in her ad brings them to the restaurant in droves."

"This is true," she agreed.

But the teen's hands dropped away from her arms and his shoulders sagged. "Aw, hell. Never mind."

Jake stared at his son and could no doubt see, as did Jenny, that this was not posturing. This was genuine dejection.

He stepped closer. "What do you say I volunteer to step in for the photographer?" Jake asked gently. "Would that help?"

Austin's head came up. "Really?"

"Yeah."

"Oh, man, that would be so dope!" He lurched forward to give Jake an awkward hug, then took a hasty step back, stuffing his hands in his pockets. "Thanks, Dad. I mean, really, thank you."

The boy may not have realized the form of address he'd just used on his father, but Jenny froze as if she'd stepped on a land mine, and her next move could be the end of her life as she knew it. And the look that flashed across Jake's face—well. For a second his expression was open and stunned. Hopeful. Vulnerable.

Then he blinked and it was as if the action punched the Drop Curtain button, because she could no longer read him at all. "That's what we'll do then…provided Jenny helps me."

"What?"

"Yeah, sure, she can do that," Austin agreed eagerly.

"Wait a darn minute, you two," she said. "I happen to have a job that's already taking up most of my time and attention."

"It's the slow season," Austin said.

"Not this weekend it isn't."

"Then we'll fit things into the weekdays." Jake looked at her. "Work around your schedule."

"Maybe we could do the team's pictures before practice or a game," Austin added. "I could let them know when."

Dammit, when the boy looked at her with his face alight with happiness, what was she supposed to do? "Why don't you go make a copy of the phone tree off my computer while I hammer out a few details with Jake?"

"Okay." He swooped to give her a big bear hug that lifted her off her feet and made her squeak. Setting her down, he grinned and stepped back. "You guys are the best."

"Of course we are. Now that you got your own way."

He shot her a cocky grin, then leaped off the porch and bolted toward home.

She turned to his father. "Seriously? You tow me into this?"

"You've been avoiding me ever since you proposed we get it on," he said, ruthlessly dragging the one subject she'd prefer left stuffed in a dark corner into the light of day. "It's either this or we go to bed and have hot sex."

"Okay, fine," she said snappishly. "Let's go to bed."

"What?" His jaw dropped. Then his eyes lit up and he stepped forward. "Really?"

"No, not really." *Dammit.*

But, no, she couldn't think that way. *No casual sex. He's leaving.*

Closing her mind to the voice whispering in her head, she gave him a poor-delusional-man head shake. "Jeez, you're easy."

"Hey, I'm a guy. It's built in our DNA."

"It's built in your *d-i-c-k*."

He grinned. "That, too. Wanna see how mine's built?"

"Pffff."

"Ouch. Dismissive. Well, never mind." He stepped closer, but the flirtatiousness disappeared. "So, how big a project is this?"

"Fairly big, although maybe not for a man accustomed to traveling to faraway places and living in primitive conditions for his assignments. Why don't we go over to the cottage and I'll dig up last year's album to give you an idea of the scope on this one." She took a breath and allowed, "I suppose it wouldn't kill me to coordinate this. There are several families who'd be happy to help, so I could delegate part of it."

"Don't forget Austin's offer."

"Oh, trust me, Austin's going to do his share."

Then she smiled. "Although, I have to admit I'm kind of proud of him for his follow-through on this. It really knocked him for a loop when he heard there wouldn't be team photos this year and no annual. Especially that, I think. The annual is unique to our team. It falls outside the range of the Little League— this is sponsored entirely by Razor Bay and the local Small Business Association."

They went over to her bungalow, where she accepted the phone tree from Austin, who had been on his way back to Jake's. She sent him to unearth the past two years' leather-bound annuals from the bookshelf in his room. While he did that and took them to Jake in the living room, she went into the kitchen to make them some coffee and cocoa and slap a dozen store-bought cookies on a plate.

A moment later, she put the tray on the coffee table and joined the two males on the couch, where they sat with their heads together, poring over last year's book. "What do you think?" she asked Jake when he closed the last one.

"I can do better than this."

She narrowed her eyes at him. "Are you insulting our photographer's work?"

"Not at all—he's not half-bad. But I'm better."

"He bragged shamelessly," she said dryly.

He shot her a cocky grin that looked an awful lot like his son's. "It's not bragging if it's true. I am good."

"Okay, you are," she conceded. "I love that photo you gave Austin."

"Me, too," Austin said, probably admitting aloud for the first time how much it meant to him.

"I think all photography rocks," Jake said. "But shooting people is what I like and do best." His eyes were alight with enthusiasm when he looked at them. "And I can make this the most kick-ass annual these kids have ever seen."

"Sah-weet!" Austin crowed and gave his dad a high five.

Jenny couldn't argue with that, so she got down to business with Jake. "You've been to enough games to have an idea how many kids are involved," she said as she rose to her feet. "I'll run off a copy of the list of participating merchants and businesses so you can get an idea of the extent of that portion of the project, as well."

Austin hopped up, too. Shoving his hands in his pockets, he all but danced with excitement. "A bunch of the guys talked about hanging at Bella T's for a while tonight. Can I go give them the news?"

"Oh, I don't know…" She glanced at Jake. One, he had just made a hell of an offer and Austin disappearing in the wake of it might seem a little less than appreciative. Two—and face it, the biggie for her—she'd just as soon not be left alone with him.

But Jake merely asked his son if he'd done his homework.

"Yeah. Did it before dinner."

"Then if it's okay with Jenny, it works for me."

Well, crap. That neatly boxed her in. "Okay. But be back by nine."

"Sweet!" It was apparently Austin's word of the day, and it hung in the air as he tore out through the kitchen.

Thighs spread wide, Jake leaned back against the couch cushions, his hands linked behind his head and elbows pointing at ten and two o'clock. "I do believe he's pleased," he said, looking pretty damn pleased himself.

"I think you can safely say that," she agreed dryly. "Well, I'll just go get the list—"

He looked up at her from his indolent sprawl. "First tell me about this write-up on the inn that Austin mentioned."

She sat down again, but this time perched on the edge of the coffee table, prepared to dash away at a moment's notice. She couldn't say why she felt so on edge. Despite his lazy posture, Jake's behavior was professional.

She exhaled a quiet breath. "Each of us gets a full page, half of which is dedicated to the ad space we buy. Basically we're paying half price for a full-page spread. The other half simply gives us an opportunity to put a personality to the advertisement."

"Who does the copy?"

"We each do our own—and those who suck at it get help from someone who doesn't. I'm sure it sounds like amateur hour to you, but it's surprisingly effective. The personal information makes it not feel so advertisey, and by boxing only the coupons we offer, it comes across more like a who's who of Razor Bay business professionals." She shrugged. "For an extra twenty-five bucks we can also have our individual pages put up on the town website. I've probably gotten more reservations through the internet than the ad in the annual, since that targets primarily team families and other locals. And as you pointed out, people who live here aren't usually in a mad rush to spend their rare night out at the inn next door. They're much more likely to go into Seattle or Tacoma or up to the Seven Cedars Casino in Sequim."

"So, why bother?"

Really? She stared at him. Wasn't it obvious?

He met her gaze expectantly, however, so she said, "To give back to the town that's given so much to me."

That elicited a grimace and she tilted her head curiously. "Why do you dislike it here so much?"

"I don't dislike it, exactly." And to Jake's amazement, he realized he was no longer experiencing the usual get-me-the-hell-out-of-here restlessness he'd felt like pepper beneath his skin the minute he'd crossed the town line. Sometime during the past couple of weeks it had disappeared—but so gradually he couldn't pinpoint when.

"Is it because your wife died here, then?"

"No. Or not entirely." *Not at all.* "Truth is, I can't

remember a time when I didn't lust after something larger than what Razor Bay has to offer."

"Still, I can only imagine how awful it must have been to lose her right after she gave birth to Austin. That had to be the last straw for Razor Bay."

He'd discussed Kari's death a little with Max, so he couldn't say why having Jenny ask questions pushed his buttons now—why it stirred up things he didn't like to think about. But it did and he focused a sharp gaze on her. "Why are you so damn interested in Kari?"

The delicate lift of her eyebrow and tiny twitch at the corner of her mouth was clear as a shrug. "I don't know. Maybe it's because I care about Austin and I'd like to get to know you better."

"Really?" *Snapping is not the way to make friends and influence people, Austin Jacob,* she'd said. Austin *Jacob.* "And you think pumping me for details about the worst time in my life is the way to do it?" How could it have escaped him that his kid had been given his name?

She blinked. Then said with stricken apology, "I'm sorry. That's not what I was trying to do."

"The hell it wasn't. Kari and I weren't fucking Romeo and Juliet. This isn't some tragic, star-crossed love story." Ugly emotions seethed beneath his skin. He had no idea where they'd come from.

But he couldn't seem to get a handle on them.

Which was why he jerked upright, shifted his butt to the edge of the couch and leaned into her space.

"Love is an illusion, sweetheart. A chimera that disappears if you look at it too closely."

"That's certainly—" she leaned back "—cynical."

"No, that's reality. You want to know what the final straw was?" he demanded in a hard voice, even as the whisper of Austin's *"Dad"* in his head felt like a reproach. "That would probably be the fact that by the time Kari died, there wasn't a speck of affection, let alone love, left between us. Or that I looked at my own kid—" Austin *Jacob* "—and the only thing I felt was a need to get the hell out of Dodge!"

She studied him for several long heartbeats, those Godiva eyes of hers searching for God-only-knew what.

Then blew out a breath.

"Look," she said. "I hate the fact that your neglect caused Austin a load of disappointment over the years."

There wasn't a reflex on earth fast enough to catch his flinch. But it didn't mean he had to parade it in front of her. He flopped back against the cushion and raised an eyebrow.

She pursed her lips and his eyes homed in on them. "At the same time," she said slowly, redirecting his attention back to her steady gaze, "you were eighteen years old. Your lifelong plans had imploded and you had a boatload of responsibility dumped on your shoulders." She examined him for seconds that felt like dog years, and his heart *thud, thud, thudded* against his rib cage. He slapped on a faintly amused smile to keep her from realizing how off balance he was.

"I'm guessing both you and Kari must have felt pretty damn trapped," she continued. "On top of that, she was dealing with seeing and feeling her body balloon into something she probably didn't recognize. I know Emmett and Kathy's propensity for spoiling, so let's say she was a young woman accustomed to being nubile and popular and getting what she wanted, and that she didn't love what was happening to her. You were working a job *you* didn't love and had had to walk away from a scholarship you'd worked toward your entire school career."

"And you would know this because...?" he asked lightly, even though forcing the careless tone was like swallowing glass.

"Emmett and Kathy told me. They didn't hate you, you know."

"Coulda fooled me. They told me to stay away from Austin."

"And this changed your life how?" For the first time her voice turned snappish. But she sucked in a breath, exhaled it and said evenly, "From what I understand you were big on saying you'd be by to see Austin, then never showing up. They finally had enough."

Bitter shame filled him. Shame at his actions, shame at the relief he'd felt at finally being cut off— if only so he could quit feeling so fucking ashamed of all his broken promises. Giving her a shrug of acknowledgment, he resisted the tell of rubbing at the ache between his brows.

"But they didn't hate you, Jake. They just didn't want to see Austin hurt."

Determined not to let her see his inner rawness any more than he already had, he yawned. "So is all this amateur psychoanalyzing your way of keeping yourself from jumping my bones again?" he drawled in a bored voice.

She shot to her feet, her cheeks flushed red. "God, you're an ass."

"And you'd love to get your hands on it, wouldn't you?"

She gave him a chilly look down the length of her pretty, exotically fashioned nose. "I think we're done here."

His own rise to his feet was much more leisurely, and he smiled at the flash of panic on her face when it brought her breasts a whisper away from touching his chest. Snaking a hand around the back of her neck, he tipped her head back, lowered his and kissed her.

Thoroughly. Not until her tongue came up to engage his as it explored her mouth, not until she quit holding herself stiffly aloof and sagged against him, not until he felt the barbarian within rush the bars of his cage, howling to get out, did he lift his lips from hers and step back.

"Now we're done," he said. Then aroused and angry and slightly sick to his stomach over his behavior, he turned and sauntered out of her house.

CHAPTER SEVENTEEN

"I'M SORRY ABOUT LAST NIGHT."

Jenny's head whipped up at the sound of the low, masculine voice just outside her door. She hadn't heard anyone come up onto the unlit covered porch, and she gaped at Jake, because of course that's who it was. He was a shadow in the dusk that crowded the other side of the screen door, but she'd know that voice anywhere.

She refused to think too deeply about why that was.

A little summerlike weather had finally arrived in Razor Bay this morning. The skies had been blue until the sun went down and were a deep, rich navy even now. The mountains were out in all their glory, the clouds that obliterated them for most of the past weeks blown away. The temperature had even climbed into the low seventies, although it had dropped significantly once the sun set. Loving the fresh air and the scent of the potted flowers that the inn's gardeners had set on her porch and planted in the border at the base of the cottage, she'd put on a sweater and left the door wide open to invite in fresh air and clear out the winter stuffies.

Who would have thought *that* might be a mistake?

Clearly it had been, however. For Jake was no longer as shadowy as he'd been at first sight and, one hand gripping the overhead door casing, his cheek against rounded biceps, he looked at her through the screen.

And the instant he saw that he had her attention he said, "You were right. I was an ass."

"You certainly are," she agreed coolly, deliberately using the present tense. "You're the only one who apparently harbors any doubt about it." But, oh, God, that kiss—no attitude in the world could eradicate that from her head. Nothing could make her forget how it had edged into something uncivilized just before he'd pulled back. A...*dominance* that had made her feel as if she were flirting with the razor edge of danger.

And as much as she hated to admit it, as much as it was contrary to her customary caution, she'd loved it. She who preferred to play it safe. Who had held on to the security of the known ever since that period in her life when everything had been one great big unknown.

Not that she had any intention of acting on the temptation that had blossomed full blown last night. She gave her head an impatient shake. No, she was going to push away the enticement of taking a walk on the wild side and continue to play it safe. To do otherwise was an invitation to disaster.

Just look at how long it had taken her to settle

down after he'd left last night. She couldn't believe
how upset she had been—all anger, arousal and frustration. She'd hardly known what to do with herself
and would have been perfectly happy never to see
him again.

At the same time, she'd longed for him to come
back long enough for her to slap him silly.

And yet…

Jake had clearly been hurting and it had been hard
to witness.

But it didn't excuse him. Not when he'd been arrogant and rude and pretty damn quick to dish out a
little pain to her, as well.

"Can I come in?"

Hell, no. She knew a bad idea, a sucker bet, when
she heard one. And she was nobody's sucker. In fact,
she contemplated rising from the couch where she
was glued to her seat to slam the door in his face.
She'd send him on his way so fast he'd be nothing
but the scent of burned rubber.

As if she were controlled by the Big Daddy of pup-
pet masters, however, she hitched one shoulder. Or
maybe it was the King of Ventriloquists, because when
she opened her mouth to tell Jake no in no uncertain
terms, her voice instead said, "Yeah, whatever."

Are you kidding me? Tossing aside the report she'd
been poring over, she shot to her feet.

But she was too late to prevent him from enter-
ing her home. The door squeaked when he opened

it, then slapped closed behind him with the meaty spank of wood on wood.

I rescind my offer! she thought frantically, then felt like an idiot. Because, really, did that work anywhere outside bad vampire movies?

Apparently not. Or theoretically not, anyhow. One would have to actually *say* it to test its effectiveness.

"Here," he said, thrusting out his hand. "These are for you."

Oh, God. He was a mess, she saw as she got her first good look at him in the light. His eyes were bloodshot, his jaw shadowed with dark stubble, and his hair suffered from a killer case of bed head, flat in some places and sticking up in others, as if he hadn't bothered to so much as pull a comb through it.

And he had flowers. A huge fistful of roses and tulips and gerbera daisies that must have been hidden behind the lower solid panel of the screen door.

She reached out to relieve him of them. She wanted to be all cool and you're-deluded-if-you-think-this-is-all-it-takes-to-get-back-in-my-good-graces. Longed to toss the lush bouquet on the coffee table to sit neglected until it moldered into dust.

Instead she buried her nose in it to take a deep sniff. Why could she never do the smart thing around this guy? She should not, not, *not* sorta love the damn flowers!

Smart would be to say, "They're lovely, thank you very much," then add a firm "Now go away."

But when he looked at her with those green eyes shadowed with misery, she simply couldn't bring herself to do it.

She blew out a sigh. Because, so much for being nobody's sucker. "I'll find a vase."

He trailed her into the kitchen and watched her dig one out of the cupboard, fill it with water, empty a little packet of preservatives into it and snip and arrange the flowers.

"Where's Austin?" he asked, glancing around him as if expecting the boy to suddenly materialize.

She looked at him over the flowers. "He's at an overnighter for Oliver Kidd's birthday party."

It was silent for a few moments as she tweaked the arrangement. Then he suddenly said in a low voice, "I really am sorry about last night. I can be an ass sometimes—but I'm not usually *that* big an ass."

She glanced up at him. "Yeah? So how did I get so lucky?"

For a moment he leaned against the counter, rubbing a thumb between his brows and merely looking at her, and she thought his response would be to ignore the question. Then he dropped his hand to his side and looked her in the eye.

"For the first time since I walked out of Austin's life, it hit home just how much I threw away." Blowing out a weary breath, he walked over to her little drop-leaf table and collapsed onto one of the chairs.

She set the vase of flowers aside and joined him,

taking the seat across the table. "You want some coffee?"

"No. Thanks. I didn't sleep for shit last night. I'd rather not screw up any chance of getting some tonight. Tossing and turning all night sucks." He stared down at his hands, fingers splayed against the warm-golden oak of her kitchen table.

Then he raised his gaze to meet hers. "The last time I saw him, back when he was a baby, he was this cranky, crying, *leaky* little stranger that I had no idea how to take care of."

"Austin?" she asked, then made a face and an erasing gesture. Because who else would he be talking about?

But Jake didn't seem to notice. "I was supposed to fall in love with him," he said in a low voice. "That's what everyone told me—that the minute they put your kid in your arms, you'll fall in love." He looked at her with haunted eyes. "So why didn't I? Why did I look at him, and the only thing I could think was that he looks sorta simian? And where the hell did he get those lungs? He exercised the hell out of those every time I came near. Kathy could calm him down. Emmett could, too. But when I had to hold him, he always screamed. Jesus."

He ground the heel of his hand into his forehead before pulling it back and staring at it as if he'd never seen a hand before. He lowered it to the table, his fingertips pressing so hard against the surface it drove all the color from his nails. "He screamed and screamed, and he was always wet and hot and stickier than a gummi bear. And all I felt was stark terror. I just wanted to get as far away from the responsibility of him as I could." Self-loathing made itself at home in his voice.

"I knew damn well I was unnatural," he said flatly. "No real father feels that way. So when Emmett said I should take that scholarship after all, that he and Kathy would take care of Austin—" He shook his head. "Man. I jumped all over it."

She stared at the palpable anguish in his face and swallowed a sigh. *Dammit.* Half of her appreciated— no, flat-out admired—his raw honesty. She loved learning that he hadn't taken his neglect of Austin lightly. It boded well for his future relationship with his son, and she genuinely wished a healthy relationship with this man for the boy she loved.

But the Jenny who was desperately scrambling to hold herself aloof in order to keep from feeling more for Jake than was wise—

Well.

She almost wished he would demonstrate some of the careless, selfish and arrogant rat-bastard father qualities she had thought defined him before they'd actually met.

She could never in this lifetime fall in love with that man.

Not that she was falling in love now!

But her heart hurt to see his self-flagellation. It was right under her nose, however—this naked grief that was so much deeper than anything she'd glimpsed last night—and she felt…something.

Something that bristled with a lot more affection than simple lust.

To refute it, she demanded in a level voice, "But you never came back."

"No. I never did." He shook his head, and the sudden bark of laughter that exploded from his throat was bitter as wormwood. "I told myself—no, hell, *promised* myself—that I would. As soon as I accomplished this or achieved that. I made dates so that I'd *have* to go back."

He looked her in the eye. "But as you know, I broke every one.

"Fuck." He pushed his chair back from the table with a force that made the legs screech against the fake terrazzo tiles of her kitchen floor. Thrusting a hand through his hair, he stared down at her. "So to answer your question—if you even remember what that was—I heard Austin call me Dad last night, I heard you call him Austin Jacob, when I didn't even know that was his middle name, and everything I managed to screw up blew up in my face. But instead of owning up to it like a man, I turned it around on you. And I'm sorry."

He about-faced and strode for the back door.

Let him go, let him go, let him go, she urged herself. She watched him twist the knob and fling open the door to the mudroom.

Watched him take the couple of long-legged strides that brought him to the exterior door.

Hugged herself as he twisted that doorknob, as well. *Let him. Go.*

Only to discover she couldn't.

"What *I* said last night still stands," she said to his back and watched him freeze with the knob gripped in one fist. "Do I wish you had handled your reaction differently—that you hadn't been such a jerk? Absolutely. But I still believe that back then you were an overwhelmed eighteen-year-old."

"That excuse is almost as shopworn as the always popular you're-doing-the-best-thing-for-Austin one I've spent the past thirteen years selling myself on."

"Maybe so. Yet they're both still true. Did you know that babies react to stress in other people?"

He looked at her over his shoulder. "What?"

"Sounds to me like Austin felt your tension and reacted by screaming his head off. Didn't Kathy or Emmett ever assure you of that?"

He slowly turned. "No."

"I'm surprised. They were parents—they must have known." A disloyal thought crept into her head that maybe they had known but liked the idea of getting Austin all to themselves for a while. She shoved it aside, however, for the mere suspicion made her feel like a traitor to two people who had been nothing but wonderful to her. And even if they had unconsciously sabotaged Jake, she doubted that their objective would have been for him to disappear entirely from his son's life. "Or maybe they didn't—we'll never know. Frankly, Jake, it's time to put the past behind you. What you do with the opportunity you have right now is what counts."

He came over to where she stood. Bent and pressed a soft kiss on her lips and straightened. "Thank you. You really are one of the nicest people I've ever met."

She made a rude noise. "No, I'm not."

"Yeah, you really are." He smiled at her.

It was ridiculous to be insulted; he clearly meant it as a compliment. But she was so tired of the Goody Two-shoes label that had been slapped on her fairly early in her residence here. In that respect, at least, she understood Jake's beef with Razor Bay. Small towns had a way of pigeonholing people sometimes.

Not that she hadn't contributed to carving out a cubby for them to stick her in. She'd always felt this town had saved her when she'd needed it most, and she'd done her best to pay it back wherever she could.

But right this moment…?

Well, maybe she was tired of playing it safe all the time.

Stepping up to him, she slapped her hands to his chest. He stilled beneath her touch as she slid them up over his shoulders, then brought them in to curl around the back of his neck. "Get this through your head," she said with soft-voiced firmness. "I am no damn Pollyanna."

And rising onto her toes, she slid her fingers up to grasp the back of his head, yanked it down to hers and kissed him.

CHAPTER EIGHTEEN

JENNY'S SUDDEN MOVE SQUISHED their noses together as she locked that sweet mouth of hers on his upper lip. It wasn't particularly salacious, as kisses went, but Jake's reaction was swift and furious all the same. No one had to tell him twice to get with the program.

Hell, he took *over* the program. Fingers plunging into her silky hair, his thumbs framing her face, he tilted her head so their noses no longer pressed together, which broke her gentle suction from his lip.

Pretty mouth still pursed and her slender eyebrows pulling together above her slowly opening eyes, she made a disgruntled noise deep in her throat and went after her target once again.

So…okay. Maybe he wasn't as in charge as he thought.

But she did retain the slight tilt he'd instigated, and inhaling through his newly liberated nostrils, Jake decided she could do whatever her little heart desired. He didn't care as long as she remained right where she was, plastered the length of his body, heartbeat to heartbeat, mouth to mouth. Hell, he was adaptable—he raked her lower lip with his teeth, yarded it into his mouth to lightly suck and just enjoyed the subtle cherry flavor that was uniquely Jenny's.

He was a take-charge kind of guy by nature, however, and when she pulled back and studied him through arousal-drowsy eyes as she slicked her tongue across the lip he'd so pleasurably toyed with, he wrapped his hands around her hips and hiked her up, grunting his approval when she wrapped her legs around his waist.

He walked her the few steps to the kitchen table, shoved the napkin holder and salt-and-pepper shakers out of the way and set her atop the table. Sliding his hands out from under her, he flattened his palms against the tabletop on either side of her, caging her in. Stiff-armed, he leaned in, satisfaction spearing him as he laid her back across the table like his own personal banquet. The napkin holder clattered to the floor, napkins fanning across the faux tiles.

"God," he whispered. And rocked his mouth over hers. This time their lips were parted and lined up the way they were designed to be, and he invaded her mouth with a lithe, muscular pump of his tongue.

They both froze for an instant—then, like alcohol poured into pure hydrogen peroxide, spontaneously combusted.

Mouth avid, Jake kissed her as if he could somehow consume her whole, moving his slightly chapped lips against hers, more fiercely and ardently with every passing second. Jenny was right there with him, her delicate hands fisted in his hair with a hold that wasn't delicate at all.

One instant he was propped above her, and the next he found himself spreading her thighs with his own and flattening her beneath the urgent press of his weight against the wooden tabletop. It wasn't until he realized he was actively grinding the back of her head into its surface with the force of his kiss that he pushed back onto his hands.

With a soft sound of protest, Jenny maintained her grip on his head to keep him in place and arched to keep her breasts in contact with his chest. It killed him to pull their bodies apart, but he needed some distance between them. Or not only was this bound to end up very uncomfortable for her, he had his doubts the table would bear up under the action.

But damn. Breath sawing in and out of his lungs, he stared down at her.

Her lips were swollen and red from the force of his kisses and, eyeing them hungrily, he licked his own. He wanted back at them in the worst way, and his head started to automatically lower.

Then he gave it a shake and pushed off her and onto his feet. "Jesus," he panted. "There's gotta be a better place for this than here."

"Oh, I don't know." Stretching her arms overhead, she undulated against the tabletop and nearly brought him to his knees. The sexual haze slowly cleared from her dark eyes, however, and she blinked. "No, you're right." Her head shake unconsciously mimicked his, and she held out a hand. "Help me up."

He hauled her off the table and straight over the shoulder he'd dipped to get under her stomach in a fireman's lift. He surged up to his full height.

"Jake!" she protested, grabbing the back of his shirt.

He stroked a placating hand down the back of her thighs. "I know—not real romantic. But trust me, it's the only safe option open to me right now. I can't be face-to-face with you or you're gonna be back on that table. Or on the floor. Or up against the nearest wall." Shit. "They're all starting to sound like perfectly fine options for our first time together, but I'm betting you'd enjoy a softer surface."

He strode over to her bedroom. Opening the door, he maneuvered her over the threshold and kicked the door closed behind him. Then he strode across the tiny room and flipped her onto the bed.

She shoved up onto her elbows and knuckled her hair out of her eyes, but Jake didn't give her time to get situated or have second thoughts. Digging a knee into the mattress, he dropped onto his hands and crawled up the bed to hang over her on all fours.

She flopped flat on her back. Arched her slender brows. "Now what?"

"Oh, honey." He bent his elbows to stroke his chest against her breasts as he planted a fast, carnal kiss on her lips. Straightening, he looked down at her. Her nipples poked hard points into her soft sweater. "Now I do all those things I've fantasized doing to you."

She insinuated her hands beneath the hem of his old Columbia U. sweatshirt and caressed the bare skin at the small of his back. For the first time since she'd launched herself at him, he recalled his less-than-pristine state and felt a moment's uncertainty.

Christ. He was hardly every woman's dream in his current condition. Had he even showered today?

But it didn't seem to bother her, for she merely murmured, "Cool," and rubbed her hands up his bare back, his ratty sweatshirt pooling in the bends of her elbows to follow the path her fingers set. "I guess that means I get to do all the things that *I've* imagined doing then, too, yes?"

His momentary doubt dissolved. "I'm counting on it." He came down on top of her.

Jenny apparently had other ideas, however, because she snapped a finger under his nose. "Back up on your hands, mister," she ordered and tugged on the sweatshirt she'd raised until it was a thick band circling his chest and upper back. "I want this off. Now."

"Pushy little thing, aren'tcha." He followed her command, however, and she pulled the garment over his head. That left it stretched across his chest from biceps to biceps and, lifting his right hand, he yanked his arm out of the sleeve, turning it inside out in the process. Then, raising his other hand, he repeated the process. But this time it bunched around his hand and he shook it sharply until the damn thing finally lost its grip and sailed over the side of the bed.

Jenny slapped her hands to his chest and shoved determinedly. He obediently fell away from her, flopping over onto his back.

She rose onto her knees, mounted him like a horse and sat astride his thighs. Perched atop him, she undulated slow and sexy, like a stripper on a sluggish mechanical bull. Pressing one clenched fist into her thigh, she raised her other arm overhead, moving it in slow counterpart with the lazy rock of her body.

She looked down at him through heavy-lidded eyes and licked her lips. "Save a horse—ride a cowboy," she murmured.

"Yee-haw." The back-and-forth motion had its predictable effect on his dick, and he gritted his teeth even as his hips cocked up to keep it aligned with the yielding friction of that soft, soft place between her legs.

Then it was gone as she slid her body down until she lay with her stomach atop his thighs, her legs stretched out along his. A discerning cock would likely be disappointed, but his was an opportunist of the equal opportunity variety. It liked every move she made and adjusted happily to nestling between her little tits.

Threading her fingers through the light fan of hair on his chest, she bent her head and nuzzled the top of his chest, then stretched to do the same to the contour of his neck where it flowed into his shoulder. Scooting up, she pushed his arms up to curl over his head on the mattress, holding them pinned with dainty fingers splayed across his forearms and the press of her inner arms against his.

It was surprisingly erotic and, feeling the need to hide how effortlessly she was heating him to the boiling point—which, okay, was a joke, considering the evidence of it determinedly prodding her—he said drily, "Dominatrix one of your fantasies?"

"You bet," she agreed. "Next time I'll dig out my leather corset."

"I'd like that. I'm—"

She sank her teeth into his triceps in a quick bite.

"Christ!" Who would have expected *that* to be such a turn-on? He shivered as she licked away the sting he only belatedly realized had startled him more than dealt much actual pain.

"Nothing egocentric about you," she said huskily against the side of his neck, where she was placing soft, openmouthed kisses. "A god, I'll grant you. But definitely one of the lower-case-g deities. Musclicious, maybe—that minor fertility god of hard bodies."

"Smart-ass."

This time she bit the ball of his shoulder and he thrust upward to rub against her nearest body part. Damn. The girl was a moving target.

So, what was it about her, anyway? He'd been with some seriously sexually accomplished women in his life—hell, with some of the world's most sexually *sophisticated* women. So how was it that the far-from-sophisticated kiss Jenny had given him a moment ago made him feel like an addict who'd just mainlined the highest-grade product in existence?

First one's on us, little boy.

Like hell. He could take over like *that!* There wasn't a doubt in his mind he was reams more experienced than she. He could have her begging for mercy in moments.

Yet he lay beneath her, still except for the jump of a muscle here, a seeking upward thrust of his hips there, desperate to see what she'd do next.

He gave up trying to swallow the occasional groan as she relinquished her grip on his arms and worked her way back down his torso in tortuous increments, exploring with her hands, her lips, her teeth and tongue. Clenching his own teeth to keep the crazy-ass pleas gathering in his throat from escaping, he looped his locked fingers behind the back of his head and crunched up to look down at her when she finally reached his waistband.

Unbuttoning it, she fiddled with the zipper head. Stared at the tense muscles in his abdomen for a moment. Then she glanced up to meet his gaze as she slowly lowered his zipper. His cock, behind the thin, stretchy cotton-and-silk blend of his boxers, made a break for it, crowding the opening.

She looked down and simply gazed for a moment where the barely concealed bulk of him was framed between wide-open zipper teeth. Then, tearing her gaze away with a clear effort, she shot him a one-sided smile. "You know, I really expected you to be a more handsy kind of guy."

He stilled. "You want my hands on you?"

"Well, of course." Running an exploratory finger down the length of the soft fabric over his hard dick, she licked the ab above his boxer's band and heaved a faux sigh, which wafted warm air to add an additional layer of torture to the mix. "Why is it that women always have to do all the heavy lifting?"

"I'll give you heavy lifting," he growled and, ripping his hands from behind his head, hooked them beneath her armpits and pulled her up the length of his torso. Wrapping his arms around her, he rolled the two of them over.

He pushed up on his elbows and grinned down at her. "I liked that domination thing you had going. Let's continue with that—we'll just reverse the spin."

She made a dismissive noise and flashed him a look down the length of her nose—a feat he had to admire, considering how hard it must have been to pull off, flat on her back with him looming over her. "Nobody likes a copycat, Bradshaw."

"Oh, you will," he promised silkily, and threading their fingers together, he replicated her earlier movements, enjoying the slide of her sweater-covered breasts against his bare chest as he pressed her arms to the bed above her head. It occurred to him that his pledge would probably carry more weight if he'd stripped her first, but he mentally shrugged. A guy could only do what a guy could do. He lowered his head and kissed her.

God, he loved her mouth. Her lips were soft and oh, so pliable. And when they opened beneath his, her mouth was hot and wet. He'd never tasted another like it, and lust pounded in his pulse points at the way her lips worked his as feverishly as his did hers. At the way her tongue tangled every bit as aggressively.

Manacling her wrists in his left hand, he lowered his right to slide beneath the thin tomato-red wool hem of her sweater. The feel of her beneath his fingers had him raising his mouth from hers and hissing in air through his teeth. "God," he breathed reverently. "Your skin is so damn soft."

Bondage lost its allure and he relinquished her wrists in favor of gripping a handful of her hair. He circled his fist to twist a slippery length around it, tilting her head back until her throat was an exposed arch. Lowering his head, he strung openmouthed kisses from the silken underside of her jaw, down the smooth-skinned column to the fragile triangular depression at its base. He lapped the flat of his tongue into the hollow, with its faint tracery of blue veins, and felt his cock jump when her pulse hammered beneath it.

Slipping his free hand beneath her top, he cupped a lace-covered breast.

Jenny arched her back, ardently pressing the small globe into his palm. "Jake?"

"I want to strip you naked and lick every inch of

you," he muttered hoarsely, inching down the bed to use his tongue to delineate the curve of her collarbone in her sweater's wide, scooped neckline. Beneath whisper-soft wool, his thumb traced circles over her beaded nipple, abrading its impudent point with the bra's lace. He wanted nothing more than to drive her as out of control as he was beginning to feel. "I want to bury myself so deep inside of you all I can feel is you coming all over my cock."

"Oh. My. God." Jenny twisted with languid sensuousness against the quilt-covered bedding. She'd gotten a kick out of being in charge—how often had that happened in her admittedly limited sexual dealings? But she liked this, too, this conceding of authority. She was accustomed to being in charge of damn near every other area of her life and hadn't known how good it could feel to let someone else take over.

And, oh, my, how Jake had taken over! She was *this* close to climaxing simply from the sound of his voice, from the inflammatory words he used. Without so much as a naked skin-to-skin touch. She couldn't discount that lace rubbing, rubbing, *rubbing* against her nipple, but still—she'd never been with a guy who talked like this. Never dreamed how sexy it could be.

But words were just the additive in the fuel; Jake didn't need dirty talk to rev her engine. That silver tongue of his was so fiery against her skin she wouldn't be surprised to find he'd branded his initials all over her with it.

Oh, God, indeed.

"I think you've got on too many clothes," he murmured. "We need to lose this sweater. I wanna see what I'm touching."

The tension holding her throat arched for his kisses disappeared as his long fingers slid out of her hair. And before you could say "striptease," he'd whipped the offending sweater over her head and off her arms, now flung over her head. She started to lower them.

"No, you don't." He was back in place, one hand spreading across both wrists, staying her. "I like having you in my power."

She snorted at the same time that tissues deep between her thighs gave a fast, sharp contraction.

Jake's gorgeous mouth quirked up on one side. "Don't see that happening, huh?"

Oh, I don't know. But, of course, she couldn't say that.

Could she?

No, of course she couldn't. "Not in this lifetime, bud."

"Oh, you never wanna say never," he murmured and rolled to his feet alongside the bed. "That'll only get my competitive juices flowing. Because I'm pretty sure that I can make you feel things—do things—you've never dreamed of."

No fooling. "So...what?" she said in a tone that said, *In your dreams.* "You have a yen to play sheik to my slave girl?"

His hands, which she suddenly noticed had lost a good deal of their tropical tan, shoved his cords down his legs and he kicked free of them. "Aw, now you're just messing with me," he said as he went to work shaking her out of her jeans. But he took his gaze off his work long enough to pin her in place with intense eyes. "I'd make a *kick-ass* sheik. I can think of all sorts of things I'd do to you—make you do to me. Honey, we'd be howling at the moon before I was done."

She swallowed hard—and squeezed her thighs together. Okay, maybe his way of talking about these things was a fuel all its own. But she managed to give him a supercilious look, complete with raised eyebrows.

"You know you like the idea," he said, but she could tell by the humor in his voice that he had no idea how much.

She forced a sigh. "I have an early meeting in the morning. You plan on talking all night?"

Jake laughed. "No, ma'am," he murmured. And thrust his boxers down.

She gawked—there was no other word for it. Not when the sudden loss of the last bit of clothing left his penis aiming like an assault rifle straight at her. "Oh. My. God."

"I know," he said ruefully. "It's not polite to point." And giving her a crooked smile, he hooked her calves in his hands and yanked her down to the end of the bed until her lace-covered butt slapped against his bare thighs. Bending her knee, he wrapped a warm hand around the instep of her right foot and pressed its sole against his penis, using it to push his sex back against his ridged stomach. "Better?"

She stared at the length that thrust out above the tips of her red-painted toes. "That's really not as long as it looks, you know. It's just that I have little feet." Instead of sounding dismissive, the pitch of her voice started rising higher with each word until "feet" cracked in two beneath its inability to reach an impossible octave. God, could she *sound* more idiotic? She had to quit trying to act all cool—it only served to bite her in the butt. Just being herself couldn't possibly sound any less ridiculous than that lie.

She cleared her throat. "Still. Maybe you're a more important god than I thought." She curled her toes against him.

His penis twitched against the bottom of her foot and he flashed her a white, white smile as he stepped back, allowing her foot to slide down his thighs. "You have to be the most fun woman I've ever met," he said, reaching for her and rearranging her back on the middle of the bed. He fetched his wallet from the back pocket of his discarded cords and tossed it on the nightstand.

Then he fell over her, catching himself on his palms and toes. Holding a plank position over her body, he lowered his head and kissed her.

Softly.

Sweetly.

With lips that moved gently, sucked lightly, licked lazily at hers. As if he had all the time in the world.

Unlike Jenny, who, just like that, went up in flames, plunging back into the conflagration that his break to disrobe them had temporarily banked. Threading her fingers through his hair, she held him to her as she kissed him back. Without nearly the softness, the sweetness or the gentleness he demonstrated.

Jake growled deep in his throat and, lowering himself to her side, reached for the front clasp of her bra. He unfastened it with a dexterous snap of his fingers and gently peeled the cups from her breasts. "Look at you," he said softly, doing just that.

No, don't. It was a knee-jerk reaction and she swallowed the words, because, really: *Show a little pride.* Her boobs might not be as grown-up looking as she'd like, but their slight roundness was pleasing and her nipples were pretty.

And, oh, God, with his hand shaping one and his mouth nipping at the other, she couldn't think straight. "Not requiring much foreplay here," she panted, shifting restlessly on the quilt and arching her back to push her breast deeper into his mouth. She felt as if he'd been teasing her for hours. Days. *Weeks.*

He released her nipple with a pop. "No? Too bad I'm in charge here, then, isn't it? 'Cause I'm all about the foreplay." His eyes locked on hers, he sucked her other nipple into his mouth and slid a hand down her stomach. Inserting it beneath the hip band of her undies, he slipped a sly forefinger between her legs, separating buttery folds to feather her clitoris.

Shooting Jenny straight into a climax, detonating her so hard and fast his name was a startled cry from her lips.

"Holy shit," he said, his eyes smoldering green sparks behind narrowed lashes. "Take note, Bradshaw," he murmured to himself. "Listen to the woman the next time she tells you what she does or doesn't need." His finger kept up its gentle circling until the last contraction faded and her hips abruptly lost their high arched rigidity and she collapsed back on the bed.

Slowly, he pulled his hand out of her panties, tugged them off and fumbled on the nightstand for his wallet. "You game for round two?"

She looked at his raging hard-on and bestirred herself guiltily. "Oh, God. For all my big talk about heavy lifting, I've let you do all the work. Give me a second and I'll rectify that." Maybe. If she could slap hands on her skeletal system, which seemed to have deserted her.

"Don't worry about it," he said, unrolling a condom down his sex, then turning on his side to face her and propping his head on his hand. He trailed the backs of his fingers down her body, from her collarbone to her navel to the tops of her thighs, coming close to but not touching what she most wanted touched. "Like you, I don't think I'm up for much foreplay. When a woman comes fast, they call it multiorgasmic, because she can turn around and do it again. When a man does, they call it premature ejaculation." He grimaced. "Not exactly what any guy wants to hear applied to him."

It startled a laugh out of her. "Ooh. Let's test that theory." She reached for the proud jut of his penis.

"Let's not." He intercepted her hand. "Let's get you back up to speed." He used her own fingers to track a reverse path up from her thighs. She tried stretching them out as they neared her erogenous zones but once again he detoured past them.

She huffed out a breath. "What's the point of this if we don't get to touch the good stuff?" But she knew. Because this sexual dodge-'em had the walls of her sex clasping at emptiness. Emptiness she wanted, needed, had to have filled.

"I want you ready," he whispered. "Ready to take me when I fuck you hard. When I go deeper than any man's ever gone before." He caught an earlobe between his teeth and expelled a breath. It was a hot rush shoving cold chills down her spine. "When I turn rough."

Oh, God, there was that voice again. That dirty talk, promising her things she'd never experienced. But she *could* not let him reduce her to sounding like a Victorian virgin again. Bringing her free hand up, she toyed with her nipple. Pinched it between her fingers. Tugged on it.

Jake's Adam's apple took a slow slide up his throat as he watched.

"Then let's go," she said with a calmness, even an edge of amusement, that made her proud, and she met his gaze when it snapped back to stare into her eyes. "This is your lucky day, Bradshaw. Because I'm ready now."

I hope, she thought as heat flared in his eyes and he rolled on top of her.

"You sure?" he asked softly. Gripping his penis, he stroked its head up and down the furrow of her sex.

Okay, she hadn't been entirely ready until she felt the head of his erection bump her clitoris. Then she didn't have a doubt. "I am." She was a little nervous, however—she couldn't deny it. Because she'd made it sound as if she were way more experienced than was true, and she wasn't sure if she was prepared to have him slam that big boy into her.

But she'd underestimated Jake. He kissed her the way he had earlier—with that you're-worth-all-the-time-it-takes gentleness—and eased his way into her body inch by inch, until he filled her like she'd never been filled before. Then he slowly withdrew, dragging tender tissues in his wake until only the head of his penis remained in her. He slipped back in with equal care.

It only took a minute or two of the tortuously slow slide method before Jenny felt as if she were about to come unglued. She drew her knees back toward her chest, and then back even further, dying for that hard, deep, *rough* he'd promised her, but unable to ask.

She didn't need to. Jake had been hanging on with everything he had, watching her for that moment when she was finally ready. Seeing it, knowing this was the real deal and not just bravado this time, he gave a grunt of approval—hell, of *thanks*—and hooked the insides of his elbows behind her knees. He planted his hands next to her shoulders, tipping her thighs back against her breasts and her hips up off the mattress.

And caution became a thing of the past. He pulled back fast, then pistoned his hips to drive in hard and fast until body slapped body. Pulled back, slammed in.

"Jake?" Jenny's nails dug into his back. "Omigawd— *Jake?*"

She was so wet and hot and *responsive*. His name on her lips an ever-escalating question, she alternated between gripping him to her as tightly as she could and clawing his back.

"That's it, baby, that's it," he grated in her ear. He didn't even hear himself, the words just poured out of him without any real consciousness. "Come for me, Jenny. God, I want to feel you come all over me." He knew she was close, *knew* it, and changed his angle fractionally, then thrust with hard, emphatic strokes.

She made a feral noise deep in her throat and *there!* Thank you, Jesus, *there.* Her wet silken sheath contracted hard on his cock, then clamped down again and again, rippling up and down its length, clasping then loosening its milking grasp only to immediately clasp him once again.

She was so good-girl tight and bad-girl relentless, and the top of his head threatened to blow off as his own orgasm roared up his cock like a ninja on crack. With a final thrust, he held himself deep and gritted out her name as he came in scalding pulsation after scalding pulsation.

They seemed to go on forever before he finally realized he was finished and collapsed atop her as if someone had just shot his legs out from under him.

Jenny's breath exploded out of her, but she wrapped her arms around him to hold him to her when he made a halfhearted attempt to lift himself off her. Thank God, because all he could do was lie there like a wounded moose and breathe heavily into her neck, knowing that what they'd just shared was different than anything he'd ever had with anyone else.

Better. It was more than simple fucking.

His heart pounded with something other than just exertion. Because, if he was feeling what he thought he was feeling…well, he couldn't be, that was all. Hell, he didn't believe in it.

And yet—God.

The *way* he felt.

It had to be the sex. The sex had him feeling—

And if it isn't? a voice he wished would shut the

hell up whispered in his brain. He buried his face in Jenny's hair. But, oh, crap. What if this was love?

No. It couldn't be. Because, well—look how great that had worked out for him in the past. Yet it sort of felt like it was.

Damn, fuck, hell.

He was in way too deep—and sinking fast.

CHAPTER NINETEEN

"I'M SO SCREWED, TASH." JENNY watched her friend chop up ingredients for her Monday pizzas. Bella T's didn't open for another forty-five minutes, and Tasha's helper Tiffany wasn't due for another fifteen.

Tasha glanced up to give her a little half smile. "So you've been saying."

A bark of laughter escaped her. "No. In more ways than that. I think I've gone and fallen in love with him."

Her friend raised a shoulder to brush back a curl that had escaped the mass piled atop her head. "Would that be such a bad thing?"

"Um, *yeah*. It'd be a disaster." Then she brightened. "Maybe it's just the sex, though. It very well could be, you know—it was really good sex." She smiled reminiscently. "I mean, Real-ly. Good. Sex."

"Sure, rub it in when it's been an age since I've gotten any, and you won't even share the details." Tasha used the flat edge of her chef's knife to scrape green peppers into a stainless steel container, then looked up to pin Jenny in place with a level look. "But you don't really believe it was just the sex."

Maybe it was the fact that Tasha hadn't phrased

it as a question that prompted Jenny's "Hell, yes, I do. I've never *had* sex like that, and it's turned my brain to mush. Probably I just have a killer crush that I only want to label *love*."

Tasha continued to meet her gaze steadily and Jenny squirmed.

Held her silence.

Then folded like a cheap suitcase.

"Okay, fine. Maybe I think it's love."

"And I repeat, that's not necessarily a bad thing," Tasha said.

"Are you kidding me? It's the dumbest thing ever. If Jake even suspects how emotionally invested I'm becoming, he'll run so fast I won't see him through the cloud of burned rubber he leaves behind."

Maybe it was the reference to burning, but Tasha's eyes suddenly went wide. "Oh, crap, the ovens! I forgot to fire 'em up." She fished an armful of wood out of the box built into her brick pizza ovens, but paused to give Jenny a serious look. "Did it ever occur to you that maybe you're underestimating him?" She turned back to arrange the wood in the first oven.

"I would *so* like to believe that's true," she said fervently. "But I've never met anyone as clueless as he is about his own capacity for love."

Tasha craned her head around, elevating an eyebrow at Jenny over her shoulder. "So, which is it? Does he have a large capacity for love? Or will he hear the word and run like hell from yours?"

"Both, Tash—it's not a contradiction. I've watched

him with Austin, and it's clear he loves that kid like crazy. But I think there's a part of him that's still afraid to own it."

"How about when it comes to you?"

"Well, I know he likes the sex. But I have no idea if it goes any deeper than that. No. That's not true— he flat-out said he doesn't believe in love. Yet there are times I think—" She shook her head. "Oh, hell, who am I fooling? It's hard to tell what he's feeling."

"And you're afraid to ask?"

"Yes." She sighed. "Which makes me the world's biggest coward, I suppose."

"No." Tasha abandoned the fire building and came over to the counter. Her stormy-sky-colored eyes were dead serious as they met Jenny's across the narrow space dividing them. "You are *nobody's* coward," she said fiercely. "Your parents—the two people who should have put you first—put you dead last instead, and I know that left scars. So if you want be to cautious, you *be* cautious." She nudged the fingertips Jenny had pressed hard against the countertop. "Do you have any idea what you're gonna do?"

She rolled her shoulders. "Say nothing, I suppose. Let Jake believe I'm content with a strictly sexual relationship."

Tasha's brows furrowed. "Do you think that's wise when you feel so much more?"

A harsh laugh escaped Jenny. "Wise?" She shrugged. "Probably not. But I do think it's realistic." She held her friend's gaze. "God, Tash. The ugly truth is, I'm going to lose both Jake and Austin come the end of the school year. And it's gonna happen whether I'm having head-banging sex or not. So I might as well grab the gusto while I can."

"And then what?"

"Then…it ends. I'm not fooling myself otherwise. But at least, when it does?" She shrugged again. "Well, I'll have the satisfaction of knowing I went into this with my eyes wide open. And I didn't miss out on the lovemaking of my lifetime because I was too damn chicken to take a chance."

JAKE TRACKED JENNY DOWN to her office at the inn later that afternoon. He'd spent some time with Austin yesterday, had heard all about the overnighter at his teammate's house the night before. But Jenny had been nowhere around—and the memory of how *they'd* spent the night had been too fresh in his mind to inquire into her whereabouts. He feared that if he so much as spoke her name, his son would somehow know what they'd been doing while he was eating birthday cake.

As he looked through the open door now, he saw her sitting at her desk, deep into one of several spreadsheets scattered across its wooden surface. He was transfixed for a moment, awash in a sensory overload of remembered sensations from their time together—the softness of her skin, the sweet slickness of her mouth against his, the throaty sounds she made as her pleasure built—and all he could do was stare. She wore her usual almost-but-not-quite sheer girly top—this one in a shimmery olive-green—and the overhead lights cast a sheen across her hair like a path of moonlight across midnight waters.

Jesus, Bradshaw. You're waxing poetic now? He tapped briskly on the doorjamb.

And smiled when, in a clear attempt to save her place, she stabbed her finger down and reluctantly dragged her attention away from the spot to look up.

"Hey," he said. "You got a minute?"

For a moment her face lit up and his heart did the jungle drum thing.

Then, even though she still smiled at him, the wattage somehow dialed back. Became…less. Vaguely impersonal.

"Sure," she said, grabbing a piece of notepaper off her desk and aligning its edge under a line of data on the report. "What can I do for you?"

Oh, the temptation, given the images that flashed through his head. He sternly shelved it. "It's more what I can do for you and Austin—or what I'd like to do, anyhow. It's gorgeous out today, and I checked the baseball calendar and saw that there's no game or practice scheduled for this evening. Could I talk you two into going on a picnic with me?"

"Really?" The wattage of her smile sparked upward several notches. "That sounds like a fabulous idea! One of us should call Austin. He didn't have plans when I saw him at the cottage after school, but you know how fast that can change."

He fished his cell out of his pocket and propped a shoulder against the jamb. "I'll do it right now."

When Austin answered, the noises in the background put him squarely in Bella T's game room. Jake laid out his proposal, and the teen greeted it with gratifying enthusiasm.

"Great," Jake said and knew he likely wore a shit-eating grin the size of Texas. "I'll be by to get you and Jenny at—what?" He cocked an eyebrow at her. "Four-thirty?"

"Make it five," she said, indicating the spreadsheets on her desk.

"Jenny says five. Right. See you then." Shoving his phone back in his hip pocket, he looked at her. "We're on."

"Excellent. Do you want me to ask the kitchen to prepare us a basket?"

"No." Tempting as the offer was. "This's my show—I'll take care of dinner."

That earned him yet another bump on the Smile-O-Meter. "Ooh. This just keeps getting better and better."

"I'm a thoughtful kinda guy." Who was tempted to cross to the desk and lay a big, warm kiss on that sweet mouth. Instead, he reluctantly shoved upright and stepped back into the hallway. "I better let you get back to work. See you at five."

She murmured an agreement and he took off.

He arrived at her cottage to collect her and his son at five on the dot, and though he wouldn't admit this for the world, he had spent the past fifteen minutes looking at his watch, willing the damn minutes to pass so they could get this party started. Loaded down with a cooler, a bag of groceries and a blanket, he lightly kicked a rhythm on the door to the mudroom.

It whipped open. "Hey!" Austin reached for the grocery bag balanced atop the cooler. "This is such a dope idea!" He lowered his voice. "I didn't tell Jenny we're gonna take my boat."

"We're going to take the boat?" Jenny said, coming into the mudroom.

Austin grimaced. "Sorry, dude."

Jake grinned at his son and gave him a companionable shoulder bump. "Nothing to be sorry about. It wasn't a deep, dark secret." He looked at Jenny, and smiled to see her dark hair now plaited in two braids, the way she had worn it the first time he'd seen her. "We were going to surprise you with a trip to Oak Head."

She smiled. "Excellent! Let me just change into my deck skimmers." She crossed the small area to the built-in cubbies and pulled out a pair of what looked to Jake like regular, if girly, tennis shoes. She toed off the shoes she had on, kicked them in an empty cubby, then wiggled her feet into the navy replacements. Bracing one up against a cubby, she leaned in, hooked a finger in the shoe's back and unbent the slight fold her foot had put in it before reseating her heel.

"Will you take me water-skiing after dinner?" Austin asked. "The water's flat as a pancake."

His head whipped back from admiring the snug pull of Jenny's jeans against her round butt to look at his son. *You water ski?* he wanted to demand, but was smart enough to swallow the question before he could remind Austin just how little he knew of his life. Instead, he said, "Isn't it still pretty cold for that?"

"Dude. Everyone and their brother has a wet suit."

"In that case—" *Shit.* Left to him, he'd say sure, but he had no idea what a responsible parent would say. So he took the safe route. "If it's okay with Jenny, it's okay by me."

"Way to cop out, Bradshaw," she said good-naturedly as she dropped her foot to the floor and straightened. She grabbed a fleece jacket off one of the hooks above the cubbies and folded it over her arm. "Make me the bad guy if I say no." She gave Austin the hip. "Luckily for you, it's fine by me, provided the water's still calm after we eat."

"Or you could take me skiing first," he said.

"I suppose we could. Go put your wet suit on and grab a beach towel. And bring your stuff with you so you have dry clothing to change back into."

"Sa-weet." He tromped out to the boat shed, where he donned his wet suit and collected his skis and towrope.

Down at the dock moments later, Jake stowed the picnic gear and turned to his son, who stood by the driver's seat pulling on his life vest. "Do you want to ski from here?"

"That would be ridiculous!" The word might be negative, but the teen's tone brimmed with enthusiasm, and Jake glanced at Jenny.

"I know, right?" Her lips curled up. "It doesn't sound like it, but in this case 'ridiculous' is actually an affirmative."

He grinned. "All right, then." Turning back to Austin, he saw the boy was already hauling his tow-rope to the back of the Bayliner. Watching the teen kneel on the back cushions to connect the rope, he said to the back of his head, "Deep water or dock start?"

"Dude. You only use deep water if there *is* no dock. Or if you fall." Pushing upright, he shot them a cocky grin. "Which I don't intend to do."

"Live and learn," Jake said agreeably and caught the little foam floater attached to the boat key that Austin suddenly lobbed his way. He stared at it in his hand for an instant, then up at his son.

"Why don't we have Jenny drive," he suggested. He glanced at her. "If you don't mind, that is. That way I can spot Austin and, more importantly, get to really see him ski." *For the first time.*

Jesus. So many firsts.

Jenny glanced at Austin and likely saw the same thing he did—his kid's face light up like a Serengeti dawn. He swallowed, so humbled by it he hardly knew what to do with himself.

Before he could go all sentimental-fool on them, however, she'd snatched the key from his hand and slipped around him. "Works for me."

Austin slid his ski out onto the dock and climbed out after it, turning to accept the bar end of the tow-rope when Jake leaned out to hand it to him.

Jenny started the engine and slowly pulled away from the dock. She glanced over her shoulder. "Tell me when the slack's all but gone."

He watched the line slowly unsnake beneath the water. "Okay, it's getting there, getting there…" The rope between boat and dock came up out of the water, and Austin poised his ski over the water. "Now!"

She slammed the throttle forward, the boat shot off like a bullet train and Austin was immediately up to speed. Jake had done some skiing with Kari's crowd back in high school. But he hadn't grown up with the sport as Austin had, and he knew within moments that his son's skills far outstripped his own. If he had tried that start, he'd probably be swallowing half the canal as he was dragged face-first behind the speeding boat.

But his son knew what he was doing and he jumped the wake with ease, then swung wide to the farthest reach of the rope, where he leaned until his elbow damn near touched the water. It turned him back toward center and he straightened as he whipped back within the wake, only to jump it on the other side.

Jake watched him with pride all the way to Oak

Head, where Jenny sped the boat to within fifty feet of the shore before cutting a sharp turn. Austin crossed the wake for the final time and, when he reached the apex closest to the beach, let go of the towrope bar.

Jenny pulled back on the throttle, and Jake let the bar skip behind the boat, in favor of watching his son skim a few more feet toward shore before gently sinking into a couple of feet of water.

Jake yelled his approval and was still cheering when Jenny brought the boat around a moment later and he jumped onto the beach. He strode straight over to his son, who was standing next to his beached slalom ski, wrapped his arms around him and hauled him off his feet in a fierce bear hug.

He set him back down. "You rocked!"

Austin looked both thrilled and a little rattled, and Jake warned himself not to push too hard. He took a casual step back. "You want to ski some more, or are you ready for a hero?"

"A what?"

"You know, a hero sandwich. Oh. A hoagie or a sub, you call them here."

"How soon we forget," Jenny said, joining them.

He hitched a shoulder. "I've lived in Manhattan a long time now."

"I could use a sandwich," Austin said. "Where'd you get 'em?"

"I bought the fixings in Silverdale. You can make your own any way you like it. I figured that was the closest I could give you to DeFonte's in Brooklyn. They make the best."

"Sweet. What all ya got?"

Jenny had snapped out the blanket he'd brought and spread it near a downed tree with an immense tangled network of sun-bleached roots. Jake would bet big bucks it was a climbing magnet for every kid who hit this beach. He and Austin joined her, and he sank to his knees atop the throw and began pulling ingredients out of the grocery bag and cooler.

"We've got ham, we've got pepperoni, we've got Genoa salami, roast beef and pastrami. We've got sliced onions and tomatoes, chopped lettuce, vinegar and oil, mayo and mustard and, of course, some kick-ass rolls. For sides I brought potato salad and fruit salad and *pepperoncini.* Oh, and chips. To wash it down we have a nice selection of bottled water, canned Coke, both high-test and unleaded, or root beer, which any aficionado will tell you is strictly high-test."

"Dude, this is so dope!"

"Yes," Jenny agreed dryly. "That oughta stave off starvation for an hour or two. Even for a teenager with two hollow legs."

They pigged out, then Jake and Austin tossed a ball back and forth on the beach and entertained themselves playing keep-away from Jenny, which was ridiculously easy to do since, 1) she was short, and 2) she had zero sport skills. At least of the ball-capturing variety.

She was pretty damn good at clambering around the root-ball, though. Her small stature stood her in good stead among the silvery twisted roots.

The days were growing longer in the Pacific Northwest, and the sun hadn't yet hit the mountain-tops when Jenny declared it time to go. Jake wanted to object the way Austin did, but he knew she was right. It was a school night.

"Pack it up, kid," he directed.

"But I don't wanna go," Austin protested. "This is fun."

Jake warmed inside, but forced himself to say easily, "And we'll do it again. But don't you have homework to do?"

"Yeah, I s'pose." Then Austin brightened. "I'm so gonna do the hero sandwiches at *my* birthday party this summer."

On June thirtieth. *Shit.* He was going to have to tell Austin soon about moving with him to New York after school got out. But what was he going to do about the kid's birthday party? Because clearly he hadn't thought this through all that well. With no school in session, Austin didn't have a prayer of making a new group of friends in the couple of weeks between school ending here and June thirtieth. He might have to extend his internal deadline.

But he didn't have to deal with that now. Tonight he got to bask in his son's approval.

When they arrived back at Jenny's, he helped Austin wipe down the ski. While Austin put it away, he stowed the towrope and hung the wet suit up to dry.

He'd just turned back when his boy suddenly flung himself at him and gave him a fierce hug. It was quick and awkward, and Austin shoved his hands in his pants pockets the instant he pulled back, studying the shed floor as if it suddenly contained a world-class hologram of his favorite video game. But Jake felt the residual effects of the hug right down to his soul.

"Thanks, Dad," the teen said. And face flushed, he hurried into the cottage.

When the door banged closed behind him, Jenny, who'd been standing in the doorway, took Austin's place in front of Jake. Reaching up, she cradled his cheek in her hand.

"You did good tonight," she said with a gentle smile. And rising onto her toes, she pressed a soft, chaste kiss to his lips. Settling back on her deck skimmers, she simply looked up at him for a moment, that slight smile playing around the edges of her lips. "Real good," she reiterated.

Then turned and disappeared into the bungalow behind his son.

AT ELEVEN-THIRTY THAT NIGHT Jenny stood outside Jake's door. Austin had been asleep for nearly an hour, and once he went out he slept like the dead. But she still didn't know quite what she was doing here.

For all she knew, one time with her was all Jake

had been looking for. It wasn't as if they'd talked about it after that cataclysmic encounter. He certainly hadn't treated her any differently at this evening's picnic, but then she couldn't actually envision him doing so in front of Austin.

For her, however, their lovemaking had been like nothing she'd ever experienced. And as she'd told Tasha, she wanted more while she still could. So, silently encouraging herself to be bold, she shook out her hands, took a deep breath and tapped on Jake's door before she could chicken out.

He pulled it open and stood in the doorway on bare feet, in the same jeans and shirt he'd worn earlier. "Hey." A smile of greeting deepened the creases bracketing his mouth. "What brings you here?"

"Booty call." It came out with amazing confidence even as she cringed inside. *Really? That's what you come up with?*

But apparently it worked for him, for his eyes lit up and he said, "Yeah?" and stepped back. "In that case, get your booty in here."

She'd barely cleared the threshold before he slammed the door shut and crowded her against it. Hands and forearms slapping down on either side of her head, he bent his head and kissed her. And just like that, she was all in.

So was he, apparently, for the kiss turned fierce and one of his hands came off the door to settle on her breast. He raised his mouth a scant quarter inch from hers.

"You've got too many clothes on," he said roughly and pulled her sweater over her head. Dropping it on the floor, he bent his knees to bring his face level with her bra and reached behind her to unfasten its back hooks. A second later, it joined her sweater.

Then he simply stared at her breasts, and she felt her nipples twist into aching points.

His tongue tip glided between his parted lips and he subtly oscillated the flat of it against the sharp edges of his top center teeth before retracting it. "You've got the sweetest tits."

As usual, his blunt speech made that sheath deep between her thighs clench tight. The sensation only intensified as he kissed each nipple and gave the right one a leisurely suck. Then he gripped her butt and hauled her up.

A startled squeak escaped her. "Okay, that's kind of embarrassing," she said, feeling the burn heating her cheeks. "I sound like a six-year-old." But she wrapped her legs around his hips and bumped squarely against the solid erection behind his fly. "Oh." Eyes fluttering shut, she slowly ground against it. "Not feeling six now."

Jake's breath exploded out of him. "What is it about you?" he demanded, doing a slow grind of his own. "I'm like the *king* of foreplay with other women, but I always end up rushing you like a fourteen-year-old."

"That so works for me."

A gritty huff of laughter escaped him. "Yeah, me,

too. God, Jenny. You're so responsive it just blows my control all to hell."

She cracked open a hopeful eye. "Does this mean you have a condom handy?"

A full-fledged laugh exploded from him. "In my wallet in my hip pocket. Or if you'd like to take this where I can display more finesse than up against the door, I've got an entire box in the bedroom."

"I like it right here." She reached around him, fumbling for his wallet. "I've never done it up against a door."

"No? Then I'm happy to be of service." He set her on her feet. "Strip," he ordered, tugging his own shirt off before reaching for his fly.

In seconds they were both naked and Jake had rolled a condom on. He sank to his knees in front of her. Leaning in, he pressed a kiss on her abdomen just above the patch of curls over her mons. "We can spare a *couple* seconds for a little foreplay," he said hoarsely and, sliding his thumbs into the wet slit between her legs, separated the lips there. "Sweet," he whispered and gently lapped the pink flesh he'd exposed with the flat of his tongue.

Choking out his name, she clenched her fingers in his hair. "You'd better stop, youbetterstop youbetterstop," she panted. But not only didn't he, he slid two fingers into her. And she came in hot, fast pulsations.

He stayed with her until the last contraction faded, then extracted his fingers, surged to his feet and lifted her back against the door. The instant her arms went around his neck and her legs locked around his waist, he reached to thumb his erection down, bending his knees until he was aligned with her opening. "God," he said. And thrust into her.

It was fast and rough and Jenny maintained a stranglehold on Jake's neck as he thrust and retreated, thrust and retreated. "Oh God, oh God, oh God," she panted mindlessly as all that sensation she'd thought satisfied sparked back to life. "Oh, God, Jake. It feels so—" He pulled almost, nearly, not quite out, then slammed back in. "Feels so—" Pulled out, slammed in. "Oh, God, I'm going to—"

"Come," he gritted and this time when he plunged into her, he stayed to grind against her clitoris. "Come for me, Jenny."

And she did, clenching and releasing around him over and over and over again.

"Jesus!" He bared his teeth, a long, gritty groan of satisfaction purling out of his throat as he, too, exploded.

Then his head thunked down on the door next to hers. "Damn. You're killing me."

"Tell me about it." She was inertia personified, lethargic from head to toe, held in place only by his body leaning heavy against hers. She retained just enough motor skills to quirk up the corners of her lips and press a clumsy kiss to the tip of his ear. She smiled again when he shivered.

"On the other hand," she breathed. "What a way to go, huh?"

CHAPTER TWENTY

"JENNY, YOUR TEN-THIRTY interview is here."

Glancing at her watch, Jenny smiled to see that the job applicant was five minutes early. It was always a bonus not to be kept waiting. "Thanks, Abby. I'll be right out."

A moment later she walked into the lobby. The only person currently there, aside from Abby behind the front desk, was a twentysomething biracial woman dressed with quirky, artistic flair in a brightly patterned jersey skirt that swirled around her boots and a long sleek tunic with a belt slung between her waist and hips.

She crossed to her. "Ms. Summerville?" She extended a hand. "I'm Jennifer Salazar, the general manager. We talked on the phone last week."

"Hello." The woman—whose first name was Harper, Jenny knew from her application—firmly shook her hand. "Thank you so much for seeing me."

She blinked. Harper might be even taller than Tasha—something she couldn't help but envy. And between the other woman's imposing stature, that latte-with-an-extra-splash-of-cream complexion, those glossily dark, loose spiral curls and large olive-green eyes, Jenny's first impression was of exotic, regal stylishness.

But rather aloof, which wouldn't do at all for the position Jenny was looking to fill.

And then Harper smiled and her face animated into something downright joyful. Her eyes narrowed to merry crescents, and those full solemn lips turned into a wide heartlike shape that exposed not only her flawless white teeth but some of the healthy gums in which they were anchored. It was a smile of singular charm that transformed her from distantly removed to not just accessible but magnetic. Jenny felt as if she were the center of the other woman's attention.

She smiled back. "I've been looking forward to meeting you. Your résumé is very impressive."

"May I quote you on that to my mother?" Harper laughed heartily even as her fingers brushed warmly against Jenny's arm with unstudied tactility. "She wants nothing more than for me to quit jumping from job to job and pick one to settle into." She grimaced. "Well, that or get married. Preferably to a doctor."

"That's mothers for you." Most people's anyway— her own hadn't demonstrated much interest in her after Lawrence Salazar's fall from grace, except to be mortified that she'd chosen to work as a maid at The Brothers.

As if, at sixteen, she'd been overburdened with choices.

Which was neither here nor there. "If it helps, you can tell her from me it was your variety of skills that struck the biggest spark with me. I'm looking for a social director, for lack of a better term, for the summer season and the number one qualification for the job is an ability to coordinate a number of activities. As it is—even with all the skills you bring to the table—this is only a three-quarter-time job. I need someone for around thirty to thirty-two hours a week."

"That was actually one of the pluses when I read your ad on Craigslist. I have some money set aside, so I can get by on less hours. It'll give me a little time to explore the peninsula." Both her delicately arched brows and the corners of her lips quirked upward. "Well, depending on what you're offering, that is. The ad didn't really specify."

Jenny named the hourly rate. "Plus room and board, of course. The accommodation isn't particularly plush—it's a little one-room-with-loft cottage up in the woods."

"Please tell me an outhouse isn't part of the package. Because that's a deal breaker."

Jenny laughed. "No. While there's nothing fancy about the cottage, it's not *that* primitive. You don't have to share with a roommate and it boasts a little bathroom. Shower only, though, I'm afraid."

"Oh." For an instant the other woman looked wistful. "I do like my baths." Then she flashed that smile again. "But I'm sure I can make do for the short summer season."

It struck Jenny that Harper's ability to make a

person feel as if she smiled for you alone was a very handy skill for someone in a people-oriented field.

She grinned back. "And on the bright side, the food in our restaurant is outstanding. If you're in the mood to whip up something for yourself, however, there's a hot plate, micro and college dorm-size fridge in the cabin."

"So...are you offering me the job, then?"

"I'm definitely leaning in that direction, but let me show you around the inn and the grounds and the cottage that comes with the position. I'll tell you what I envision for this position, and you can fill me in, in a little more detail than I got from your application, on your own vision. And don't be afraid to speak up, because often instructors, with their superior experience in a given activity, come up with ideas that never in a gazillion years would have occurred to me. I do love it when someone has ideas for making things better."

"Sounds good to me."

"Excellent. I have to tell you—I've never met a Harper before. I love the name."

"Thanks. Mama adored *To Kill a Mockingbird*." Harper grinned. "She considers Harper Lee a genius to this day."

"It's both unique and pretty—it suits you." Then she got down to business, indicating the area around them with a sweep of her arm. "This, as you can see, is The Brothers' lobby...."

AUSTIN STOPPED DEAD where the lightly wooded path from the parking lot opened into the ballpark. He gaped at the scene in front of them. "Are you kidding me?"

"Whoa." Nolan looked as taken aback as he felt. Still, he turned to Austin and grinned, clearly happy to be out and about at last. "Good thing we're still having summer preview weather, huh? Because it looks like everyone and their freakin' brother turned out for—" his voice dropped into stentorian tones "—Jake Bradshaw Photo Day."

The entire town had been saying those exact words like wannabe sports announcers ever since the Razor Bay Blog had shouted, in bold-font headlines earlier in the week and again this morning, that *National Explorer* photographer Jake Bradshaw would be shooting the Bulldogs' team pictures and yearbook. Nolan's voice returned to its usual register. "WTF, man." He stared at the dense mob swarming the stands. "Why are all those people jockeying for space on the bleachers?"

"Beats the crap outta me. Except for a couple, I don't see anyone who's got zip to do with the team." He shook his head. "I've never seen so many people in the stands!"

"I know. You'd think team pictures were a spectator sport or something."

"Yeah." Austin snorted. "We should get such a turnout at our games." But he feared he might break out in an embarrassing giggle at any minute. Because for all his playing it cool, he was killer excited about today. And now that the initial shock was wearing off, he secretly got a charge out of the whole damn town being here. His dad was a big-deal photographer, he was taking *their* team photos and everyone wanted to see! How kickin' was that?

His stock at school had shot up ever since he'd brought in two issues of *National Explorer Magazine* and shown off the photos his dad had taken to the kids who had drawled a bored "So?" when he or someone else on the team had boasted that Jake was taking their pictures.

But that wasn't the only thing that had him pumped today. He was also beyond relieved at how happy he was to be hanging out with Nolan again. He knew he'd spent a lot of his friend's bout with chicken pox wishing that it'd take its own sweet time clearing up. But now that Nolan had gotten the green light, Austin was totally jazzed. For a while he'd lost track of how good it felt to be around him.

The thing he wasn't looking forward to was having to come clean to his best friend about his feelings for Bailey. But he figured he owed him that.

The question was, did he tell him before they got their pictures taken? Or after?

Now, he decided, taking a deep breath. He was just gonna feel like dog crap until he did, so he might as well get it out of the way. He exhaled with gusto. "I got something to tell you."

"Yeah?" Nolan gave him an expectant look—and he chickened out.

"Where's your cousin? I thought she'd be here."

"She was on the phone with Aunt Debbie when I left, so Mom's gonna bring her over."

"Cool." Then he sucked in and blew out a breath. "I, uh…really like her."

"Sure." Nolan shrugged. "Who doesn't?"

"No, I mean I *really* like her. Like in wanna-kiss-her like her."

Nolan stopped dead to stare at him. "You want to *kiss* her?"

"Jeez, dude, keep your voice down." He looked around to see if anyone was paying attention. Still, when he looked back at Nolan, he refused to back-pedal like his inner chickenshit was screaming at him to do. He gave the other teen a jerky nod.

Nolan was quiet for a moment. Then he, too, nodded. "Okay. I guess I sorta get that. I had a massive crush on her last year."

Austin felt his jaw sag and he firmed it up. "That's perverted, dude. She's your *cousin!*"

"Oh, get a grip. It's not like I wanted to make cross-eyed babies with her. But she's pretty and funny and she plays baseball better'n half the guys I know. Plus, I don't know if you've noticed this, but she's got boobies." He raised his hands in a *whataya gonna do* gesture. "So, I wouldn't have minded kissing her once or twice myself, ya know?"

"Did you try?"

"Nah. One day it just…I don't know…no longer seemed like the best thing ever, the way it had up until then. The point is, though, for a while I *did.* So I get that you wanna."

Austin was grateful for Nolan's easy acceptance— but also nursing a major case of discouragement that had been growing the past couple of days and dampening his mood. "Yeah, like I've got any chance of actually doing it," he admitted glumly. He wanted it so bad he could taste it. At the same time, he had an equally strong fear of making a fool of himself. "I've been making myself crazy trying to figure out how to go about it."

"You oughta ask Jenny."

"What?" The question was rhetorical, however, and appalled, he stared at his friend. "I can't ask her!"

"Why not? She's a girl—who better to know about these things?"

"I just can't. Dude, she's…*Jenny!*"

"I can't help you, then, man, because that's it— that's all I've got." He shook his head with a little glumness of his own. "Face it, unless there's a spinning bottle involved, it's not like *I've* had any success in the lip-lock department, either."

"Who the hell would've thought I'd have to do crowd control at Little League picture day?"

"Not me." Jake looked up at Max from where he squatted next to the third-base coach's box. He felt a little crowded by all the people tramping over the field and diamond. He hadn't even started yet and already the damn circus playing out around him had his schedule messed up. "Pass me that gray bag."

"Where the hell is Jenny?" Max demanded, leaning down to snatch up the bag in question, then swinging it over to Jake. "I thought you blackmailed her into being your assistant."

"Good question. I expected her by now. Hell, I let her off the hook already when I took all the ad shots without her help."

"Well, there's your problem right there." His brother gave him a pitying look. "What kind of candy-ass blackmailer are you—you violated the first rule! Shit, Jake, demonstrate a weakness like that and you've blown any chance you ever had of controlling the sitch. I'm ashamed to call you broth…" His voice trailed away.

Jake, who was arranging lenses on a piece of felt in the order he'd need them, had no trouble ignoring the critique on his blackmailing technique, but glanced up at the sudden silence.

"Holy Jesus," Max breathed, but since both his tone and expression were reverent as a monk's seeing the Shroud of Turin, Jake guessed it wasn't a blasphemy. "Who *is* that?"

He followed the general direction of Max's gaze, but too damn many people were trampling the ballpark to pinpoint who Max was staring at. "You'll have to narrow it down for me a little," he said drily. "Who's who?"

"The babe with Jenny."

That got his attention. "Jenny's here?" He rose to his feet.

"Yeah. Over there, see? Just this side of the path from the parking lot."

Narrowing his search, Jake locked in on her.

"Woman's a fucking goddess, right?" Max said.

Jake's head whipping around, his eyebrows slamming together, he gave his brother an incredulous stare. "Jenny?" What the hell was Max doing looking at the woman he'd warned *him* against?

"What? No, you dumb shit. *Her!*" Max stabbed his forefinger in Jenny's direction and for the first time Jake noticed the woman with her.

"Oh. Wow." Max was right. The mixed-race woman towering next to Jenny was a looker, if you went for the stick-up-the-ass exotic princess type.

But his attention drifted back to the petite brunette at her side, and he watched Jenny look around the grounds. When her eyes tracked in his direction, he set off the flash. It attracted her gaze and he raised an arm to cement her attention.

She strolled over, the woman who had Max all hot and bothered—which was kind of a kick, now that he thought about it—at her side.

Jenny flashed them both a friendly smile as she fetched up in front of them. "Hey, there. Sorry I'm late. I was showing Harper around the inn." She laughed. "Where are my manners—let me introduce you. Harper, this is Jake Bradshaw, the reason today's turnout is such a spectacle, and his brother, Max Bradshaw—"

"Half brother," Max interrupted, and Jake gave him a shot to the shoulder. He put some power behind his fist, too, but Max, being Max, didn't even rock back on his heels.

"Time to let it go, bro," Jake said.

Max merely hitched a big shoulder, and Jenny picked up as smoothly as though there'd been no interruption, "—Jake's half brother, Max, who is Razor Bay's favorite deputy. Jake, Max, meet Harper Summerville, The Brothers' brand-new fun and games director."

"Seriously?" Jake stared at Jenny. "You're honest-to-God calling her the *fun and games* director?"

"Okay, fine. She's our summer activities coordinator." She shot him a speaking glance from between narrowed lashes. "If you have to be so damn literal about it."

Harper laughed, and Jake noticed it totally negated his first impression of her. That cool-princess vibe disappeared beneath a truckload of warmth.

"She can call me whatever she wants," the woman said in a blues-singer-smooth contralto. "I'm just excited to get to work here. It's a great area. Hi." She offered her hand to first Jake, who was nearest, then Max. "It's nice to meet you both." Letting go of Max's hand a moment later, she patted his forearm where he'd pushed back his uniform sweater, snatched her hand back rather quickly, Jake thought, but then gave Max a megawatt smile.

"Goodness. If all the men in Razor Bay are as big as you two, there must be one heck of a growth hormone in the water."

Jake laughed, but to his surprise, Max not only didn't crack so much as a smile, he merely gave the woman he'd all but been drooling over a clipped nod.

"Ma'am," the idiot said, as if he'd just written her up and was handing back her license and registration along with a spanking-new parking ticket.

Harper's we-are-not-amused princess vibe made a red-hot reappearance, and Jenny, shooting Max a look as perplexed as Jake felt, said hastily, "Well, listen, I'm going to see if Tasha showed up with the rest of the town so I can introduce her to Harper. Then I'll be back to give you a hand with the photos."

"It was nice meeting you, Harper," Jake said. His socially inept brother gave her another, if this time fractionally less stiff, nod and said again, "Ma'am."

Jake watched the two women walk away. Then he turned and smacked the back of Max's head with his palm. "*Ma'am?* What the fuck, man?"

Max shoved his hands in his jeans pockets, his muscular shoulders hunched. "I know. I'm not very good with women like that."

A bark of laughter escaped Jake. "Ya think?"

"Fine, all right?" Max said sullenly. "I *suck* when it comes to them. You happy now?"

"Why?"

"Well, let me think—because you live to see me cut off at the knees?"

"No, you ass—why do you suck with women like her?" And just what did his big bro consider *women like her,* anyway?

Max shrugged, but Jake had a sudden flash of his brother's perpetually unhappy-looking mother. When they were kids, he'd been pleased as punch to see someone giving Max a rash. It had never occurred to him to wonder what her problem was—or how it affected Max. Now he did.

"You used to do okay," he said. "I remember you strutting around with Judy Ziegler tucked under your arm. Man—" he shook his head, remembering "—she had like the best tits of any girl in school."

"And the T-shirts and sweaters to showcase 'em." Max cracked a reminiscent smile.

One that was all too brief. "I don't have a problem with the flash girls," he said. "They make it easy by doing all the talking—even if it is all about stuff that you don't really care about. That's a trade-off, since they don't seem to mind all that much if you're not real good with the chitchat shit."

His gaze sought out Harper across the field, where she stood with ramrod posture talking to Jenny and Tasha. Jake watched Max's frustrated interest as he watched her.

"The silver-spoon girls are different," his brother said without taking his eyes off the apparently fascinating Ms. Summerville. "They freeze me up every time."

An altercation broke out over in the stands, and Jake witnessed the relief scudding across Max's expression.

But his brother merely said gruffly, "Damn that Wade. When's he going to get it through his head that Mindy is well and truly married to Curt? Five'll get you ten he came straight here from the Anchor, too."

"And that never helps."

"No shit. I'd better go intercept him before Curt decks him and I've got to arrest the pair of them." He strode off, happy, no doubt, to be out of the "feelings" biz and back in his natural element.

Jenny returned a few minutes after Max's departure and promptly began organizing the boys—and Bailey, whom the coach and team had insisted on including—first for the team photos, then their individual ones. In the lags between shooting the latter, some of the adults he'd already photographed for the album stopped by to exchange pleasantries.

Jake found he was enjoying himself every bit as much as he did on professional shoots.

He didn't know why that should make him uneasy when he thought about it again later that night, after Jenny had slipped from his bed to go back to her own. But as he lay there, hands stacked behind his head, staring up at the ceiling, he acknowledged it did. So he switched his focus to Jenny, wondering when they could get together again and what he'd do to her when they did.

But that just made him scowl. Because for some damn reason, her apparent contentment with the strictly sexual arrangement they had going itched under his skin like a bad rash. He refused to dig too deeply into the reasons why.

Hell, she was giving him exactly what he demanded in a relationship. And if *this* one felt different from the rest—well, he knew better than to trust all these emotions roiling beneath his surface. Bradshaw men just didn't do the happily-ever-after thing. They didn't settle down—and after his didn't-last-a-month-beyond-the-I-do's with Kari, he for one had never been tempted to profess undying love to any woman.

Yet, okay, he was tempted with Jenny. And he could almost, maybe, see himself professing.

Realizing where his woolgathering had taken him, he felt his heart pound as a cold sweat filmed his skin. *Think of something else, think of something else.*

Okay, how about this? Today at the ballpark, for practically the first time ever, he hadn't wished he was anywhere but in Razor Bay, Washington.

Somehow the realization didn't do a damn thing to calm him.

CHAPTER TWENTY-ONE

"I GUESS YOU'VE PROBABLY kissed, like, a million girls in your life, huh?"

Jake looked up from the line he was untangling. He and Austin had been lazily trolling the canal in one of the inn's small aluminum outboard boats. Austin had chosen it because, he said, it was better than his Bayliner for fishing, a sport at which Jake didn't exactly shine. His kid knew what he was doing, though, and had taught him a trick or two, a fact that seemed to tickle him no end. "Nowhere close. But I guess you could say I've kissed my fair share."

"Yeah?" Austin grunted. "So, how old were you the first time?"

His overly casual gaze made Jake's newly developed dad warning system go off in silent alarm. Oh, man, he thought as he baited the hook with a fresh herring and dropped the now straightened-out line overboard. It had to be the girl, Bailey, that Austin had been spending so much time with. He fit the pole in its holder, rinsed his hands in the frigid canal and met his son's eyes. "I don't remember exactly. Around your age, I think."

"You were probably pretty dope at it, huh? Knew 'zactly what to do?"

He snorted. "You kidding me? I wasn't what you'd call a natural. The fishing you're teaching me? I'm better at it than I was at kissing."

Austin winced. "Oh, man. Not good."

"Tell me about it. We bumped noses, our teeth clashed. But funny thing—Mary Beth Brimmyer didn't seem to notice my less than smooth moves." He gave his son a wry smile. "Probably because she didn't have any more experience than I did. Still, we both enjoyed ourselves. And little by little, with each other, and over time with other partners, we improved." He bounced his fist off his chest. "I'm like *king* of the good kissers these days, if I do say so myself."

Some of the tension went out of Austin's shoulders. "How did you make your move the first time?"

A corner of his mouth quirked up. "Oh, I was suave, kid. You'd do well to take notes on this."

His son sat straighter in his seat, and Jake continued, "We went to a movie in Silverdale. My mom drove us, which was kind of lowering, but—hello!—thirteen."

Austin made a *whatcha gonna do* face.

"I bought Mary Beth popcorn and a Coke and waited for the theater to go dark and the movie to get under way. Then I made my move."

"How?"

"I did the prestretch warm-up so I could get

my arm up in the air. You know, like this—" Faking a yawn, he raised his hand to his mouth and brought his elbow up. "Then, just as I was starting to straighten it out so I could casually drop it over her shoulder, I caught her right in the ear with the pointy end." He tapped his elbow. "Made her spill half her popcorn."

"No way."

"'Fraid so. Learn from my mistakes, buddy. Make sure to get that sucker behind her head before you make your move. Practicing with a soccer ball placed at the right height might not be amiss."

"Dude."

"I know. Geeky. But think about the embarrassment it might save."

Austin's grin did something to Jake's insides. But, as had been happening more and more frequently lately, along with the warmth in his heart came an accompanying low-grade panic.

"I'll have to give that some thought," Austin said. He picked up his pole and fiddled with it. "So," he said to the reel. "You gonna live here from now on?"

Shit. Jake gave his own pole a hopeful look, but it was still just sitting in its holder, line slack and in no apparent need of adjustment. In no need of attention of any kind.

His son, however, was a different matter, and Jake pulled himself up in his seat. It wasn't as if he hadn't known this moment was coming. And he sure as hell couldn't fob it off on Jenny. It wasn't her job to break the news that he intended to drag Austin out of town with him when he went.

His kid, his responsibility.

"Turn off the motor for a minute," he said quietly.

"Huh?" Austin had clearly comprehended, however, because even as he made the inquiring sound, he twisted the throttle of the little seven-horse to shut it down. The boat drifted gently, riding its own wake when the soft swell caught up with it.

Jake took a deep breath, then let it out. "I have a life I need to get back to in New York."

"Oh." The boy swallowed. "Sure."

The disappointment in his eyes nearly brought Jake to his knees and he hurried to say, "But I want you to come with me."

"Yeah?" Austin's eyes lit up. But then he scowled. "What the heck am I supposed to do in New York?" he demanded, and Jake's heart sank.

Still, he said calmly, "Are you kidding me? There is *so* much to do there. That city never sleeps." Which, okay, wasn't exactly a selling point, considering there was no way in hell he'd let his thirteen-year-old stay out all night. *You can't think of anything better than that?*

Before he could, Austin, with a mulish slant to his mouth, said flatly, "All my friends are in Razor Bay. *Jenny's* here—and so is the girl I wanna kiss." He sat up so abruptly the aluminum boat rocked. "My Bayliner! What am I supposed to do with my boat in *Manhattan?*"

The teen said "Manhattan" as if it was Sodom and Gomorrah, but Jake said neutrally, "I'd have to think about that, but there are lots of other great things to do. NYC is home to a superior baseball team for starters."

Austin calmed some. Nodded. "That's true. The evil empire's won something like twenty-seven World Series and forty American League pennants."

Jake gazed at his clasped hands between his spread thighs for a moment before raising his head to look at his son. "I know what I'm asking of you isn't small spuds. Leaving everything you know will be a huge adjustment. But I'm hoping you'll find the trade-off—" *Me* "—worth it."

"Jeez, I really don't wanna live in New York," Austin said, and this time Jake's stomach thudded right to the bottom of the aluminum boat. He watched his boy as he gazed out toward the mountains, then at two eagles circling and swooping overhead, then finally back at him.

Austin gave him a diffident smile. "At the same time, you just came back into my life like yesterday. And I want to be with you. So, I suppose if I have to put up with New York City to get that—well…" Looking uncertain yet resolute, he squared his shoulders and met Jake's gaze head-on. "Then I guess I will."

That low-grade panic he'd been struggling with bloomed into the real deal. Suddenly he couldn't breathe. *What the hell is your problem, man? You're not happy no matter which way the kid jumps. Is this how it's going to be from now on—damned if you do, damned if you don't?*

But, oh, Christ, it wasn't that at all. It was reality setting in. What the fuck had he been thinking? The kid was placing his future happiness in his hands, and no way in hell was he cut out to be a dad! The fact that it'd been in the back of his mind all this time to install Austin in his house with a hired companion while he went back to trotting the globe for weeks at a time simply proved it.

Somehow, though, he managed to pull in a couple of shallow breaths and paste a pleased smile on his face.

"Great," he said—and just hoped to hell it didn't sound as weak to his son as it did to him. "That's... great. It's settled then. That's what we'll do."

JENNY WATCHED AUSTIN push his corn around his plate. He held his homemade taco in his other hand, but had only taken two bites out of the thing—and usually tacos ranked in his top-ten favorite dinners. He'd been quiet last night, too, now that she thought about it.

"Are you feeling all right?" she asked, rising half out of her chair to reach across the table and feel his brow. Her concern ratcheted up another degree when he not only didn't yank impatiently out of reach, as was his usual reaction to her mothering moments, but actually leaned slightly into her touch the way he had when he was a little guy. Oh, damn, oh, God. He *was* sick.

His forehead, however, felt perfectly cool. She slowly sat back in her chair and gave him a steady look.

Setting his fork and taco on the plate, he looked up at her. "Did you know that Dad's moving me to New York City?"

The few bites she'd eaten took an oily roll in her stomach. Oh, God. This was no longer a coming-soon-but-at-least-not-here-yet-so-I-can-ignore-it issue. The queasy feeling dug itself what she feared might be a permanent pit in her belly, and she set her own taco back on her plate.

It was official—she was losing both of them. She'd thought she'd known that, yet apparently she hadn't fully believed it until this moment. She gave him a jerky nod of acknowledgment. "I did."

He narrowed his eyes at her. "And you never said anything to me?"

"I didn't, no. And I told Jake not to, either, when he first told me his plan. I thought he should give you time to get to know him before he sprung a life upheaval of this magnitude on you."

"Yeah." He sagged back in his seat. "That was probably a good idea."

"Are you…okay with it?"

"Like I told him, I'm not thrilled to be moving away from home—especially not to a big freaking noisy city where I'm not going to know anyone except him." His newly wide shoulders hitched. "But I want to be with him, Jenny. I want to know what it's like to have a dad."

She nodded slowly. "Of course you do. That's completely understandable." She leaned across the table and gripped his hand. *I will not cry, I will not cry!* "But I'm going to miss you like crazy."

He gave her a stricken look. "I've been trying real hard not to think about that. Crap. Crap!" Shoving away from the table, he surged to his feet. "I can't go. I'm gonna have to tell him that I just can't go."

She, too, rose to her feet and circled the table to put her arms around him, her heart hitching as he trembled against her. "Shh. Shhh, now. Yes, you can go. It's not like either of us is going to drop off the face of the earth. We'll talk on the phone all the time. We'll email and text and, and...Skype, even. I can learn to do that. And you'll come back to see everyone, to dazzle us all with your big-city sophistication. And maybe I can come visit you, too."

One by one, his muscles relaxed against her, but he kept his head bent, his face buried in her updo. "Yeah," he muttered, nodding against the crown of her head. "Yeah."

"It'll be fine, you'll see. Once you make a few new friends, I think you'll probably start to enjoy yourself. Manhattan has a lot to offer."

"I'll miss my boat."

"Yeah. I don't know how much it costs to moor

one in the East River or wherever one does that, but maybe there's a way to take yours with you."

"It wouldn't be the same, though. I know these waters like the back of my hand. Everything there is gonna be new and confusing." His noise wrinkled. "And noisy."

Oh man, she so agreed. But she sucked up her own misgivings and said firmly, "Well, I can't argue about the noisy part. But as for the new and confusing? It won't be for long, big guy. You're smart and a fast learner, and if I know you—which I do, buddy—you'll own that city in no time."

And she would just have to keep how desperately empty her own life was going to be with him and Jake clear across the country to herself.

She could and would do that. Even if it killed her.

"COACH, I GOTTA DO something. I'll be back in five minutes." Austin didn't give Mr. Harstead time to say "fine," "forget it" or "WTF, Bradshaw." He was a man on a mission, and he vacated the baseball field to head straight over to Bailey, who was reading a textbook on the bleachers, which she had to herself for once.

"Can I talk to you for a sec?"

"Sure." She closed her social studies book and looked at him expectantly.

"Not here. Come with me."

One of the things he really liked about Bailey was the way she never seemed to feel the compulsion to talk something to death before she'd move an inch, like so many girls did. She just gave him an agreeable smile, set her book down next to her backpack, then rose to her feet. She loped down the risers.

Stopping in front of him on the grass, she smiled. "What's up?"

He took her hand and led her around to the back of the bleachers. "Under here."

She blinked but followed gamely enough as he bent and sidestepped through the cross braces. When she straightened beneath the highest risers, he lurched forward and grabbed her. He lowered his head to hers.

They bumped noses, but he reminded himself his dad had done the same thing the first time *he'd* kissed a girl, too, and he adjusted for the miscalculation. Then his lips found hers. And they were soft and warm and...*wow.*

Just about the dopest thing in the world.

Bailey's hands came up to his shoulders and he tensed, bracing himself to be shoved away. But she curled her fingers to grip them instead. And she kissed him back—even opening her lips a little beneath his.

He touched his tongue to her bottom lip and her mouth opened a little bit more.

"Bradshaw!"

They jumped apart at Coach's bellow. "Crap," he whispered and licked his bottom lip, picking up a faint taste of Bailey. Man, he'd made up his mind to do this today because his window of opportunity for a chance with her had narrowed with his dad's announcement. But now that he'd kissed her he was *really* conflicted about moving away. "So, uh, would you like to go to a movie with me Friday night if I can get Jenny or my dad to drive us? I know it's not a lot of notice but—"

"I'd like that," she said, then winced when Coach Harstead yelled his name again.

"It's a date, then. I'll give you a call after I talk to Jenny and Dad." He leaned forward and gave her another quick kiss on the lips. Then he turned and loped away.

And couldn't have erased the big grin on his face to save his life.

CHAPTER TWENTY-TWO

FRIDAY NIGHT AND HARBOR STREET was already jumping—at least by Razor Bay standards—when Jake drove through town just before six on his way back from Silverdale. He'd dropped Austin and Bailey off at the Kitsap Mall, and the kids were probably eating at the food court even as he contemplated his son being on a date. A *date!* He was going to miss out on so much when he—

He chopped off the thought, and went back to mulling over what two thirteen-year-olds might be doing at this moment. If they weren't eating, they were likely killing time in the mall before they caught the seven-twenty movie at the multiplex.

Either way, his dad duties were done for the night, thanks to Rebecca Damoth, who had offered to pick them up when the show was over.

He'd found himself breaking speed limits driving back here. And the minute he powered off his SUV in the parking lot between his place and Jenny's, he headed over to her cottage. He hadn't seen her in two long nights and he found himself…needing to.

He didn't know what the hell that was all about

but was too impatient to worry about it tonight. He rapped out a rapid tattoo on her front door.

When Jenny opened it, he watched something flicker across her face. Whatever it was came and went so quickly he didn't have time to pin it down, so he let it go and stepped into her house, her *space,* without awaiting an invitation. Sliding his fingers into her hair, he framed her cheekbones with his thumbs, tilted her head back and kissed her.

Gently.

With a host of feelings he didn't care to examine too closely.

She wrapped her arms around his neck, drawing a satisfied sound from deep in his throat. Every muscle in his body loosened as he felt the tension he hadn't even realized he'd been carrying in his neck and shoulders release its grip. Kicking the door closed behind him, he swept her up in his arms and, without breaking their kiss, carried her into the bedroom.

Laying her on her queen-size bed a moment later, he stretched out atop her and focused on learning every cushioned curve of those sweet lips as if they were brand-new and he had all night to explore them. For some reason, it *felt* brand-new—maybe because the sex they'd shared before had invariably been hot and hard and urgent.

Not that he wasn't every bit as hot and hard now. But a new element had been added with this bone-deep desire he had to take his time with her, to take *care* of her. He went with it, keeping his grip tender and his mouth slow and thorough.

After several satisfying moments, he raised his head. "Where've you been hiding?" he murmured, brushing a silken strand of hair off her cheek. "I missed you." He didn't wait for an answer, but instead dove back into the kiss.

But even as their mouths meshed, that damn sharp edge of unease, that unscratchable anxiety that burned like a hot itch just below the surface of his skin anytime he got too close to a happy state, muscled into his consciousness.

Because he had no business missing her. No business thinking he could be a father.

Hell, he had no business thinking any relationship he touched would last.

Yeah, because how's that worked for you so far? Your daddy walked, your wife—well, there's no doubt that if she hadn't died that's a relationship that would have ended in divorce court—and you abandoned your kid. Face it, man. Bradshaws just don't have what it takes for happily-ever-afters.

It was why he'd come to the decision about his— and Austin and Jenny's—future.

"Hey." Jenny threaded her fingers through his hair and pulled his head back. "Where'd you go?"

He looked down at her, at those dark, caring eyes, and pushed everything else away. "Nowhere," he said, then shook his head because she knew better. "That is, we've experienced a temporary blip in the attention-span portion of our program. But I'm back. Right where I want to be." And, feeling her fingers loosen their grip, he lowered his head again.

It was true, he was where he wanted to be. With these damn Bradshaw genes, he might lack what it took for the long haul, but for the next hour or so?

Well, he'd at least have this.

FOR THE PAST COUPLE of days—ever since she and Austin had had that talk over dinner—Jenny had done her damnedest to avoid Jake. She wasn't a rip off the Band-Aid kind of woman—she was more a peel it gently from all directions girl. So rather than continue having sex with him up until the day Jake left town—and, oh, incidentally, took the only person she'd ever thought of as a brother with him— she'd decided to start distancing herself. That wasn't possible with Austin, but she could sure as hell attempt it with Jake.

There was no distancing herself from this, however. It had never *been* like this. Not that it hadn't been great, because, oh God, it had—all hot and exciting and the best sex of her life.

But this…*this* was even better. The tender enough to bring her to tears kisses that at the same time made her feel like stretching like a cat in a patch of sunlight. The slow, oh-so-capable hands that stripped them both of their clothing, then took an unhurried journey over her body, leaving no curve, no dip or hollow untouched in his explorations. The caring that came off Jake with such near-palpable energy it threatened to capsize her composure. For maybe the first time ever, she felt so, oh Lord, so—dare she even think it?—cherished.

Swamped in sensation, she absorbed his kisses, writhed languorously beneath his touch and moaned when he pushed up onto his palms, widened his muscular thighs between hers to spread her legs and slide inside her. Her arms twined around his neck to cling, her body arched in an attempt to get nearer.

And still he moved at a glacial pace, sinking in, then pulling back centimeters at a time. As that achy sheath deep between her legs tried to grip the iron-hard invader that made her feel more wonderful, yet greedier, than she'd ever felt in her life, words began crowding up her throat.

Words she'd be smart to keep to herself.

But as he brought her closer, closer, some began to escape despite her best attempts to swallow them. Thank God they were just the generic ones everybody said when their bodies grabbed the reins. As the sensations grew more imperative, however, she sank her teeth into her bottom lip. Because her control was slipping and it became more and more difficult to bottle up all the keep-it-to-yourself words threatening to spill.

Then she climaxed in an attenuated wave that made her see fireworks—and her self-censoring abilities hit the skids. "Oh, God, Jake, I love you," she panted. "Love you, love you, love you."

He cried out and thrust deep; then he, too, came with a deep, primal groan. After a moment he slumped heavily atop her.

Where he lay ominously still and quiet.

Crap, she mentally lambasted herself. *You just couldn't keep it to yourself, could you?* She opened her mouth to backtrack, to assure him it was only heat-of-the-moment sex talk. But she bit back the words.

Because, dammit, it wasn't.

She did love him. God knew she hadn't gone looking for it, but she did. She'd loved before, of course; she adored Austin and Tasha. But she hadn't been sure she believed romantic love between a man and a woman was more than a word that people flung around and businesses used to sell their products. She'd certainly never seen proof of it up close and personal.

And in truth, it didn't resemble the romantic legends that books and movies hyped. For instance, this was no love at first sight. *Her* love had built over the course of their acquaintance, given impetus by Jake's actions, as a father, as a man, and strengthened by the character she hadn't expected him to possess but which she'd delighted in watching him unveil a little more each day.

So, yes, she loved him. Period, end of story. Damned if she'd trivialize it just to spare them an awkward moment.

He pushed up on his elbows and smoothed her hair back from her face. "We need to talk."

His expression was carefully noncommittal, and her heart took a nosedive. But what could she do but nod and say, "Okay." Still, she didn't have to be completely passive. She raised her hands to his shoulders to push him back. "Move."

"Huh?"

"I need you to get off me. Given your no-expression expression, I believe I'd like to be dressed to hear this."

He pulled out of her and rolled to his feet to stand alongside the bed. Apparently not suffering from the self-consciousness she abruptly felt, he stood with his legs braced apart and his long-fingered hands propped on his hips. He opened his mouth to speak, but not wanting to be gently let down while she was buck naked, she shook her head at him, then climbed from the bed, as well.

"Hey, this isn't necessarily a bad thing," he protested as she located her panties and pulled them on. She found her bra in a different location, her sweater in yet another and had to search a moment to track down her Levi's, which Jake had apparently tossed over the end of the bed. The comforter had slipped off sometime during their lovemaking and pooled atop them.

With each article she located, she felt a little more armored. Finally she faced him, her own expression as neutral as his as she watched him swipe his own pants up off the floor. Stepping into them, he pulled them up his legs and zipped up, but left the waistband button unfastened.

She took a deep breath. "Okay. Let me have it."

Jake had been giving the matter a great deal of thought since his talk with Austin, and it *wasn't* a bad thing. Hell, if you asked him, he was about to be downright noble.

So why was his stomach so jittery and his heart doing the jungle-drum thing again?

It didn't help that his assurance had fallen on deaf ears. Jenny stood on bare feet that struck him as unaccountably vulnerable, with one hip cocked and her arms folded over those little cupcake breasts of hers. Giving him the stink eye.

Making him feel that he was in the wrong.

Anxious to change that, he shifted slightly. Cleared his throat. "I've been giving this a lot of thought in the past couple days," he said slowly. "And I came to the conclusion that the right thing to do is leave Austin here with you."

Knowing how close she was to Austin, he kind of expected her to be thrilled. She didn't look it, though. In fact, her eyes narrowed between dense, dark lashes and her lips tightened.

Her silence unnerved him. "Look, I admit I didn't think it through real well before, okay?" God, he hated the idea of acknowledging the plan he'd always had in mind. He knew, though, that it was the only way she'd understand. "My work takes me away for chunks of time—and he'd be left in a strange city with nothing but a companion."

"You're going right back to work?"

He shifted again. "I have to—and sooner rather than later. I've already turned down two jobs, and my editor's been calling every damn day."

She simply looked at him and his defenses rose. He raised his brows at her. "What? You didn't expect me to give up my job, did you?" He flashed her a smile edged with an amusement he didn't feel.

She returned one edged with a contempt he was pretty damn sure she felt right down to her bones. "No, I didn't," she said with stone-cold composure. "But neither did I expect it to be an all-or-nothing proposition. For instance, I'd totally get you leaving Austin with me for the summer, then arranging for a block of time when the new school year starts in New York, so you can be there to help him acclimate. That would give him time to make a new friend or two, so he'd have more support in place than just a companion when you have to travel. But this—you blowing him off after you made him fall in love with you—that I don't get at all."

It was such a good, logical plan—and one that had never once occurred to him. The additional guilt over his failure put his back up even further.

But he was a pro at slapping on an ask-me-if-I-give-a-rat's-ass face. He'd had years of practice, after all, and he donned one now. Then subjected her to a slow up-and-down for good measure. "Are we still talking about Austin, Jenny? Or you?"

His chest hurt when she flinched. But he had to hand it to her—she didn't let it slow her down. Not from the first day they'd met had she let anything do that, he acknowledged with an odd pride.

She returned his sin-on-a-stick once-over with interest before looking him in the eye. "Oh, are you acknowledging that I said the *L* word? And here I thought you were going to ignore it to death. Sorry to disappoint you if I'm supposed to be embarrassed by it, but I try to own my feelings." Her face softened slightly. "I'd sure like to know why you're in such denial about yours."

His heart pounded, pounded, pounded and he forced a laugh. "What? You think I'm in love with you?"

"I was actually talking about Austin—I think you love that kid with every fiber of your being. But for some reason it makes you all—I don't know—tense and twitchy and scared spitless."

"I'm not afraid of anything!" He couldn't deny the tense and twitchy, though.

"I'm sure you aren't…when it comes to your average physical threat. But I'm talking about the emotional stuff, Jake. About the connection—to Austin, to me—and the idea of commitment. I bet *those* scare you right down to the ground. And you know what?" She planted her feet apart as if bracing herself. "I do believe you have strong feelings for me."

He rubbed at the squeezing pain in his chest. Jesus, was he having a heart attack? He was proud, however, of the amused tolerance he essayed when he drawled, "Do you, now?"

"Yes," she said with exaggerated patience. "I do. But if I'm mistaken?" She gave a slight shrug. "Well, hey, I'm a grown-up, I'll get over it."

Her voice hardened. "I wish I could say the same for Austin. That might have been possible if you hadn't already told him you wanted him with you—" She broke off, shaking her head. "But you did, and there's no unsaying it." She met his gaze head-on. "Have you even told him your big plan?"

That was it? She was an adult and she'd get over it? Then her question sank in and he shook his head. "Not yet, no."

She sighed in disgust and his honed-through-experience defense machine barricaded guilt firmly behind the walls he'd spent years erecting. He squared his shoulders. "It wasn't like he was thrilled at the prospect of moving to New York in the first place, Jenny. No doubt he'll be relieved."

Her jaw dropped, but she quickly snapped it back in place. "Really. That's the best you can come up with. My *God,* you're an idiot."

It was a direct jab at some of the reservations he'd felt himself but had shoved down and tried to bury, and he scowled at her. "Is name calling really necessary?"

"Can you honestly say it's *not?*"

"Hell, yes. I'm trying to do the best thing for him *and* you. And it's not like I'm abdicating my responsibilities here. I'll provide for you both, and I'll come by when I can between *National Explorer* gigs."

For the first time, he saw genuine fury cross her face before she about-faced on her bare heel and strode out to the living room. Hotfooting it after her, he found her perched stiffly on the edge of the couch, pulling on socks and a pair of shoes she must have kicked off earlier. He opened his mouth, but didn't really know what to say. Which, as it turned out, probably didn't matter, because in the two seconds he had to think of something, she'd furiously surged to her feet.

"You. Can. *Keep.* Your stinking. Money. That's never been what Austin needed from you—and neither do I." Her eyes burned like hellfire, but her voice was more frigid than an arctic winter as she stepped close. If she were a taller woman, she would have been nose-to-nose with him. "As for swinging by as the spirit moves you?" All that fury abruptly disappeared and she stepped back, her eyes eerily un-Jenny distant.

"If you're going," she said flatly, "you should just go. Because Austin might've been leery about moving away from Razor Bay, but he was willing to do it anyhow. Everything that he loves here was outweighed by finally having the one thing he's always longed for more than anything else—a father."

He jerked. Oh, Christ. The very last thing he'd

ever wanted was to bring Austin more pain. And yet—in the long run the kid would probably thank him.

Jenny clearly didn't give a shit about his anguished regret, nor was she finished. "Trying to do your best for him would be you busting your ass to make this relationship work. You're either in or you're out, Bradshaw. Austin deserves better than a half-assed father who will drop by when he can fit it into his oh, so important schedule."

She took a sudden big step back. "And you know what? So do I. It took me way too long, but I finally vowed this year that I was through accepting the crumbs of other people's affection." She thrust her chin up at him. "So, excuse me if I won't take them from you—a man who refuses to commit to anyone because he had a few things go wrong in his life."

He was grateful for the fury that snapped to life. "A few things? I had a brother who hated me, a dad who walked out, leaving Mom and me flat, and a wife who died, all before I was nineteen years old."

"Oh, boo-hoo, Jake! Tasha grew up with a mom who's an addict. Before I was seventeen, I had a father who was only available to me when it suited him and a mother who took to her goddamn bed, leaving to me the responsibility of finding a roof to put over our heads and earning a living to keep it there. And not because my dad was a crook, mind you, but because her fucking tony friends *knew* he was. Who the hell doesn't have issues? Most of us just suck it the hell up and get on with it! We don't use our troubles to dodge responsibility for the rest of our lives."

He stared in stunned fascination at the passionate conviction on her face—even as her words took a sledgehammer to the wall he'd thought he'd so solidly built around his heart. That in turn thundered in his chest like a charge being set off as his fortifications began to crumble piece by piece.

Hugging herself, she looked around. "I've gotta get out of here." She strode over to the coat tree by the front door, grabbed a thin windbreaker from it, then turned to look him in the eye as she pulled it on. "If you go, don't come back. You'll be leaving wreckage in your wake, and I will not subject Austin to that again. And don't you dare leave it to me to break the news. You can damn well look your son in the face and see firsthand what it does to him when you tell him you rescind your invitation to be a family. Because I swear to God, Jake, if you just sneak off—" She sucked a deep breath in through her nose, then gustily exhaled it.

"There will be no place on earth you can hide. And make no mistake, when I find you, I *will* hurt you." She whirled and banged through the door.

Staring at the solid panels that still quivered from the strength of her slam, Jake didn't doubt her claim for a second.

CHAPTER TWENTY-THREE

JENNY STORMED DOWN the porch stairs, stalked several yards along the path toward the beach...then stumbled to a halt when it hit her that she didn't have the first idea what to do next. She'd left Jake in possession of her cottage, for God's sake, when she should have pointed the righteous finger of wrath at the front door and demanded that *he* get out of her house. But she'd been so damn furious she simply hadn't been thinking straight.

Nor were her abilities along that line improving as she stood there. What did she do now?

Okay, there was never a shortage of things needing her attention at the inn. Except...what was the point? It wasn't as if she'd be able to concentrate worth a damn. And God knew she wasn't up to being around people and carrying on actual conversations. Not when all she really wanted to do was howl.

She supposed she could take her troubles to Tasha, since that was always comforting. But it was Friday night, and her best friend was no doubt up to her eyeballs in the weekend rush. Plus friends and neighbors liked to stop by to say hello at Bella T's, and just the thought of having to pretend she was okay added to her urge to howl.

Hell, even if she had Tash to herself, a bottle of red to drown her sorrows and total privacy for a heart-to-heart, she wasn't up to talking about this yet.

Not without falling to pieces—something she felt treacherously close to doing as it was.

Straightening her backbone, she sucked in a calming breath and reminded herself that she'd known the end was coming. Well, she couldn't have guessed Jake would suddenly reverse his decision to take Austin with him to Manhattan. But she'd certainly known his time with *her* was finite and that the day was rapidly approaching when he'd pack up his bags and leave. What she hadn't known—and for some reason had never once even considered—was that when the don't-examine-it-too-closely day arrived, it would break her heart.

Boy, did I miss the mark on that one. She stared dejectedly at the path beneath her feet. Of course, neither had she realized she was in love with him until the words left her mouth and she'd recognized the sheer…rightness of them. Up until then, heartbreak hadn't been part of the equation.

Now it was a part wider than the canal she couldn't even summon the energy to look at.

A bitter laugh escaped her. Make that wider than the solar system, she thought. Because her heart wasn't simply broken. She was pretty sure if she looked, she'd find an honest-to-God hole in her chest where it had been before Jake ripped it out. In truth it was taking every ounce of strength she possessed not to drop to her knees, curl tightly into the fetal position and bawl her eyes out until she had no tears left. Which, given the way she was feeling, might be the week after never.

Her breath hitched, then shuddered as she clung tightly to her quickly eroding composure. In rising desperation, she realized she had to find a place to vent her sorrow without witnesses. But with her home occupied by the author of her misery, she simply couldn't think where to go.

Her head snapped up as the obvious solution came to her. Doing her best not to think beyond putting one foot in front of the other, she strode down the path to the dock where they moored the inn's boats. She was going to Oak Head.

They were still a few weeks shy of the season for bringing most of the inn's half-dozen Crestliners out of winter storage in the boathouse. But because the weather had been pretty decent recently, two of the twelve-foot aluminum boats, each sporting a small motor, were tied up at the dock where Austin moored his Bayliner. Striding out onto the wharf, she stopped at the boat tied nearest the end. She stooped to unwrap the line from the front cleat.

To her horror, being this close to making an escape weakened the iron grip she'd been maintaining on her emotions. The tears she'd held back by willpower alone began to roll silently down her cheeks.

Ignoring them as best she could, she worked faster.

She was in the midst of tossing the line, which she ordinarily would have taken the time to neatly coil, onto the tiny bow seat when a male voice boomed, "Excuse me! Miss!"

"Crap," she whispered and, with a sniff, surreptitiously swiped her fingers beneath her eyes. Then she looked over her shoulder.

Dan, the inn's longtime head of maintenance, strode down the dock with a purposeful stride, a slight frown on his weather-beaten face.

It was replaced by a look of surprise and perhaps some embarrassment as he pulled up short with an abruptness that rocked him onto his toes. "Oh. Hey, Jenny." The heels of his Carhartts returned to the decking with a solid thump. "Sorry, I didn't realize that was you. I just saw a girl getting ready to take the boat and wanted to make sure she was a guest."

"Not a problem. You probably knew we don't have any young women in residence at the moment." Or maybe not. She really didn't care; she just had to get the hell away from here, to get to a place where she didn't have to pretend everything was hunky-dory.

Still, she forced herself to say calmly, "Austin's out with friends, and I thought I'd take advantage of the calm evening to go out on the water for a bit." To her mortification, her voice cracked on the last words and those damn tears spilled over once again.

Dan's already ruddy face went ruddier. "Uh,

sure." He reached over the skyward-pointing bill of the ubiquitous faded brown John Deere baseball cap he wore and gave the crown a rub. "That is... you okay?"

"Yes." She dashed away the tears, then fanned her face with her fingers. "Don't mind these. It's just...that time."

He backed away in horror. "Oh. Hmmm. Well." He cleared his throat. "You enjoy yourself." No doubt reconsidering that last piece of advice given her damn tears, he flushed scarlet.

"Sure." *That time? Really?* Avoiding his gaze, she squatted to unfasten the rear line, then climbed in the boat and grabbed the life vest on the middle seat. Putting it on, she moved to the back to take the rear seat and gave Dan a little wave. She made sure the shift lever was in neutral, pulled out the choke, then gave the starter rope a yank.

It failed to catch, so she poured every ounce of her humiliation and rage into giving it another. This time the motor rumbled to life and she pulled away from the dock. The moment she cleared the last buoy marking the inn's recreational water, she opened the throttle to get the full horsepower out of it.

Breathing a sigh of relief to be out where nobody could get to her, she pointed the bow toward Oak Head. She was going to be okay. She just needed time. Time to think, time to get herself together, then she'd be just...fine.

She kept telling herself that over and over—and was beginning to almost believe it.

Until she hit the shores of Oak Head, climbed from the boat and, with a throat-scouring sob, her defenses abruptly abandoned all pretense of anything being the least bit fine.

JAKE BANGED THROUGH the front door of the Sand Dollar. She wanted him gone? By God, that's what she would get! The minute he made Austin understand that he wasn't abandoning him, but rather trying to preserve the boy's way of life, he was so out of here. And screw Jenny's mandate that he'd better not come back. She wasn't the final arbiter of all things Austin, and he wasn't about to walk out of his son's life entirely.

Austin might've been leery about moving from Razor Bay, but he was willing to do it anyhow. Everything he loves here was outweighed by finally having the one thing he's always longed for more than anything else—a father.

Jenny's voice in his head stopped him in his tracks temporarily, but he shook it off and took the stairs to the second floor two at a time. He was still going to *be* a father. He just wasn't willing to have his kid left alone in a strange city for chunks of time while he did his job. Not when Austin already had everything he needed right here.

He headed for the little bathroom he used as a darkroom, hitting the overhead light switch as he cleared the door. He'd start boxing up his equipment and supplies for shipping.

The first thing he saw, however, were the prints he'd made of Team Day, hanging on the drying line. Turning on the halogen desk lamp he'd set up on the minuscule bathroom counter, he studied each photo beneath its light as he unclipped it.

And smiled.

He'd been blown away by how much he'd enjoyed taking these, and that enjoyment showed. It seemed to be the guiding principle of Bradshaw Images that the more he was engaged, the better his work. He'd clearly been engaged big-time the day he'd taken this batch. Because they'd turned out great.

His work with the album wasn't done, though. He'd agreed to ready the layouts for the printer and hadn't even started that yet. Hell, he couldn't leave tonight, after all. He had work to do.

Plus, his kid was on his first date. Jake couldn't do anything to take the shine from that. He'd let Austin have his big night. And he'd finish up the work he had promised.

He ignored the odd warmth the reversal of his plans seemed to spread in his chest. Because, *then* he'd go. But not on a forever basis. And if Jenny had a problem with that, well, she could just—

The shot he'd just unclipped from the line and brought down to view under the light erased his train of thought. *Aw, hell, Jenny.*

His heartbeat drummed a furious rhythm. This

wasn't just any photo of her, it was the money shot. He'd managed to capture her very essence in this one. Caught her midlaugh and her shiny dark hair in midswing as she'd turned her head in his direction after someone had said something, which to anyone else likely wouldn't have seemed more than moderately funny, but to Jenny, with her generous, inclusive spirit, had been riotously amusing.

"Jake, I love you. Love you, love you, love you."

"Christ." Scrubbing his knuckles over the ache in his heart, he stared at the photo. Hearing the words from her lips had thrust him over the edge, had made him come in the most mind-bending, screaming pulsations of his life.

"Well, hell, that's just because—"

No. He chopped his prevarication off midsentence. No lies. He had to match her honesty, if only to himself. Had to own his feelings for once.

And admit she'd also been right when she'd said hearing the *L* word had shaken him—okay, scared him…a little. Because just how much he'd needed to hear it had leveled him. Love had never exactly been his friend.

Still. Did he hide behind that excuse forever? Or did he face some home truths like a man?

Maybe he needed to have a conversation with her that was more honest than the last one had been. It might not change anything, but she deserved that. Hell, she deserved so much more than he could ever give her.

But at the very least she merited a truth for truth.

He crossed to the upstairs bedroom to look down on the back of her bungalow. The sky was turning that deep midnight-blue that preceded full night, and her place was dark.

His truth would have to wait. She clearly wasn't back from wherever she'd gone when she'd left him in her home rather than spend another minute in his presence.

He rubbed his chest again.

He made himself go back to work on the layout, but had a hard time concentrating and found himself pausing way too often to check her place again. It remained unlighted, and his mood began to reflect the stygian gloom over there. Where the hell *was* she?

His trips to the front bedroom grew so frequent it verged on absurd. He was heading downstairs to grab a beer in hope of getting his brain out of this walk/stand/stare loop, when he heard footsteps coming up the steps and onto the porch.

He loped down the final stairs and ripped open the door before the knock that sounded on it quit reverberating. He'd hoped to see Jenny on the other side, but it was the inn's maintenance man, Bob or Dave or—

Dan. The guy's name was Dan. "Hey," he said, trying not to sound impatient. "Can I help you?"

"Yeah, look, I'm sorry to bother you," the man said uncomfortably and scratched at his thinning hair, pushing his worn cap even farther to the back

of his head than it already was. "But I'm a little worried about Jenny."

Jake snapped erect. "Why?"

"I saw her down at the docks getting into one of
the Crestliners earlier. And she was crying."

No. His gut iced over.

Oblivious, Dan continued, "She said it was—"
his face reddened "—that time of month. But the
thing is, Mr. Bradshaw, you two seem close…and
she's not back yet."

Where the hell could she have gone? The question had barely entered his mind before he knew the
answer. "I have an idea where I might find her," he
said, stepping out on the porch and closing the door
behind him. "Let me see if I can find the keys to Austin's Bayliner. I wonder why she didn't take it herself." He gave his head an impatient shake, because
what did it matter; she hadn't. "If she's not where I
think she is, I'll call Max to contact the coast guard
or the navy."

Dan blew out a relieved breath. "Okay, good.
That's a good plan."

"Yeah. Assume I've found her unless I call to tell
you otherwise." He went down the stairs, but stopped
to look back at the other man before he headed across
the lot. "Thanks for letting me know, Dan. I appreciate you looking out for her."

The maintenance man shrugged. "It's Razor Bay,
son," he said as if it were a no-brainer. "Looking out
for our neighbors is what we do."

STUPID, STUPID, STUPID! The bottom of the Crestliner scraped the pebbled shore at Oak Head for the second time that evening as Jenny leaned back on the rope and hauled the bow of the boat onto enough solid beach to keep it from floating away. Because *that,* she thought as she found a good-size rock to hold it in place, would just slap a pretty blue ribbon on the idiocy that had led her to strand herself here.

Aside from donning a life vest, she'd already managed to neglect every boating safety measure that Emmett had ever taught her. She hadn't bothered to check the boat's fuel level before she'd taken it from the inn's dock, for starters. It was maintenance's job to keep the tanks topped off...when a guest checked out an inn boat. But when a family member or employee used one, it became that person's responsibility. The same applied to making sure there were oars in the craft.

Only a few guests had used the boats recently, so the kind of too-few-hands, too-much-to-do situation that might allow maintenance to let the upkeep of one slip through the cracks was highly unlikely. It wasn't a stretch then to assume this was the boat Austin and...*he* had taken fishing the other day.

Which was neither here nor there. Because even if they'd neglected to fill it up when they were through, it didn't let her off the hook. Anytime you took a boat with an engine out, rule one was always, *always,* to make sure it had a full tank.

Rule two was that each boat contain a full set of oars—in case you screwed up rule one.

She had not only ignored both rules, she'd also stormed off without her cell phone. She'd come straight over here to have her breakdown.

And boy had she. She'd wallowed in her grief, refusing to get a grip until her head was so stuffed from sobbing she could barely breathe. That's when she'd decided to head back to the inn so she'd have time to apply enough ice and makeup to conceal her misery from Austin. Because if his father hadn't run like a thief, the teen would no doubt be riding his own Misery Express tonight. He wouldn't need hers, as well.

She hadn't made it more than half a mile across the canal before the boat had started sputtering. A moment later it was flat out of gas. Realizing what had happened, she'd planned—despite the growing choppiness of the water—to row the rest of the way home.

Only to discover she was missing an oar. Then the smarter option had become returning to Oak Head, since it was both closer and not bucking the tide.

So here she was, if not shipwrecked, exactly, then marooned for who knew how long, chilled, hungry and feeling like a colossal fool on so many fronts it was impossible to narrow them down. She could see Razor Bay's and The Brothers' lights, but they might as well have been a hundred miles away instead of the two she knew it was.

The only saving grace of this entire gawd-awful evening was that she'd put the kibosh to her damn crying jag over he-who-would-not-be-named. Given the far from bright night, however, she sure wished she had a lighter or a book of matches so she could build a little fire for some warmth and comfort and—more importantly—to guide whoever ultimately came looking for her. The moon was out, but it wasn't even half-full and was playing peekaboo with the clouds.

With a pitiful sigh, she rubbed her tender, tearswollen eyes and killed some time balancing rocks atop each other, building two short but fairly complicated cairns. She wasn't sure how long she'd been pacing the beach to keep warm when she heard a boat roaring across the canal in her direction, it's bow *slap, slap, slapping* against the chop. As its running lights grew nearer, she raced down to the water, waving her arms and screaming her head off, but the moon had gone behind a cloud again, and calling out was probably a waste of breath, given the noise the powerful engine made. She damn near started bawling again at the thought of it speeding by.

But miracle of miracles, the driver turned before reaching Dabob Bay and cut the engine to drift ashore. He landed up the beach near the spot where she'd picnicked with Austin and…him.

Unable to believe her luck, she started running. "Hey!" she yelled, waving her arms overhead again. *"Hey!"*

She was met with silence for a moment. Then feet hit the beach. "Jenny? Jesus, are you all right?"

She stopped short. Dear God, the hits just kept coming. Didn't it *figure* it would be Jake?

All the feelings she'd managed to bury beneath her more immediate problems resurfaced with a vengeance, and she pivoted to storm back the way she'd come. The last thing she needed right now was to be rescued by *him*. She'd rather be stranded. She'd rather spend the night alone.

Her pace faltered as common sense took over. No, she really wouldn't. She was cold, exhausted and hungry and she wanted the hell *off* this peninsula. If accepting a ride from him was her ticket home, well, then, so be it.

But she wasn't saying one word more to him than she had to.

She turned around and started back up the beach again, heart thundering in her chest to see that, while her back had been turned, he'd gotten very close.

He strode right up to her and grasped her upper arms, his gaze all over her, just as the damn traitorous moon broke through the clouds.

For God's sake, was there *no* justice in the world tonight? Because, of course she wasn't one of those women who cried all pretty. So was it truly necessary to shine a spotlight on her blotchy skin and swollen, tear-ravaged eyes?

"Are you okay?" he demanded again.

"Yes." She wanted to shake his hands off her, but

something in his eyes made her stand very still beneath them.

"Jesus," he breathed. "Ever since Dan told me you'd taken a boat out and hadn't come back, I've had every horrendous possibility that can happen in a boat—and a helluva lot more that can happen anywhere—running through my head. What the *hell*, Jenny!"

He hauled her into his arms. "I made a decision on my way over here," he said, roughly stroking her hair, her back, with blessedly warm hands. "I'm moving my base of operations to Razor Bay."

Jenny's heart stopped, only to immediately resume in triple time. But she told herself not to read more into it than was there. Disengaging herself from all that lovely heat, she took a giant step back. "I thought you didn't like it here."

He made an aborted move as if to reach for her, but then dropped his hands to his side. "It's grown on me."

"That's...good," she said with commendable calmness, all things considered. "It will mean the world to Austin." It might mean hell on earth for her, being so close to Jake on a physical basis while worlds apart emotionally, but she'd just have to do what she'd told him and suck it up.

"I didn't make the decision strictly for Austin, Jenny." Shoving his hands in his pockets, he stepped closer. "I wasn't kidding when I said I had a rough ride over here hoping to hell I'd find you here but fearing you'd been drowned or injured or, hell, kidnapped or raped." He shook his head as if to clear those images. "It made me realize you were right. I *was* an idiot."

Her heart was so firmly lodged in her throat she could barely breathe. "Was?" she croaked.

"Yeah. I'm a helluva lot smarter now." He took another step closer, and one hand came out of his pocket to stroke a strand of hair away from the corner of her mouth. His thumb followed up the gesture with a soft circular rub against her lower lip. "It's funny how fast a good scare can cut through the bullshit. And bull is what I was slinging earlier at your place. You were right. You saying you love me scared the bejesus out of me. Because, God, I love you, Jenny. I likely have for a while now, but I was so damn busy protecting my heart in case you didn't love me in return." His dark brows slanted. "Or even if you *did,* what if you changed your mind?"

He shook his head. "This was all subconscious, you know? I'm not real big on psychiatry, but in this case, the panic attacks I had every time I felt the least bit happy were clearly trying to tell me *something.* I think I had so many ways it could go south running like a ticker tape at the bottom of my screen that I refused to let what I really *wanted* work its way to the surface. I'd already decided we needed a more honest talk than I'd given you. But then, when Dan came by and I heard you were crying and had gone out on the canal, I thought of all the awful things that could've happened when you didn't come home. And I simply…knew."

And just like that she could breathe again. But it had been a rough night for her, too, and she wasn't quite ready to let him off the hook. "What makes you think those things *won't* happen?"

He shrugged. "They might. But one thing about being in the midst of the longest fifteen minutes of your life, it teaches you not to throw away the best thing that ever happened to you because of something that might never take place."

He stepped close, wrapped a hand around the back of her neck and bent to rest his forehead against hers. "I'm sorry I hurt you," he said in a raw voice. "I can't promise I'll never do it again, b—"

She dipped her chin in solemn agreement. "Because you're a guy."

Drawing his head back to look at her, he gave her a crooked smile. "Right," he agreed drily. "But a guy who will love you as long as he draws breath. And I'll do my damnedest to keep my crap to a bare minimum."

"Okay," she said. "So will I."

"Do your best to keep my crap to a minimum?"

She slung her arms around his neck and laughed up at him. "I meant my own, actually, but that works, too."

He gave her a look so full of love her heart clutched. "Nah, you haven't got any," he said with marvelous sincerity. "You're like the most perfect person I've ever met."

"Oh, honey, you go into a relationship thinking that, you're probably gonna be disappointed. I have my share of issues. Still." She raised onto her toes to press a kiss against his lips, before settling back on her heels. "I love you," she said softly. "So, so much."

Then she shot him a cocky smile. "And an imperfect man who thinks I'm ideal?" She hitched herself up to wrap her legs around his waist. "I can so live with that."

EPILOGUE

Sunday, July 8

"So, you're leaving town tomorrow, huh?"

Jake's hand, in his cargo pants pocket, ceased rolling a small box end over end. He gave his brother a solid punch to the biceps with his free fist.

Holy Mary, mother of—

He resisted shaking his hand, but *damn*. He kept himself in shape, but Max was like the proverbial brick shithouse. "Tuesday," he corrected. "And it's only for three weeks tops, then I'll be back home." He turned the box over once more and looked around as Jenny, Tasha and Rebecca banged through the back door, chatting and carrying covered dishes out to the table he'd helped set up for the *come-back-soon* barbecue they were throwing him in Jenny's tiny backyard.

At his side, Max said, "It's odd to hear that word coming from your mouth."

"What, *home?*" Tearing his attention away from Jenny, he grinned. "Yeah, surprised me, too. But you can forget everything I ever said about Razor Bay, because for the first time in my life it really feels like home." Catching one of the box's rounded corners with his thumb, he rotated it in his palm.

Max's miss-nothing cop eyes tracked the motion. "You have something you'd like to share with the class, Mr. Bradshaw?"

"No, ma'am." Closing his fist around the tiny box, he pushed his hand deeper into his pocket. "But damn decent imitation of Ms. Harris," he said drily, naming the humorless history teacher from high school. "Man, that woman was so buttoned-up, I spent part of every class trying to visualize her doing that take your glasses off, let your hair down, turn into a bombshell thing that was so popular in the old black-and-white movies."

Max looked as if he were trying to visualize it for himself. He shook his head. *"Naaaah."* He shot Jake one of his rare grins. "No way I can make that fly."

"I never could, either. But I always tried."

Nolan Damoth's little brother, Josh, speeding on a sugar high, shot around the corner of the cottage, zigzagging ahead of his dad and shrieking maniacally. The kid's behavior could be laid directly at the feet of Austin, Nolan and Bailey, who were practicing bike tricks in the small parking area. Until the women had put a stop to it, the teens had wasted a lot of pop by opening a can, taking a few sips then wandering away. And the next time they were thirsty, instead of expending effort looking for the ones they'd left behind, they'd simply grabbed fresh sodas out of the cooler. Josh had managed to help himself to several of the abandoned cans before Jenny and Rebecca had caught on, and was now solidly wired.

Max's massive body abruptly blocked the wild-eyed kid from Jake's view. Finding his left forearm gripped, he looked down to find his brother's hard hand firmly wrapped around it. "What's your problem, man?"

"Let's see what's so damn interesting in your pocket," his brother ordered.

Jake kept his hand firmly in place but arched his eyebrows. "Sure you want to go there? Maybe I'm just happy to see you."

Max's grip loosened as he threw back his head and laughed.

It was such a great and infrequent sound that Jake relaxed his guard, and the next thing he knew Deputy Dawg had pulled his hand from his pocket.

Max's laughter died and his fingers went slack, then dropped away as he stared at the ring box in Jake's fist. "Jesus. Is that what I think it is?"

"Dunno. What do you think it is?"

"An *engagement* ring?"

Jake gave the small velvet box a fond look and smoothed his thumb over its slightly curved top. "Give the man a cigar."

"Jesus, Jake, you haven't even known Jenny three whole months."

He shrugged. "Damn near. Long enough, at any rate, to recognize she's the best thing that's ever happened to me. You said it yourself, bro—she's special. And I want to marry her." He narrowed his eyes. "You wanna take a big step back if you've got a problem with that. Because I'll fight you right down to the ground over this. I'd hate to do that, because we've been getting along real well, but I will."

His brother stared at him for a moment. Then his wide shoulders relaxed and he nodded. "I think she probably *is* the best thing to happen to you—along with my nephew, of course." He thrust out a hand. "Congratulations."

Jake ignored the hand and hauled his brother in for a hug—or as close to it as guys got, since it was more a bumping of chests and a slap on the back. "Thanks," he said, stepping back. "But keep this under your hat. I haven't actually asked her yet, and for all I know she might agree with you and think it's too soon."

"What's too soon? And were you two *hugging?*"

His heart stumbled. Thrusting the ring box back in his pocket, he turned to slide an arm around Jenny's shoulders as she walked up to them. He hugged her to his side and felt his heart level out beneath a wash of warmth as she wrapped her own arm around his waist and leaned against him trustingly.

"Hell, no," Max said. "The clumsy fool tripped."

"Okay." She gave him a skeptical look, then turned to Jake. "I just caught the tail end of your conversation. What's too soon?"

"Something I want to discuss with you later."

"'Discuss,'" Max marveled. "Listen to you, sounding all mature. Who'da thought we'd ever see that day?" Then he looked past Jenny, his humor fading. "Oh, hell, what's she doing here?"

Jenny glanced over her shoulder and a wrinkle formed between her delicate brows when she turned back. "Who, Harper? I invited her. She's only been in Razor Bay a week, so I thought this would be a good opportunity to meet a few locals." She gave Max an assessing look. "Do you have an objection to that for some reason?"

"Huh?" He pulled his gaze back to her and a dull flush climbed his cheeks. "No, of course not. It just…caught me by surprise." He looked at his watch. "Hey, it's almost five—I think I'll have a beer." He shot Jake a look. "You want one?"

It was rare to see his brother rattled and Jake was tempted to prolong the treat. But this was about women and attraction and feeling outclassed, and sometimes guys just had to stick together. "You bet."

Max beat a hasty retreat.

Jenny looked up at him. "What was that all about?"

"Beats me." Hey, he really didn't know for sure.

"O-kay. Let's talk about what you plan to discuss with me."

"We'll definitely do that—later." Jake leaned down to plant a kiss on Jenny's lips and didn't raise his head until gagging noises started issuing from behind him. He looked over his shoulder.

"Dude! Get a room," Austin ordered. "It's bad

enough I see this action going down all over my house and yours, too—you gotta start in in front of the neighbors?" But the boy's green eyes were alight with the same joy that had been shining in them ever since Jake had told him they were staying in town.

"You wanna talk action?" Jake inquired smoothly, sending a pointed glance toward Bailey.

Austin took a hasty step back. "Nah. It's a party. That was just a little FYI, dude. They build walls for just this sort of thing." And, laughing, he turned back to his friend and his girl.

Jenny turned to Jake—and promptly revisited the previous conversation. "Why not discuss with me now?"

"What—oh, the something I wanna discuss with you that you only know about because you eaves-dropped earlier?"

"Yep. That." She grinned at him without a shred of discomfiture. "Why not discuss it now?"

"Because, my darling Jenny, we've got company and we're going to do it later."

She sighed. "Fine. But don't think I'll forget."

He laughed. "Trust me. The thought never even crossed my mind."

IT WAS CLOSING ON MIDNIGHT when Jenny walked into her living room. Jake was sprawled out, eyes closed, in the overstuffed chair and she went over and climbed aboard, wedging a knee on either side of his thighs.

He cracked an eye open. "Hey. Austin finally crashed, huh?"

"Yeah. I hated to separate you two, because I know how much he wants every minute he can get with you before you leave. But he was running on fumes."

"So now it's just you and me." Looking up at her with heavy-lidded eyes and a sleepy smile, he rubbed his hands up and down her thighs.

"Yes, it is." She arched beneath his touch, put her hands over his—and held them still. "It's also later. Let's discuss."

With a wry smile, he slid his fingers out from beneath hers and arched his left upper torso as he dug a hand into a deep pocket in his cargos. "This isn't exactly the way I envisioned doing this," he murmured, pulling his hand out of his pocket. He held a little velvet box up to her, snapping open its top with his thumb. "Jennifer Salazar, will you marry me?"

She could almost swear an electric shock jolted through her heart, and she gawked at the marquise-cut diamond that winked up at her from its simple platinum setting. Her heart drummed with both joy and panic. Without taking her eyes off the ring, she said, "Jake, it's too soon. You said so yourself."

"No. *Max* said."

That snapped her attention away from the ring, and she looked at him through slitty eyes. "You told him about your plans before you told *me?*"

"Not deliberately." He shook his head. "Guy's got

a nose like a bloodhound. And I'm not proposing we get married next month—a long engagement is fine. You're in charge of the where and when. But what I feel for you, Jenny? It's like nothing I've ever known. Plain ol' vanilla *love you* just doesn't cover it. And I want everyone to know you're mine."

"That's very…"

"Primitive," he interrupted with a baffled laugh. "Tell me about it. Hell, if I were a dog I'd be pissing circles around you to warn off the other hounds. This is a huge departure from my usual relationships with women. I've spent my entire adult life seeking affairs with finite shelf dates—the more temporary, the better. And now…"

He shook his head. "I don't want to own you, and I sure as hell have no ambition to control you." He shot her a crooked smile. "Like *that* would be possible if it *were* my intention. I just wanna see the proof that you consider yourself taken shining from your finger."

Jenny looked down at the ring again. "And this rock certainly does shine." Her panic couldn't have sunk faster if it had been fitted with cement boots. Only thrilled joy remained.

"It's only a three-quarter carat," Jake said with a shrug. "You've got delicate fingers—I didn't think something you'd need a sling to support would suit you."

Okay, really, what woman *didn't* appreciate the man she loved taking things like the size of her fingers into consideration? Didn't like hearing how much he wanted to inform the world of the depth of his love?

Her fingers suddenly itched with greed. "Well, I don't know," she murmured. "I think I should be the judge of that, don't you?" She held out her left hand.

Jake's face lit up. "You definitely should." Plucking the ring from the box, he slid it onto her finger.

And stilled. "Damn. That looks so…right."

She held her hand at arm's length to get the full effect. "It really does. It fits, too." She tore her gaze away to look at him. "How did you manage that?"

"I borrowed that little silver ring you sometimes wear from your jewelry box." He rubbed his finger over the band of the ring. "So…will you wear mine?"

Curling her fingers, she brought her hand to her heart. "Just try and take it from me!"

He whooped and crunched up to kiss her. When he finally pulled back, it was only to press his forehead against hers, so close that he was all laugh lines and white teeth as he grinned at her. "You and me, Jenny? Whether we get married right away or sometime down the road, we're going to be so. Damn. Good together."

Her own grin felt every bit as big, and her forehead rocked against his as she nodded her agreement. She knew they'd have adjustments to make and that they might not always see eye-to-eye. But none of that mattered in this moment. Because when it came right down to it—

"Oh, man," she said. "We absolutely will."

* * * * *

Summer love can last a lifetime....

A charming new romance from
New York Times **bestselling author**

SUSAN MALLERY

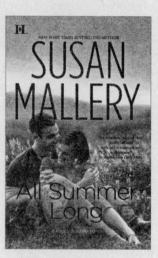

Former underwear model turned entrepreneur Clay Stryker has loved, tragically lost and vowed that he'll never risk his heart again. After making his fortune, the youngest of the rugged Stryker brothers returns to Fool's Gold, California, to put down roots on a ranch of his own.

Clay finds an unexpected ally, and unexpected temptation, in tomboyish Charlie Dixon, the only person who sees beyond his dazzling good looks to the real man beneath. But when Charlie comes to him with an indecent proposal, will they be able to overcome their pasts and find a love that lasts beyond one incredible summer?

All Summer Long

Pick it up today!

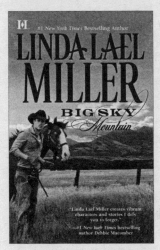

REQUEST YOUR FREE BOOKS!

2 FREE NOVELS
FROM THE ROMANCE COLLECTION
PLUS 2 FREE GIFTS!

YES! Please send me 2 FREE novels from the Romance Collection and my 2 FREE gifts (gifts are worth about $10). After receiving them, if I don't wish to receive any more books, I can return the shipping statement marked "cancel." If I don't cancel, I will receive 4 brand-new novels every month and be billed just $5.99 per book in the U.S. or $6.49 per book in Canada. That's a saving of at least 25% off the cover price. It's quite a bargain! Shipping and handling is just 50¢ per book in the U.S. and 75¢ per book in Canada.* I understand that accepting the 2 free books and gifts places me under no obligation to buy anything. I can always return a shipment and cancel at any time. Even if I never buy another book, the two free books and gifts are mine to keep forever.

194/394 MDN FELQ

Name	(PLEASE PRINT)	

Address		Apt. #

City	State/Prov.	Zip/Postal Code

Signature (if under 18, a parent or guardian must sign)

Mail to the **Reader Service:**
IN U.S.A.: P.O. Box 1867, Buffalo, NY 14240-1867
IN CANADA: P.O. Box 609, Fort Erie, Ontario L2A 5X3

Not valid for current subscribers to the Romance Collection
or the Romance/Suspense Collection.

Want to try two free books from another line?
Call 1-800-873-8635 or visit www.ReaderService.com.

* Terms and prices subject to change without notice. Prices do not include applicable taxes. Sales tax applicable in N.Y. Canadian residents will be charged applicable taxes. Offer not valid in Quebec. This offer is limited to one order per household. All orders subject to credit approval. Credit or debit balances in a customer's account(s) may be offset by any other outstanding balance owed by or to the customer. Please allow 4 to 6 weeks for delivery. Offer available while quantities last.

Your Privacy—The Reader Service is committed to protecting your privacy. Our Privacy Policy is available online at www.ReaderService.com or upon request from the Reader Service.

We make a portion of our mailing list available to reputable third parties that offer products we believe may interest you. If you prefer that we not exchange your name with third parties, or if you wish to clarify or modify your communication preferences, please visit us at www.ReaderService.com/consumerschoice or write to us at Reader Service Preference Service, P.O. Box 9062, Buffalo, NY 14269. Include your complete name and address.

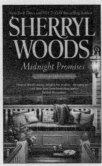
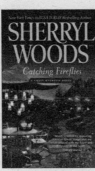
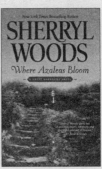

Susan Andersen

77589	PLAYING DIRTY	___ $7.99 U.S.	___ $9.99 CAN.
77574	JUST FOR KICKS	___ $7.99 U.S.	___ $9.99 CAN.
77498	BURNING UP	___ $7.99 U.S.	___ $9.99 CAN.
77457	SKINTIGHT	___ $7.99 U.S.	___ $9.99 CAN.
77419	HOT & BOTHERED	___ $7.99 U.S.	___ $8.99 CAN.
77393	BENDING THE RULES	___ $7.99 U.S.	___ $8.99 CAN.

(limited quantities available)

TOTAL AMOUNT $ _____
POSTAGE & HANDLING $ _____
($1.00 FOR 1 BOOK, 50¢ for each additional)
APPLICABLE TAXES* $ _____
TOTAL PAYABLE $ _____

(check or money order—please do not send cash)

To order, complete this form and send it, along with a check or money order for the total above, payable to Harlequin HQN, to: **In the U.S.:** 3010 Walden Avenue, P.O. Box 9077, Buffalo, NY 14269-9077; **In Canada:** P.O. Box 636, Fort Erie, Ontario, L2A 5X3.

Name: _____
Address: _____ City: _____
State/Prov.: _____ Zip/Postal Code: _____
Account Number (if applicable): _____

075 CSAS

*New York residents remit applicable sales taxes.
*Canadian residents remit applicable GST and provincial taxes.

HARLEQUIN® HQN™
™ www.Harlequin.com

PHSA0812BL